ANDRE FREEMAN

LittyVerse

A Fractured Awakening

First published by UNLTD CO 2026

This novel is entirely a work of fiction. The names, characters and incidents portrayed in it are the work of the author's imagination. Any resemblance to actual persons, living or dead, events or localities is entirely coincidental.

Andre Freeman asserts the moral right to be identified as the author of this work.

First edition

ISBN (paperback): 979-8-90220-011-6
ISBN (hardcover): 979-8-90220-012-3

This book was professionally typeset on Reedsy.
Find out more at reedsy.com

Contents

Chapter 1

L ITTYVERSE — BOOK 2
Fracture of Reality

CHAPTER 1 — "THE SKY DID IT AGAIN"

I f you've never watched the sky blink, count yourself lucky.

Most people think a blink is a cute little moment. Eyes close, eyes open, life keeps moving. But when the sky blinks, it's not cute. It's not poetic. It's not a metaphor your English teacher can overhype into a TED Talk.

It's a warning.

The first time it happened, everybody acted like it was some freak weather thing. An "optical illusion." A "power grid glitch." A "mass hallucination." The news spun it into a whole buffet of excuses because that's what the world does when it's scared—feeds you explanations until your fear gets tired and falls asleep.

But I didn't forget.

I couldn't.

Because after the blink, reality didn't feel stitched up right. Like somebody rushed the job and left loose threads hanging out of the universe.

And if you tug the wrong one?

Everything unravels.

I learned that the hard way on a night I should've been asleep.

It was around 2:17 AM—yeah, I remember the exact time, because my phone had been stuck on 2:17 for twenty minutes like it was protesting time itself. I was on my mattress (don't judge, I'm not living in some penthouse yet), staring at the ceiling, trying to convince my brain to shut up.

I'd been hearing it again.

The sound.

Not a voice. Not exactly. More like... a pressure. Like someone pressing a finger into the back of your skull from the inside, trying to tap out a message in a language you don't know.

Tick. Tick. Tick.

Not a clock. Not my heartbeat. Something else.

The room was hot, but the air felt cold in patches. Like invisible doors were opening and closing around me. My fan was spinning on high, but the sound kept warping— normal, then underwater, then normal again.

I sat up and said the first thing that came to mind.

"Alright bro," I told the empty room. "If the universe wants to talk, it can at least pay rent."

The walls didn't answer.

But the window did.

A thin crack of white light slid under the blinds—bright enough to draw a clean line across the floor. That didn't make sense. Streetlights don't flicker like that. Not in a straight, surgical line like someone was aiming a flashlight from the sky.

I got up. Barefoot. Quiet. Like being quiet mattered.

I pulled the blinds.

Outside, my neighborhood looked normal. Same old street. Same tired cars. Same shadows where the trees leaned over the sidewalk like they were gossiping.

But the sky...

The sky looked too flat.

Like someone painted it and forgot to add depth.

No stars. No clouds. Just a dark blue-black sheet stretched tight over everything. It felt close, like if I threw a rock hard enough it would bounce back.

I whispered, "Nah."

Because the first blink? It had a vibe. You could feel the world holding its breath like it knew something was coming.

This felt worse.

This felt like the world already knew it lost.

Then my phone finally changed.

2:17 became 2:18.

And the moment it did, the sky blinked.

It wasn't like lightning. It wasn't like a flash.

It was like someone shut the whole universe off for a split second.

Everything—gone.

Not dark. Not black. Not "night."

Just... nothing. Like the concept of "light" got deleted from the file.

I felt my stomach drop.

The street, the houses, the air—everything vanished, like I'd blinked and opened my eyes inside a void.

Then the universe came back.

Lights. Street. Trees. Shadows.

Normal.

Except it wasn't.

Because the second time the sky blinked, it left behind a ripple.

I saw it—actual ripples in the air, like heat waves, but sharper. The kind you see above asphalt in the summer, except these were vertical, slicing through space in long, invisible curtains. They moved slow, like they were trying to decide which way time was supposed to flow.

I stumbled back from the window.

My heart wasn't racing. It was skipping. Like it couldn't keep rhythm in a world where rhythm had stopped making sense.

I tried to laugh it off, because if you don't laugh, you scream, and if you scream, you admit you're not in control.

"Okay," I muttered. "That's... that's new."

My fan made a choking noise and stopped.

The lights didn't go out. The power was still on. My phone was still glowing. But the fan stopped like somebody told it, personally, to shut up.

Then the tapping in my skull got louder.

Tick. Tick. Tick.

The pressure pressed in behind my eyes, and suddenly I had a thought that wasn't mine.

LOOK UP.

I froze.

I didn't want to.

But my body moved like it had been given a command by something older than free will.

I turned back to the window.

The ripples were still there, bigger now. One of them passed over a parked car and for a second the car looked... wrong.

7

Not like it disappeared.

Like it was a different version of the same car.

Same shape, but the paint was a different shade. The license plate letters weren't the same. The bumper had a dent that wasn't there before.

Then the ripple moved on, and the car snapped back.

I stood there, gripping the blinds so tight my fingers hurt.

"What are you?" I whispered.

The air shimmered.

And something shimmered back.

Not a person.

Not a creature.

More like... an outline. Like the absence of a thing pretending to be a thing.

It hovered above the street, about twenty feet off the ground, right where the ripple lines crossed.

It didn't have a face.

It didn't need one.

I could feel it looking at me anyway.

The tapping turned into a single, clean sensation.

A message. Not spoken.

DOWNLOADING.

I grabbed my head like that would stop it.

My eyes blurred.

And then the world did something I can't explain without sounding insane.

The neighborhood overlapped with another neighborhood.

For a breath, I saw two streets at once. Two versions of the same place layered together like two videos playing on the same screen.

One version was mine—normal, dim, tired.

The other version looked... upgraded.

The street was cleaner. The houses were sharper. The air had a faint glow like the atmosphere itself was lit from within. The parked car was the dented version. The street signs had slightly different names, like somebody changed a couple letters and hoped no one would notice.

And in that other version...

There were people.

Standing still.

Not moving. Not blinking.

Like NPCs frozen mid-animation.

They were all looking up, too.

At the same place in the sky.

The outline above the street shifted.

I felt a new thought slam into my mind.

FOUND YOU.

My legs almost gave out.

"Found me?" I whispered. "Who the—"

The outline pulsed.

And the other neighborhood flickered away like a dying screen.

My neighborhood returned to normal.

Except the outline stayed.

I backed away from the window, stumbling over my own feet, knocking my knee into the side of the bed frame so hard I saw stars.

Real stars.

Which was extra disrespectful, because the sky still had none.

I fumbled for my phone and opened my camera. If I could capture it, maybe I could prove I wasn't losing it.

I pointed it at the window.

The screen showed the street.

The trees.

The shadows.

No ripples.

No outline.

Nothing.

I lowered the phone and looked with my eyes.

The outline was still there, hovering like a glitch in reality.

11

My phone was blind to it.

Or maybe it wasn't blind.

Maybe it was blocked.

Because suddenly, my phone buzzed.

Not a notification.

A full-body vibration like it was being possessed.

The screen went white.

Then black.

Then a single line of text appeared.

WELCOME BACK, LITTY.

My throat went dry.

Nobody calls me that unless they know me. And even then, it's not like some official greeting.

This felt... official.

Like I'd just logged into something.

I stared at the message.

"Who is this?" I whispered. My voice sounded too small in my own room.

The phone screen flickered.

NEW OBJECTIVE: REMAIN CALM.

I snorted, because whoever—or whatever—wrote that had never met me.

"Remain calm? You got jokes."

The tapping became a slow drumbeat.

Not tick-tick-tick.

More like...

Knock. Knock. Knock.

My bedroom door rattled.

I froze.

I wasn't expecting a knock. I wasn't expecting anything.

Another rattle.

Then the handle turned, just a little, like someone was testing it.

13

But nobody had knocked like a person.

No voice. No "yo." No "you up?"

Just... the door trying to open itself.

I stepped back, phone in my hand like it was a weapon.

"Who's there?" I called, keeping my voice steady. "If it's the universe again, tell it I'm closed."

The handle stopped moving.

Silence stretched.

Then my phone buzzed again.

WARNING: DO NOT OPEN.

My eyes snapped from the door to the phone.

"Cool," I muttered. "So you can warn me but you can't, like, explain? Love that."

The door handle turned again.

Harder.

The door shook like someone on the other side was leaning their whole weight into it.

Except... I didn't hear footsteps.

I didn't hear breathing.

I didn't hear anything you'd hear from a human standing outside a door.

It was just the door reacting to force.

I backed away until my shoulder hit the wall.

My room felt smaller, like the air was shrinking.

And then something changed.

The outline outside the window dipped lower, like it was descending. The ripples in the air intensified. I could see them even in my room now—thin distortions crawling across the walls like invisible snakes.

The fan, still off, slowly began to rotate again.

Not because power returned.

Because something was turning it.

Slow.

Slow.

Slow.

A whisper slid across my mind.

NOT SAFE HERE.

I clenched my jaw.

"Where is safe?" I whispered back, because at this point, talking to my own brain felt like the least crazy option.

The phone screen flickered.

SAFE ZONE: NONE.

I laughed once, sharp and bitter. "Oh, so we're just doing horror mode."

The door handle jerked so violently I thought it would snap off.

Then the door didn't open.

It... glitched.

That's the only word.

For a blink—no, not the sky blinking, but reality—my door was open and closed at the same time. Like it couldn't decide which state it was supposed to be in.

In that half-second, I saw the hallway.

And I saw something standing in it.

Tall.

Too tall.

Its head nearly brushed the ceiling, but the ceiling didn't look like it was touching it. Like space itself was politely making room.

It didn't have eyes.

It didn't have a face.

But it was shaped like a person the way a shadow is shaped like a person—technically correct, spiritually wrong.

It tilted its head.

And I felt it recognize me, the same way the outline outside did.

FOUND YOU.

My muscles locked.

My phone buzzed so hard it nearly flew from my hand.

RUN.

I didn't think.

I moved.

I bolted toward the window, because my bedroom door was now an argument between open and closed, and the thing in the hallway was too wrong for my brain to process.

I yanked the window up.

Cold air hit my face like a slap.

Outside, the street rippled again, and for a heartbeat, I saw the upgraded neighborhood. The frozen people. The strange glow.

The outline outside shifted toward me, like it was pulling me.

My phone flashed one more message.

JUMP.

I stared down. I wasn't on the ground floor.

I was on the second story.

Not crazy high, but high enough to mess up a leg if you land wrong. High enough to regret it.

Behind me, the bedroom door made a sound like tearing fabric.

18

I turned my head.

The door was finally open.

The thing in the hallway stood there, and it was closer than it should've been. Like distance didn't apply to it the same way it applied to me.

It lifted one arm.

The air in my room rippled outward.

Everything on my desk—papers, pens, random junk— lifted an inch off the surface like gravity just got muted.

My lungs tightened.

The phone buzzed again.

NOW.

So I jumped.

I didn't jump like a superhero.

I jumped like a guy with rent and anxiety and no plot armor who just watched reality glitch in his doorway.

I dropped fast.

The night air rushed past me.

And right before I hit the ground, the ripples caught me.

Not physically.

More like... I fell through a seam.

The street below wasn't my street anymore.

It was the other one.

The upgraded one.

I hit pavement—hard—but not as hard as I expected. Like the ground had a slightly different physics setting.

My knees buckled. My hands slapped the road. Pain shot up my arms.

But I was alive.

I looked up.

The sky above this version of the neighborhood wasn't flat.

It wasn't empty.

It was full of stars—too many stars, packed close together like the universe here didn't believe in subtlety.

And the people I'd seen frozen?

They were moving now.

Slowly turning their heads toward me like I'd just walked into the wrong classroom in the middle of an exam.

They all had the same expression.

Not fear.

Not anger.

Recognition.

Like they'd been waiting.

A voice—an actual voice this time, not in my head—spoke from somewhere behind me.

"Litty," it said, calm as a teacher calling roll. "You're late."

I turned.

And saw a girl standing under a streetlight that didn't exist in my world.

She looked around my age. Hoodie. Sneakers. A chain that shimmered like it had tiny galaxies trapped in the links. Her eyes were sharp, like she'd seen this kind of impossible before and got tired of being surprised.

She held something in her hand that made my stomach

drop.

It looked like a phone.

But not like mine.

It was thinner. Darker. The screen wasn't glass—it looked like liquid night.

And on it, glowing in clean white letters, was the same phrase I'd seen twice already.

FOUND YOU.

She tilted her head and smirked like she was trying not to laugh.

"Welcome to the fracture," she said. "Try not to die in the first five minutes. That would be embarrassing."

I stared at her, chest heaving, palms stinging, brain screaming.

"Who... who are you?" I managed.

She stepped closer, and the streetlights flickered as if they were nervous.

"My name?" she said. "Right now, you don't need my name. You need a rule."

She held up one finger.

"Rule one: if the sky blinks again while you're in the fracture—don't look up."

I swallowed.

"Why?"

Her smirk faded.

"Because the last time somebody looked up," she said quietly, "the universe looked back."

And right on cue...

The stars above us shuddered.

The air rippled.

And the sky began to close its eyes.

....

CHAPTER 2 — "RULES ARE REAL WHEN YOU BLEED"

T he sky blinked.

But I didn't look up.

Not because I'm disciplined. Not because I'm brave.

Because the girl said "don't," and her voice had that tone like she'd already watched somebody ignore her and pay for it. And something in my bones—something older than my opinions—agreed with her.

So I stared straight ahead at the streetlight glow, at the pavement, at the people who were slowly turning their heads like they were tracking a scent.

My breathing came out in short bursts. My palms burned. My knees felt like they'd swallowed gravel.

The girl grabbed my hoodie and yanked me sideways,

behind a parked car that looked like the "other" version I'd seen for that split-second back home—cleaner paint, sharper edges, like the whole world got a graphics upgrade.

"Stay down," she hissed. "And don't be stupid."

I wanted to say something smart. Something like, "Define stupid," or "That ship sailed," or "Who are you and why is the universe messing with me?"

But the air changed.

It got heavier, like gravity leaned in to listen.

A faint crackling drifted over us—the sound you hear right before a thunderstorm, except there was no storm. Just that vibrating hush of something big moving through reality.

The streetlights flickered.

The shadows stretched wrong.

Across the street, one of the frozen-NPC people—an older guy in a neat jacket—jerked like a puppet whose strings got yanked. His head tilted upward.

My stomach turned over.

He wasn't looking at the sky.

He was looking through it.

Like it was a window.

The girl pressed a finger hard against my shoulder, holding me down.

"Eyes forward," she whispered. "If you look up, it sees you faster."

"It?" My voice came out like a squeak. I hated that.

She didn't answer. She didn't need to.

Because something answered for her.

A sound that wasn't sound.

A presence that wasn't presence.

It rolled overhead like the shadow of a planet passing in front of a sun.

Even without looking up, I could feel it—the shape of attention, sweeping across the fracture like a scanner.

I swallowed.

My phone—my normal phone—buzzed in my pocket like it was panicking. I didn't pull it out. I didn't want to.

The girl's weird liquid-night phone lit up anyway. The screen didn't glow; it absorbed light around it.

New text appeared.

SCAN IN PROGRESS.

She clicked her tongue, annoyed like she got a parking ticket.

"Of course."

"What is it?" I whispered again, because my brain was doing that thing where it repeats the same question until it gets an answer, like a toddler.

Her eyes flicked to me. Sharp, calculating.

Then she did something that made me trust her more: she told me the truth the way you tell a kid the stove is hot—fast, simple, no sugar.

"It's a watcher," she said. "A hungry one."

"That's not simple."

"It's simple enough," she snapped. Then softer: "Listen. This place—this version of your neighborhood—it's not a dream. It's a layer. A spillover. A crack between realities. We call it the fracture."

She said it like it was common knowledge. Like everybody had a class on "How To Survive The Universe Being Broken."

"I didn't sign up for this," I muttered.

She almost smiled. "Nobody does."

Overhead, the pressure moved.

The scanning sensation passed directly above us.

I held my breath so hard my lungs hurt.

The parked car's windows fogged.

Not from heat.

From fear.

Across the street, another person jerked and stared upward. Then another. Like dominoes tipping in slow motion.

The girl's phone buzzed again.

SCAN: ANOMALY DETECTED.

My heart slammed.

She stared at the screen. Then at me.

Then her eyes narrowed like she wanted to punch the universe.

"...You."

"What?" I whispered. "Me what?"

"You brought attention," she said. "You're loud."

"I'm literally whispering."

She shook her head. "Not like that. Your signal. What-ever you are—whatever you have—you're bright in the fracture."

I started to protest.

Then a shadow fell across the hood of the car we were hiding behind.

Not the watcher shadow.

A different one.

Smaller.

Closer.

Something walked between the streetlight pools on the sidewalk. The pavement didn't crunch. The air didn't shift. It moved like it didn't need permission from physics.

The girl's body stiffened.

She reached into her hoodie pocket and pulled out some-thing that looked like a coin at first—round, metallic, etched with a pattern that hurt to focus on. Then she flicked it in the air.

The coin unfolded.

Literally unfolded, like it had hinges in dimensions my brain wasn't built to understand.

In her hand, it became a short blade.

Not a knife. Not a sword.

A shard. A piece of something that shouldn't exist.

It shimmered with that galaxy-chain energy.

I stared, because wow.

She noticed and rolled her eyes like she was tired of being impressive.

"Don't freak out," she whispered. "If you freak out, you get loud."

"Noted," I whispered, still staring. "So that's... a—"

"Shhh."

The thing on the sidewalk stopped.

My skin prickled.

I could feel it sniffing with no nose.

The girl leaned closer to my ear.

"If it checks under this car, don't move," she said. "If it finds you—"

She didn't finish.

Because the thing spoke.

Not in words.

In static.

A burst of broken sound and feeling, like a radio station turning into a scream.

My vision flashed.

For half a second, I saw my bedroom door again—open and closed at the same time—the tall faceless thing in my hallway.

This sidewalk thing felt related.

Like a smaller tooth from the same mouth.

It stepped closer.

My muscles locked.

Then my phone buzzed again, and it wasn't a normal buzz. The vibration felt like it shook my bones.

The sidewalk thing snapped its head toward my pocket.

The girl swore under her breath.

"You gotta be kidding me."

The thing drifted closer to the car.

The air around it rippled like water.

Its outline sharpened.

It was humanoid, but wrong in the same way the hallway thing was wrong—like a person-shaped hole cut out of reality.

Where its face should've been, there was a smooth dark surface that reflected the streetlights like oil.

No eyes.

No mouth.

But when it "looked" at the car, I felt it pressing into my thoughts.

FOUND YOU.

The girl moved fast.

She rose from behind the car in a single clean motion, like a dancer who learned violence instead of ballet. The shard-blade flashed.

She slashed the air in front of the thing.

The blade didn't hit its body.

It cut space.

A bright line ripped open between them, like a zipper in the world.

The faceless thing recoiled—not in pain, but in offense, like she'd insulted it.

It released another burst of static.

The girl grimaced. Blood beaded in her nose.

That's when I realized the fight wasn't physical.

It was... conceptual.

Like arguing with a nightmare using a knife.

The thing reached out.

The air thickened and bent toward its hand.

33

The streetlight above us flickered out.

Darkness poured down, heavy and cold.

The girl hissed at me, "MOVE."

I didn't need to be told twice.

I scrambled backward, out from behind the car, then immediately regretted it because the sidewalk people— those moving NPCs—had started walking toward us.

Not running.

Walking.

Like sleepwalkers drawn by a magnet.

Their eyes were blank.

Their mouths hung slightly open.

They moved in a slow, steady ring, circling.

"What are they doing?" I shouted—okay, I didn't whisper. My bad.

The girl shot me a look that could kill a small animal.

"They're anchors," she said. "The watcher uses them to hold the fracture stable. If they touch you, they lock you."

"Lock me where?"

She slammed her blade into the pavement.

The ground cracked—not physically, but like the texture of reality split. A narrow seam opened at our feet, showing darkness beneath.

"You don't wanna know," she said. "Now run."

The faceless thing surged forward.

The darkness it carried washed over the street like an ink spill.

The ring of anchors tightened.

My mind raced.

In my world, if somebody chases you, you sprint. You weave. You hop fences. You pray your cardio isn't fake.

Here?

The rules felt different.

The girl grabbed my wrist and dragged me toward an alley.

We ran past houses that looked like my neighborhood but not—different mailboxes, different porch lights, different graffiti tags.

My lungs burned.

Behind us, the anchors followed—still walking, still steady, like they didn't need to hurry because time belonged to them.

The faceless thing glided after them, faster than it should've been without moving its legs much.

We hit the alley.

The girl stopped, slammed her palm against the brick wall.

Symbols flared across the bricks—faint, gold, like someone drew them in light.

A door outline appeared.

"Go," she barked.

"A door?" I panted. "You're making doors now?"

She shoved me toward it. "It's not a door. It's a cut. Go."

I hesitated for half a second, because stepping into glowing brick-door magic is not on my normal checklist.

Then the faceless thing entered the alley behind us, and the air tasted like metal and panic.

So I stepped forward.

36

The brick wall turned soft.

Not squishy.

More like... the concept of "solid" got politely moved out of the way.

I fell through.

For a heartbeat, there was nothing.

No up. No down.

Just pressure and darkness and the feeling of a thousand radio stations whispering your name.

Then I hit a floor.

Hard.

Wooden boards. Dust. Old air.

I rolled, coughing.

The girl dropped through after me, landing on her feet like she'd done this a hundred times.

The glowing door seam in the wall zipped shut behind her.

Silence slammed down.

No anchors. No faceless thing. No scanning pressure.

Just... a room.

An old storage space maybe. A place with stacked crates, hanging tarps, and a single dim lightbulb that flickered like it was nervous to exist.

I lay there, panting, staring at the ceiling.

"Okay," I said between breaths. "We are officially not in Kansas. Not that I was in Kansas. I was in—"

"Pittsburgh," she said, cutting me off.

I froze mid-breath.

I sat up.

My eyes narrowed.

"How do you know that?"

She stared back, unimpressed. "Because your file says it."

"My file?"

She held up her liquid-night phone.

On the screen, a profile card glowed like a hacked ID.

SUBJECT: LITTY
  ORIGIN: PRIME-LAYER
  STATUS: UNSTABLE
  RISK: HIGH
  NOTE: SKY-BLINK SURVIVOR

I stared at it like it was a death certificate.

"That's not real," I said. "That's… that's—"

"Welcome to the fracture," she said again, but this time she sounded less sarcastic and more… tired. "Reality has paperwork."

My mouth opened.

Nothing came out.

She crouched near me, her eyes sharp again, studying.

"You want to live?" she asked.

I blinked.

"What kind of question is that?"

"The only kind that matters," she said. "Because you're going to get hunted now. Not just here—in your world too."

I swallowed.

"By the watcher?"

"By worse," she said.

Then she leaned closer, voice low.

"The first blink opened you. The second blink tagged you."

I felt cold spread across my chest.

"Tagged... like a GPS?"

She shook her head. "Like prey."

I stared down at my hands, still trembling.

"What do I do?" I whispered, and I hated how small my voice sounded again.

She exhaled like she'd been carrying too much for too long.

"Rule two," she said. "You don't go back alone."

"Back?" I said. "To my world?"

She nodded. "If you try to go back solo, they'll be waiting. You need cover. You need a mask."

"A mask?" I repeated. "Like... metaphorically?"

She tilted her head and her galaxy-chain glinted.

40

"Like literally."

Before I could ask, she reached into her pocket and pulled out another coin.

This one had a different symbol on it—like an eye crossed out, or a star with a crack through it.

She tossed it to me.

I caught it.

The metal was warm.

It pulsed faintly, like a heartbeat.

"What is this?" I asked.

"A hush," she said. "It dulls your signal. Makes you less loud in the fracture."

I turned it over in my hand.

"So... I keep it on me?"

She nodded. "At all times. Sleep with it. Shower with it. Marry it if you want."

I snorted once despite myself.

Then my expression fell.

"But it didn't work before."

She frowned. "Because you didn't have it before."

I looked up.

"Who are you?" I asked again, more serious. "What's your name?"

She hesitated.

Just a flicker.

Then she said, "Nova."

I didn't know if it was her real name. It sounded like a code name. A brand. A star.

But it fit her.

Nova sat back on her heels.

"Rule three," she said. "Never trust a stable world. Stability is how the fracture lies to you."

"That's not a rule," I said. "That's paranoia."

Nova's eyes hardened.

"No," she said. "That's experience."

The lightbulb flickered again, and for a second the room shimmered.

Like it tried to become a different room.

My stomach flipped.

Nova stood instantly, blade appearing in her hand like it was part of her.

"Hold the hush coin," she ordered.

I clutched it tight.

The warm pulse synchronized with my heartbeat.

The shimmer eased.

Nova's jaw tightened.

"They're searching," she said.

"Here?" I whispered.

She nodded.

"But... the door is closed," I said.

Nova's expression turned grim.

"Doors don't stop them," she said. "Only delays them."

The wooden boards beneath us creaked—not from weight.

From tension.

Like the building itself was bracing.

Nova looked at me.

"Listen," she said. "I didn't plan to babysit you. I have my own problems. But you're here now, and that makes you my problem too."

"I didn't ask—"

"I know," she snapped. Then she softened slightly. "But you're not useless. The watcher didn't blink at you twice for nothing."

I stared at her.

"What does that mean?"

Nova leaned closer, lowering her voice.

"It means there's something inside you," she said. "Something that can either seal the fracture... or tear it wide open."

My mouth went dry.

"No pressure."

She gave me a look like pressure was the only thing keeping the universe from falling apart.

Then she said, "We're going to find out which one you are."

And somewhere above us—far above, beyond wood and brick and reality—

The sky blinked again.

....

CHAPTER 3 — "THE WORLD DOESN'T RESET FOR YOU"

T he hush coin kept pulsing in my hand.

Not loud. Not dramatic.

Just enough to remind me I wasn't dreaming.

Nova stood near the far wall, blade gone now, arms crossed like she was trying to hold the room together by attitude alone. The storage space smelled like dust, old paint, and something electric underneath it all—like the air remembered storms.

I sat up slowly.

My head felt full.

Not in a headache way.

In a "my brain just met new physics and needs a minute" way.

"So," I said carefully, "I'm tagged. I'm loud. I'm prey. And the sky has personal beef with me."

Nova snorted. "Pretty much."

"That's insane."

"Yes."

"I want a refund."

"Join the club."

I rubbed my face with both hands.

When I lowered them, Nova was watching me like she expected something to happen.

"What?" I asked.

She shrugged. "Sometimes people crack by now."

"Give me a minute," I muttered. "I'm still buffering."

She almost smiled.

Almost.

I looked at the crates stacked around us.

"What is this place?"

47

"A hinge room," she said. "It exists between stable struc-tures. Old buildings are easier to hide in. Reality doesn't update them as often."

"...Reality updates buildings?"

"Sometimes," she said flatly.

I nodded like that made sense.

Silence stretched.

Then I asked the question I'd been avoiding.

"You said my second blink tagged me."

Nova's eyes sharpened.

"Yeah."

"I don't remember a second blink."

She tilted her head. "Exactly."

My stomach dropped.

She walked closer and crouched in front of me.

"When the sky blinks," she said, "most people see it. A flash. A distortion. Then their brains protect them by forgetting the impossible parts."

"And me?"

"You didn't forget," she said quietly. "You absorbed it."

I swallowed.

"So what happens now?"

Nova leaned back against a crate.

"Now your world isn't just your world anymore," she said. "You're standing in overlap territory. The fracture can reach you easier. And things inside it can reach out."

"Like the hallway thing," I whispered.

Her jaw tightened. "Yeah."

I stared at the floorboards.

"I thought I was losing my mind," I admitted.

"You weren't," she said. "You were waking up."

That didn't comfort me at all.

I looked at her again. "You said I shouldn't go back alone."

"You shouldn't."

"But I can't just stay here."

49

"No," she agreed. "You're not built for this layer yet."

"Yet?" I repeated.

Nova raised an eyebrow. "You planning on dying early?"

"Preferably not."

"Then yet."

I exhaled slowly.

"Okay," I said. "Then what's the plan, Nova-from-the-fracture?"

She considered me for a moment.

Then she said, "We stabilize you."

"That sounds medical."

"It's not," she said. "It's worse."

She reached into her hoodie again and pulled out a thin, flexible band that looked like metal pretending to be fabric. Symbols pulsed faintly along it.

"This goes around your wrist," she said. "It anchors your presence between layers."

I stared at it. "And if I don't wear it?"

"You'll start slipping," she said. "Dreams will feel too real. Reality will feel too thin. You'll see things you shouldn't. Hear voices between thoughts. Lose track of time."

"...Oh."

She held it out.

I hesitated.

Then I remembered the hallway.

The faceless thing.

The static.

I took the band.

It was cool against my skin when I wrapped it around my wrist.

It tightened itself gently, like it recognized me.

The symbols dimmed.

The pressure in my head eased.

I blinked.

"...That helped."

Nova nodded. "Anchor confirmed."

I stared at my wrist. "I don't like that sentence."

"You'll get used to worse ones."

A distant hum rolled through the building.

Not loud.

Not close.

But present.

Nova stiffened.

"They're mapping again," she muttered.

"Who?" I asked.

"Watchers don't hunt alone."

Great.

She grabbed her bag from the corner and slung it over her shoulder.

"We move soon."

"Where?" I asked.

She looked at me.

"Back to your world."

My chest tightened. "Is it safe?"

"No," she said honestly. "But it's yours."

She walked to the wall where the hidden door had been.

"This time," she said, "we do it clean. Controlled."

She placed both palms against the bricks.

Symbols flared again—different this time. More stable.
More careful.

The wall softened.

Light spilled through the seam.

Not bright.

Normal.

Streetlight yellow.

My heart jumped.

"That's... my street," I whispered.

Nova glanced back at me.

"You ready?"

"No," I said immediately.

She smirked. "Good. Means you're thinking."

She stepped through first.

I followed.

The world folded.

Then unfolded.

I was back in my neighborhood.

Same houses.

Same street.

Same night.

But everything felt… thinner.

Like a sheet of glass sat between me and reality.

Nova stood beside me, blending in now. Her clothes looked normal. Her chain dim. Her phone looked like a phone.

To anyone else, she'd just be a girl standing too close.

I breathed in.

The air smelled like home.

I almost cried from relief.

Then I saw it.

Across the street.

At the end of the block.

A man stood under a streetlight.

He wasn't moving.

He wasn't looking at us.

But I knew.

I just knew.

Nova saw my expression.

"Don't stare," she whispered.

"Is that—"

"An anchor," she said. "Left behind to watch."

My chest tightened.

"So I'm not free."

She shook her head. "You're not owned. That's different."

I swallowed.

My house stood right there.

My door.

My porch.

My normal life pretending it hadn't shattered.

Nova leaned closer.

"Listen carefully," she said. "From now on, you live two lives."

"I didn't agree to that."

"You didn't agree to the sky blinking either."

Fair.

She straightened.

"I'll find you again," she said. "Soon."

"How?"

She tapped the hush coin in my pocket.

"When you dream too clearly."

Then she stepped backward.

And the space behind her... wasn't space.

It was absence.

She faded into it like she was stepping out of a reflection.

And she was gone.

I stood alone on my sidewalk.

My heart pounding.

My wristband warm.

My pocket humming.

Across the street, the anchor man finally moved.

He turned his head.

And for the first time—

He looked directly at me.

I felt something inside me answer.

Not fear.

Not curiosity.

Recognition.

I walked toward my house anyway.

Because rule one of survival, I realized too late—

The world doesn't reset for you.

It just waits.

....

CHAPTER 4 — "YOU DON'T OUTRUN A SIGNAL"

I didn't sleep.

I lay on my bed staring at the ceiling like it might blink too.

The hush coin was warm in my pocket. The wristband pulsed slow, steady, like it was counting for me. Every time I closed my eyes, I saw ripples. Every time I opened them, I expected the world to look... thinner.

It didn't.

That was the problem.

Morning came like it always did. Birds. Traffic. Somebody arguing on a phone outside. A trash truck clanging like it hated its job.

Reality acted normal.

And after everything I'd seen, that felt fake.

I finally sat up and checked my phone.

No messages. No warnings. No glowing cosmic notifications.

Just a cracked screen and low battery.

I exhaled.

"Okay," I muttered. "So maybe I'm still allowed to brush my teeth."

I walked to the bathroom.

The mirror looked back at me like it always had.

Same face. Same tired eyes.

But when I leaned closer...

For half a second, my reflection blinked a split-second after I did.

Not enough for anyone else to notice.

Enough for me.

I stepped back.

"Nope."

I turned away from the mirror and washed my face, pretending the water was normal and not a universal reset button.

When I left my room, the house was quiet. Too quiet. Not eerie quiet—just "everybody's asleep or gone" quiet.

I went to the kitchen.

The clock on the microwave read 9:11.

Of course it did.

I grabbed a bottle of water and leaned against the counter.

That's when I felt it.

The pressure.

Not inside my head this time.

Outside my skin.

Like the air was paying attention to me.

I froze.

The wristband tightened slightly.

The hush coin pulsed once.

Nova's voice echoed in my memory.

You're loud.

I walked slowly to the front window.

Carefully.

Like the world might jump.

Outside, the street looked normal.

But the man under the streetlight was gone.

In his place stood a different man.

Same height.

Same posture.

Different jacket.

Different face.

Same feeling.

Anchor.

I stepped back.

My phone buzzed in my hand.

Not a normal vibration.

A deliberate one.

I looked.

A message sat on my screen.

UNKNOWN CONTACT:
   You returned faster than expected.

My chest tightened.

I typed back before I could think better.

WHO IS THIS?

The response came instantly.

Someone who watches you try to pretend you're normal.

My fingers hovered.

I typed:

STOP.

Three dots appeared.

Then disappeared.

Then a new message came.

You think the fracture is behind you.
    It's not.

I swallowed.

Another message.

You brought part of it back.

I typed:

LEAVE ME ALONE.

The typing dots returned.

Then a pause.

Then:

We can't.

My phone went black.

Not off.

Black.

The reflection in the screen wasn't my face.

It was the sky.

Blinking.

I dropped the phone.

It hit the floor with a dull thud and the screen returned to normal.

I stared at it, heart racing.

Then the doorbell rang.

I jumped so hard I almost kicked the fridge.

I stood frozen.

The doorbell rang again.

Slow.

Polite.

Like whoever was outside had time.

I checked the window again.

The anchor man was still there.

But he wasn't looking at me anymore.

He was looking at my door.

I backed away.

The doorbell rang a third time.

"Litty," a voice called through the door.

My blood went cold.

It wasn't Nova.

It wasn't anyone I recognized.

But it said my name like it had known me longer than I'd known myself.

I didn't answer.

The voice continued, calm and friendly.

"We're not here to hurt you."

Lies always sound nice.

"We just want to talk."

I stayed silent.

The wristband pulsed faster.

The hush coin heated.

The air thickened.

I heard something shift behind the walls.

Like the house was remembering it wasn't just wood.

"Litty," the voice said again. "You don't belong in only one layer anymore."

I finally spoke, my voice low.

"Go away."

A pause.

Then:

"You already invited us when you survived the second blink."

My heart pounded.

"What do you want?" I asked.

Silence.

Then the voice softened.

"We want what's waking up inside you."

My door handle turned slightly.

Not opening.

Testing.

I backed away into the hallway.

"Don't," I warned.

The voice laughed.

Not mean.

Not loud.

Just... amused.

"You still think doors are boundaries."

The walls shimmered.

Not visibly.

I felt it.

I turned and ran.

Up the stairs.

Into my room.

I slammed the door behind me, locking it even though I knew better now.

My window shimmered faintly.

Not enough to open.

Enough to promise it could.

My phone buzzed again on the floor below.

I ignored it.

My ceiling rippled.

My bedframe creaked.

Then my closet door slid open slowly.

I didn't scream.

I didn't move.

A shadow stretched out from inside the closet.

Not connected to anything.

Just a shadow.

It crawled along the floor like spilled ink.

I backed into the corner.

My wristband pulsed hot.

The hush coin burned.

And something inside me—

Something I didn't know I had—

Answered back.

The shadow stopped.

It hesitated.

Then recoiled.

Like it felt me.

The air around me vibrated.

My chest tightened.

My heartbeat slowed.

Not from calm.

From alignment.

I whispered without realizing it:

"No."

The shadow folded inward.

Not destroyed.

Dismissed.

It pulled back into the closet like it had been embarrassed.

The closet door shut.

Hard.

The room went still.

My breathing shook.

I slid down the wall, sitting on the floor.

"What am I?" I whispered.

My phone buzzed again downstairs.

I stood slowly and walked down.

Picked it up.

A message waited.

UNKNOWN CONTACT:
   Now you understand.

I typed back with trembling fingers.

UNDERSTAND WHAT?

The response took longer.

Then finally:

You don't just survive fractures.

You enforce them.

I stared at the words.

My reflection in the phone screen didn't blink late this time.

It blinked with me.

Perfectly.

And for the first time since the sky blinked...

I felt something inside me smile.

END CHAPTER 4
   ....

CHAPTER 5 — "NOVA NEVER LEAVES CLEANLY"

I knew Nova wasn't really gone.

People like her don't vanish. They reposition.

I locked my door, sat on my bed, and stared at the hush coin resting in my palm. It pulsed once—soft, warm—like it was breathing.

The house was quiet again. Too normal.

I hated that.

Normal felt like camouflage now.

I checked my wristband. The symbols were dim, but alive. Not glowing. Waiting.

I whispered, "You still there?"

No answer.

But the air shifted.

Not dramatic. Not cinematic.

Just... heavier. Like a thought had weight.

Then my closet door creaked.

I froze.

Slowly, the door slid open again.

But this time, there was no shadow.

Just Nova.

She stepped out like my closet was a hallway she'd been using for years.

"Okay," I said flatly. "So closets aren't real anymore."

She smirked. "They are. Yours just has bad boundaries."

My heart finally caught up with itself.

"You scared the hell out of me."

"You were supposed to be scared," she said. "Means the anchor still works."

She shut the closet door behind her and leaned against it

like this was normal.

"You left."

"I tested distance."

"You didn't say goodbye."

"I don't do emotional transitions," she replied.

I shook my head. "You're impossible."

She tilted her head. "You jumped into a fractured layer because your hallway tried to eat you. Don't judge my social skills."

Fair.

She walked closer, studying me.

"You stabilized fast," she said.

"I almost lost my mind twice."

"Still counts."

She reached out and touched the wristband.

The symbols brightened slightly.

"You're syncing," she said quietly.

"With what?"

"With yourself."

I stared at her.

"That sounds like something people say before something terrible happens."

She didn't deny it.

Instead, she sat on the edge of my bed like she owned the lease.

"Litty," she said. "You need to understand something now."

I swallowed.

"When you rejected the shadow in the closet, you didn't push it away with fear."

"So?"

"You commanded it."

My stomach flipped.

"I didn't—"

"You didn't speak," she interrupted. "You enforced."

Silence stretched.

I looked down at my hands.

They looked normal.

That scared me more than anything else.

Nova continued, "Most people react to the fracture. You... respond to it."

"I don't want that."

She sighed. "Nobody ever does."

She stood and walked to my window, peeking through the blinds.

"The anchors are rotating," she muttered. "They're con-fused."

"Why?"

"Because you're not acting like prey."

She turned back to me.

"You're acting like a variable."

I frowned. "That's not comforting."

"It's powerful."

I exhaled slowly.

"So what am I supposed to do now? Just live my life and pretend the sky didn't blink twice?"

Nova smiled softly.

"No," she said. "You learn."

She reached into her pocket and pulled out another object.

This one looked like a thin ring made of shifting metal. It didn't reflect light correctly.

"What is that?"

"A key," she said. "Not to a door. To perspective."

She placed it in my hand.

The moment my skin touched it—

I saw.

Not visions.

Not images.

Possibilities.

Thousands of versions of the same moment layered on top of each other like transparent slides.

I gasped and dropped it.

The world snapped back.

I stumbled onto the bed, dizzy.

Nova caught my shoulder.

"Too much," she said softly.

"What the hell was that?"

She met my eyes.

"That's what the Architects see."

My breath caught.

"You said they were real."

"They are," she replied. "And now... they're curious about you."

I laughed weakly.

"Why me?"

Nova didn't answer right away.

Then she said, "Because you weren't chosen."

I blinked.

"They don't like unpredictability," she continued. "They prefer design. You weren't designed."

"So I'm a glitch?"

She smiled.

"You're a rebellion."

The air vibrated faintly.

Not danger.

Not yet.

But awareness.

Nova looked up.

"They felt that."

I swallowed. "Felt what?"

She pointed at my chest.

"That."

My heartbeat echoed in my ears.

"Rule four," she said quietly. "Never believe you're small just because you started normal."

I stared at her.

"And rule five?"

She smiled—real this time.

"You don't walk this alone anymore."

Outside, the anchor across the street slowly turned away.

Not because it lost interest.

Because something else had become more important.

And far above us—

The sky did not blink.

It watched.

END CHAPTER 5

....

CHAPTER 6 — "THE ARCHITECTS DON'T MISS"

N ova disappeared again.

Not dramatically.

Not with sparks or portals.

Just... not there anymore.

One second she was leaning against my wall like she owned the lease on reality, the next second the air forgot her shape.

I stood there for a long moment, listening to my own breathing.

Then I checked the room.

Normal.

Too normal.

I hated that word now.

I sat on my bed and stared at my hands.

They still looked like hands.

No glowing. No cracks. No cosmic tattoos. No chosen-one upgrades.

Which somehow made everything worse.

Because whatever I was becoming wasn't cosmetic.

It was structural.

My phone buzzed.

I didn't jump this time.

Progress.

I picked it up.

UNKNOWN CONTACT:
  They noticed your rejection.

I typed back immediately.

WHO?

Three dots.

Then:

The Architects.

My chest tightened.

Nova's voice echoed in my head.

Reality is a server. Someone has admin access.

I typed:

WHAT DO THEY WANT?

The reply came slower this time, like it was being considered.

You.

I swallowed.

WHY?

Because you're not following your probability lane.

I frowned.

PROBABILITY LANE?

A new message.

Every human moves along weighted paths.
    Choices feel free.
    But outcomes are guided.

I stared at the screen.

That felt... too real.

I typed:

AND ME?

You diverge.

I looked up at my ceiling.

I could almost feel lines stretching out from me in every direction.

Different futures.

Different versions.

All trying to pull.

Another message appeared.

You are a fracture point.

My phone vibrated again.

We do not allow uncontrolled fracture points.

My jaw clenched.

SO WHAT, YOU DELETE ME?

A pause.

Then:

We correct you.

The word made my skin crawl.

I typed back:

I'M NOT BROKEN.

Another pause.

Longer.

Then:

You will be.

The lights in my room flickered.

Not power flicker.

Reality flicker.

My walls shimmered faintly, like someone turned down their resolution for a second.

I stood up.

My wristband tightened.

The hush coin warmed.

My heart didn't race.

It steadied.

I typed one more thing.

TRY ME.

The phone went black.

Not off.

Black.

Then a ripple passed through my room.

Not like wind.

Like memory being edited.

I felt pressure in my skull.

Not pain.

Alignment.

Then the air in front of me folded.

And three figures appeared.

They didn't step in.

They *resolved*.

Like a video buffering into clarity.

Tall.

Humanoid.

Smooth surfaces where faces should be.

Their bodies were made of layered transparency—like multiple realities stacked into one shape.

They radiated authority without emotion.

Without cruelty.

Without mercy.

The middle one tilted its head.

Its voice did not use sound.

It used certainty.

LITTY.

I felt the name inside my bones.

You are outside your allowed outcome.

I swallowed.

"I don't care," I said out loud.

That surprised even me.

The figure's form shimmered.

CARE IS NOT REQUIRED.

Another one stepped forward.

You will be returned to compliance.

My fists clenched.

"With what?" I asked. "A reset? A memory wipe? A personality patch?"

The third one moved.

You will be optimized.

My stomach twisted.

I felt something rise in me.

Not anger.

Not fear.

Recognition.

Like my bones remembered a rule the universe forgot.

I whispered, "No."

The word didn't echo.

It *pushed*.

The air bent outward from my chest.

The Architects paused.

Not stunned.

Not confused.

But... recalculating.

IMPOSSIBLE.

I stepped forward.

"You don't own choice," I said. "You just manage fear."

Their forms shimmered harder.

This entity is developing outside approved parameters.

I felt heat in my wrists.

The band glowed faintly.

My pocket pulsed.

My heartbeat synchronized with the hum in the room.

"You built lanes," I continued. "But you forgot one thing."

Their voices layered together.

SPEAK.

I lifted my eyes.

"You forgot people learn how to walk off roads."

The middle Architect raised its arm.

Reality tightened.

I felt gravity lean in.

Time thicken.

Then something inside me snapped into place.

Not violently.

Correctly.

I raised my hand.

Not like I knew what I was doing.

Like I remembered.

The air folded around my palm.

Not torn.

Not broken.

Rewritten.

The pressure released.

The Architects recoiled.

Not in pain.

In denial.

This cannot be occurring.

I smiled.

Small.

Tired.

Certain.

"It is."

The room stabilized.

The flicker stopped.

The three figures faded—not destroyed, not defeated.

Withdrawn.

Before they vanished completely, the middle one spoke one last time.

You are no longer classified as human standard.

You are now—

Nova's voice cut through the room like a blade.

"—A problem."

She stepped out of thin air beside me.

The Architects disappeared completely.

Silence dropped.

I turned to her, breath shaking.

"They're real."

Nova nodded.

"Yeah."

"They want to correct me."

"Yeah."

I looked at my hands.

"I pushed them."

She smiled.

Not proud.

Not scared.

Relieved.

"Welcome to the war nobody remembers starting," she said.

My heart pounded.

"What am I now?"

Nova met my eyes.

"A fracture king," she said quietly.

"And they don't miss."

I swallowed.

Then I smirked.

"Good."

Because neither do I.

END CHAPTER 6

....

CHAPTER 7 — "THE FIRST TIMELINE BREAKS QUIETLY"

The Architects didn't come back right away.

That was the first sign something had changed.

Nova stood near my window, arms crossed, eyes scanning the street like she expected the world to glitch any second.

"They never retreat without rewriting something," she said.

"What did they rewrite?" I asked.

She didn't answer.

Instead, my phone buzzed.

Not with a message.

With a memory.

I blinked—

—and suddenly I was standing in my kitchen three weeks ago.

Same counter. Same microwave clock. Same bottle of water.

But this time, I wasn't alone.

Malik stood beside me.

Alive.

Laughing.

My chest slammed so hard I nearly fell.

"What—" I whispered.

The scene played like a recording.

Malik talking about something stupid. Me rolling my eyes. A joke I remembered making.

Except...

I didn't remember this version.

I remembered him leaving that night.

I remembered the other version.

I stumbled backward.

The kitchen dissolved.

I was back in my room, gasping.

Nova grabbed my shoulders.

"They touched your past," she said.

"They can do that?" I choked.

"They already did," she replied.

I shook my head. "No. That's not right. That's not how memory works."

Nova's voice hardened.

"Memory isn't storage anymore," she said. "It's access."

My phone vibrated again.

Another memory slammed into me.

This time I was standing at Malik's funeral.

Except the casket was open.

And empty.

People were whispering.

Confused.

The mural on 7th Street showed a different face.

Not Malik.

Someone else.

Someone I didn't recognize.

I dropped to my knees.

Nova caught me.

"They're trying to replace outcomes," she said.

"Why?" I asked, barely breathing.

"Because if they can't delete you," she replied, "they'll rewrite the reason you exist."

I squeezed my eyes shut.

When I opened them, tears blurred everything.

"They're stealing him," I whispered.

Nova knelt in front of me.

"They're trying to," she said gently. "But you still remember him. That means the timeline isn't fully overwritten."

I swallowed hard.

"What do I do?"

Nova held my face so I had to look at her.

"You anchor him," she said. "You remember him harder than they can forget him."

"That's not a power," I said. "That's grief."

She shook her head.

"In the fracture, grief is gravity."

My phone buzzed again.

This time, it wasn't a memory.

It was a notification.

TIMELINE ADJUSTMENT COMPLETE.

I screamed.

The room shook.

Not violently.

Subtly.

Like a building settling after an earthquake.

Nova stood instantly, blade forming in her hand.

"No," she whispered. "Too fast."

I felt something tear inside my chest.

Not physical.

Relational.

Like a cord snapped between moments.

I looked at my wall.

The photo of Malik I had taped there—

Was gone.

Just clean wall.

Tape marks still there.

But no photo.

My throat closed.

"They took him," I whispered.

Nova looked at me.

"They can't fully," she said. "Not while you're still remembering."

I stared at my empty wall.

Then something happened.

I felt Malik.

Not memory.

Not imagination.

Presence.

A pressure behind my heart.

A warmth in my chest.

A voice that wasn't sound.

Kai...

I gasped.

Nova froze.

"You heard that," she said.

I nodded.

My hands trembled.

"He's not gone," she whispered.

"He's between," I said.

I stood up slowly.

The air around me tightened.

Not hostile.

Focused.

The wristband flared brighter.

The hush coin burned.

My phone screen cracked down the middle.

Not shattered.

Split.

Two identical screens showed two different versions of my room.

One with the photo.

One without.

I looked at Nova.

"They didn't delete him," I said.

"They displaced him."

Nova smiled.

Not happy.

Proud.

"You're learning."

I raised my hand.

The air bent.

Not aggressively.

Deliberately.

The two screens began to merge.

The wall shimmered.

The photo faded back into existence.

My knees buckled.

I laughed and cried at the same time.

Nova exhaled.

"You just repaired a micro-timeline breach," she said.

I stared at my hand.

"That's... insane."

She nodded.

"And they felt it."

The sky outside flickered once.

Not a blink.

A flinch.

Nova looked up.

"They just realized," she whispered.

"Realized what?" I asked.

She met my eyes.

"That you don't just survive fractures."

"You fix them."

I swallowed.

"What does that make me?"

Nova smiled slowly.

"A threat."

Outside, somewhere far beyond clouds and stars and probability lanes—

The Architects updated their classification.

SUBJECT LITTY
   STATUS: CONTAINMENT PRIORITY

And for the first time since the universe learned fear...

It aimed it at me.

END CHAPTER 7

....

CHAPTER 8 — "THE FRACTURE FIGHTS BACK"

The sky didn't blink.

It pulsed.

Once.

Low.

Like a heartbeat you only notice when it's about to stop.

Nova stood beside me, eyes lifted just enough to read the movement without meeting it directly.

"They're not observing anymore," she said.

I swallowed. "They're preparing."

She nodded.

My wristband tightened. The hush coin burned like it

wanted out of my pocket.

The air over the street bent—subtle, but undeniable—like heat over asphalt. Windows along the block shimmered. Reflections delayed themselves by fractions of a second.

The fracture wasn't opening.

It was *pressing through.*

People stepped outside their houses one by one. Not all of them. Just enough.

Not panicked.

Not confused.

Empty.

Their movements were synchronized but not robotic— more like they were following a rhythm they couldn't hear anymore.

Nova whispered, "They're using your layer to stabilize the breach."

"Through people?" I asked.

"Through belief," she replied. "Through memory. Through identity."

A woman across the street turned and looked straight at me.

Her eyes weren't blank.

They were *edited.*

Like someone had rewritten what her fear was allowed to recognize.

She smiled.

That broke me more than if she'd screamed.

I stepped back.

"No," I whispered.

Nova grabbed my arm.

"You don't get to look away," she said firmly. "This is where fracture kings are forged."

"I didn't ask for that title."

"None of us ask for power," she replied. "We survive into it."

The woman began walking toward us.

Not fast.

Not slow.

Perfectly paced.

Behind her, others followed.

Not zombies.

Not monsters.

People.

Normal people whose realities had been gently hijacked.

I shook my head.

"They're not enemies."

Nova's jaw tightened. "No. They're collateral."

The air thickened.

I felt the fracture breathing through them.

I felt the Architects' pressure again—distant, calculating, patient.

This wasn't an attack.

It was a demonstration.

The woman stopped five feet away.

Her smile widened unnaturally.

"You're not supposed to be here," she said calmly.

Her voice layered—hers and something behind it.

I felt the hush coin vibrate violently.

"You're not supposed to exist unindexed."

Nova stepped forward.

"She doesn't belong to you."

The woman tilted her head.

"You misunderstand," she replied. "He belongs to causal-
ity."

I felt something inside me snap again.

Not rage.

Not pain.

Resolve.

I looked into the woman's eyes.

"I belong to choice."

Her pupils dilated.

The fracture rippled outward.

The people behind her froze mid-step.

The street bent—not physically—but relationally. Like the meaning of distance changed.

Nova whispered, "Do it."

"Do what?"

"Rewrite the rule."

I exhaled.

I didn't push.

I didn't command.

I remembered.

I remembered Malik.

I remembered grief.

I remembered my hallway.

I remembered the sky blinking.

I remembered fear turning into refusal.

I spoke quietly.

"No one here is yours."

The fracture responded.

The woman gasped—not in pain—but in release.

Her smile vanished.

Her eyes flooded with confusion.

Tears welled.

"I—I don't know why I was walking," she whispered.

The others behind her blinked.

Reality resumed.

The ripple collapsed inward.

The street returned to its original shape.

Nova let out a shaky breath.

"You just severed a mass anchor," she said in awe.

I felt weak.

But alive.

The pressure retreated.

The Architects didn't.

They simply adjusted.

A voice rolled through the sky—not sound, but intention.

SUBJECT CONFIRMED: FRACTURE AUTHORITY.

Nova looked up.

"They've upgraded you."

"That doesn't sound good."

"It never is," she said softly.

The sky darkened—not night, but depth.

Stars shimmered through daylight.

The fracture began to widen above us.

Nova grabbed my hand.

"You ready to stop reacting?"

I looked up.

At the universe watching itself lose control.

"No," I said.

Then I squeezed her hand.

"But I'm ready to lead."

The fracture pulsed.

And for the first time...

It didn't resist me.

END CHAPTER 8

....

CHAPTER 9 — "INSIDE THE FRACTURE, AWAKE"

The fracture didn't open.

It invited me.

Not with light. Not with noise.

With understanding.

The space above the street softened, like the universe loosened its grip on itself. Stars bled through daylight. Colors lost their loyalty to objects. Gravity felt... optional.

Nova stepped closer to me.

"This time," she said quietly, "you're not falling in."

"I'm walking," I replied.

She searched my face.

Then nodded.

The fracture widened.

Not like a hole.

Like a thought deciding to become real.

I stepped forward.

And the world... let me.

The moment I crossed, sound dropped out first. Then heat. Then weight. Then time stopped pretending it was linear.

I wasn't floating.

I wasn't falling.

I was *present*.

Around me stretched a city that had never been built.

Structures shaped like ideas. Bridges made of light and shadow. Towers that existed only when you believed in their purpose. Rivers that flowed upward, carrying reflections instead of water.

People moved through it — not walking, not flying — transitioning between positions like pages turning.

Some looked human.

Some looked like possibilities.

All of them felt aware.

Nova stepped in behind me.

Her voice sounded layered now, like it came from multiple directions at once.

"Welcome to the fracture awake."

I swallowed.

"This is real."

She smiled faintly. "This is what reality looks like when it's honest."

I looked down at my hands.

They weren't glowing.

They weren't altered.

They were *clear* — sharper, more defined, like my existence had been rendered at higher resolution.

My heartbeat echoed through the space like it mattered.

Something inside me settled.

Not excitement.

Not fear.

Belonging.

A ripple passed through the fracture.

Entities turned toward me.

Not hostile.

Not welcoming.

Assessing.

Nova leaned close.

"They feel you," she whispered. "You're not hidden here."

"I don't want to hide," I said.

She studied me.

Then nodded once.

We walked.

Each step rewrote the space beneath us. Not destructively

— creatively. Like reality preferred my weight.

We passed a group of fractured beings clustered around a floating structure made of memory-light. They paused when they saw me.

One of them stepped forward.

It looked human until it didn't.

Eyes too deep.

Skin too smooth.

Voice layered like Nova's.

"You are the divergence," it said.

I met its gaze.

"I'm the choice," I replied.

The being tilted its head.

"Then you will break us."

I shook my head.

"No," I said. "I'll free you."

It studied me.

Then stepped aside.

Nova exhaled slowly.

"You don't realize what you just did."

"I talked," I said.

She smiled.

"You redefined authority."

We reached the center.

A massive structure hovered there — not a building, not a machine — a *convergence*. All timelines passed near it. All outcomes whispered through it.

And at its core...

A light.

Not bright.

Certain.

Nova stopped.

"This is as far as I go."

I turned.

"Why?"

"Because you're not following me anymore," she said. "I'm following you."

I stared at the convergence.

"What happens if I touch it?"

She answered honestly.

"You stop being only human."

I stepped forward.

The fracture held its breath.

I placed my hand against the light.

And everything I had ever been...

Everything I could become...

Everything the Architects tried to restrict...

Aligned.

Not into power.

Into clarity.

I saw the probability lanes.

I saw the corrections.

I saw the erased lives.

I saw Malik — not dead, not alive — but preserved in possibility.

I saw Nova's past.

I saw the Architects' fear.

And I saw myself…

Not as a king.

Not as a god.

As a bridge.

The light accepted me.

The fracture stabilized.

The universe exhaled.

Nova whispered behind me:

"He's awake."

And somewhere beyond all layers...

The Architects realized they were no longer designing the future.

They were negotiating with it.

END CHAPTER 9

....

CHAPTER 10 — "THE ARCHITECTS HIT WITH PAPERWORK... THEN WITH FIRE"

T he first thing I learned about being "awake" in the fracture is this:

Nothing dramatic happens when you expect it.
Everything dramatic happens when you finally breathe.

I pulled my hand away from the convergence-light and expected—I don't know—sparks, a halo, a glowing tattoo that says "CONGRATS, YOU'RE SPECIAL," maybe a choir of invisible angels doing background vocals.

Instead, the fracture got... quiet.

Not peaceful quiet.

Administrative quiet.

Like the universe had just opened a spreadsheet and started

sorting your life into columns.

Nova's silhouette sharpened behind me. In the fracture, she looked more like herself—less "girl in a hoodie," more "storm with a pulse." The galaxy chain around her neck wasn't just jewelry here. It was an orbit.

"You did it," she said.

I stared at my hands again. They were still mine. Same scars, same fingernails, same "I've carried groceries up three flights of stairs" palms.

"I touched the giant cosmic lightbulb," I said. "If I didn't do it, I at least offended something."

Nova huffed a laugh. "You definitely offended something."

The fracture around us shifted, and I realized we weren't alone anymore.

Not "there are monsters in the shadows" alone.

More like "the crowd just realized you're on stage" alone.

Entities drifted closer—fractured beings, half-human shapes, probability silhouettes. Some looked like people with slightly wrong edges. Some looked like statues that forgot to be solid. Some looked like options—like if you chose a different life, you'd be standing where they were.

They didn't speak.

They watched.

And when they watched, it felt like they were reading.

Not my face.

My trajectory.

Nova leaned in. "Don't flinch."

"I'm not flinching," I whispered.

My knee jerked anyway because the convergence behind me pulsed once, low, like it had a heartbeat now—and I felt it answer inside my ribs.

Nova's eyes narrowed. "Okay. That's new."

"What's new?"

"That it answered you back."

I swallowed. "Is that... good?"

Nova's expression said the same thing her mouth didn't.

Nothing is good. Everything is useful.

The fracture's air thickened again. The quiet spreadsheet

vibe escalated into something else.

A presence slid into the space, and everything that wasn't stable stepped aside like it knew its place.

Then the Architects arrived.

Not the three I'd faced in my room.

These were different.

More refined.

More... official.

They formed without moving—appeared as if the fracture itself was forced to accommodate them.

Their shapes were clean and symmetrical, like they'd been designed by someone who hated imperfections. Their "faces" weren't blank this time. They had surfaces— smooth planes that reflected the fracture city in fragments, like broken mirrors trying to assemble a picture.

And their voices didn't feel like static.

Their voices felt like law.

SUBJECT LITTY: FRACTURE AUTHORITY DETECTED.

Nova's blade snapped into her hand with a quick fold of

reality.

I held my hands out slightly—less "hands up," more "I'm not trying to start something, but I will finish it."

An Architect stepped forward. The fracture dimmed, like it didn't want to be caught choosing sides.

You have interfaced with restricted convergence.

Nova spat. "He touched it. He didn't steal it."

The Architect didn't look at her. That told me everything.

NOVA: OUTCOME-REDIRECTOR. SECONDARY PRIORITY.

Nova's jaw clenched. "Cute label."

My heart steadied. The convergence behind us pulsed again. A thin ripple expanded outward like the fracture was breathing in and out through me.

I said, "If you came to arrest me, at least explain the charges."

The Architect tilted its head.

Humor: irrelevant.

"Yeah," I said. "Everybody says that until the jokes win."

Nova shot me a look like, "Now is not the time," but she didn't stop me.

The Architect's voice layered into something sharper.

You are not indexed. You are not compliant. You are not within acceptable probability.

I shrugged. "And yet... here I am."

For a fraction of a second, I felt something like irritation from it.

Then it did the worst thing possible.

It stopped trying to scare me.

It started trying to convince me.

Correction offer initiated.

A panel of light unfolded in the air between us—clean, elegant, impossible. It looked like a floating menu, the kind you'd see in a sci-fi movie right before someone makes a bad deal.

OPTIONS PRESENTED:
   1) MEMORY REALIGNMENT
   2) LANE REASSIGNMENT
   3) IDENTITY REBINDING
   4) CONTAINMENT (NONLETHAL)

5) ERASURE (ABSOLUTE)

I stared at it.

Nova hissed. "They're negotiating."

"They call this negotiating?" I said. "This is a hostage menu."

The Architect spoke, calm.

Select correction. Preserve your existence.

My pulse thumped.

The fracture beings around us leaned in. Even the air felt like it was waiting to see if I'd fold.

I looked at Nova. "What happens if I pick one?"

Her face tightened. "You become predictable."

"And if I don't pick?"

She exhaled. "Then they enforce."

I looked back at the menu.

Option five glowed faintly, like it was the default when you annoyed them.

I said, "What if I offer you a sixth option?"

The Architect paused.

Option six: cease.

"Not that," I said. "Option six: you back off."

The Architect's voice cooled.

You do not negotiate with your designers.

Nova muttered, "Told you."

I felt the convergence behind me pulse hard—like it didn't like that phrase.

Designers.

The word hit me weird.

Because it implied the universe was engineered, not grown.

And if it was engineered...

Then someone wrote the code.

And code can be changed.

I kept my voice steady. "You designed lanes. That's cute. But you didn't design me."

132

The menu flickered slightly.

Nova's eyes widened.

I felt it again—clarity.

Like the fracture wasn't giving me power; it was giving me access.

The Architect's head tilted.

You are a defect arising from rare convergence overlap.

I laughed once, sharp. "I'm a defect? That's your best insult?"

Nova whispered, "Litty..."

But it was too late.

I leaned forward and spoke like I was talking to the universe's customer support line.

"If you built a system where a human's choice is just a weighted path, then you're not protecting reality. You're controlling it."

The menu's text jittered.

The Architect's voice hardened.

Control is stability.

"Control is fear," I said. "Stability is earned."

The fracture beings shifted, like they'd never heard anyone say that out loud.

The Architect raised its arm.

Enforcement initiated.

The menu collapsed into a single symbol—an eye made of fractured lines.

The symbol shot toward me like a stamp.

Nova moved to intercept—

—but my wristband flared and the hush coin burned, and something in my chest answered faster than either of us could react.

The symbol hit an invisible barrier in front of me.

It didn't shatter.

It... stopped.

Hovered.

Confused.

Nova stared. "You blocked a correction stamp."

I stared too. "I didn't know I could do that."

The Architect's voice changed.

Containment required.

The fracture around us tightened like a fist closing.

Gravity increased. Air thickened. The space between my thoughts got narrower.

Then the Architects did something worse than trying to crush me.

They tried to rewrite me.

A pressure pushed into my mind—not like a headache, like a hand reaching into your memories and flipping through them.

I saw flashes—

Me on my block.
   Me in school.
   Me laughing.
   Me angry.
   Me alone.

Then I saw a version where I wasn't there.

135

Like my life had a missing file.

I gritted my teeth. "Get out of my head."

The pressure intensified.

Nova surged forward, blade flashing, but her strike cut the air and nothing happened—as if the Architects weren't "there" to be hit.

"They're operating from above-layer," she snapped. "Litty, you have to answer it from inside!"

"Inside WHAT?" I gasped.

Nova's eyes locked on mine.

"Inside your authority."

That phrase clicked something in me.

Authority.

Not power.

Permission.

I stopped trying to fight the pressure like it was a force.

I treated it like a policy.

Like a rule that could be refused.

I inhaled.

Then I said, calm and clear:

"Denied."

The word wasn't loud.

But it landed like a gavel.

The pressure paused.

For the first time, the Architects hesitated—not because they were scared, but because they weren't used to resistance that wasn't chaos.

Nova whispered, almost smiling, "Yeah. That's it."

I repeated it, stronger.

"Denied."

The pressure snapped back, like a hand touching a hot stove.

The fracture breathed again.

The air loosened.

The Architects' forms shimmered.

UNAUTHORIZED.

"Exactly," I said, voice steady now. "Uninvited. Unauthorized. Unwelcome."

Nova stood beside me, blade up.

"This is his lane now," she said.

The Architect replied:

This lane is not permitted.

I looked at the convergence behind me, felt it pulsing like a second heart.

Then I spoke the truth that had been forming since Book 1—since the first blink.

"Your permission doesn't matter if the universe recognizes me."

For a split-second, everything went still.

Then the convergence flared.

Not bright.

Clear.

A wave rolled outward, and the fracture city rippled, like it was syncing with my heartbeat.

The Architects reacted instantly, their shapes sharpening into something more dangerous.

They dropped the negotiation.

They chose violence.

Not explosions.

Not lasers.

They changed the rules.

All at once, the fracture beings around us froze.

Like time hit pause.

Nova froze too—mid-breath, mid-blink.

I tried to move—my arm felt heavy, like the air had turned to stone.

Only my eyes moved.

Only my thoughts moved.

The Architects stepped forward in the paused world like they owned time itself.

You have been granted a temporary anomaly window.

The voice slid into my mind like cold metal.

We will now demonstrate consequence.

The Architect raised its hand.

A new panel unfolded—this one not a menu.

A map.

My world.

My street.

My house.

And then—like someone pinched the screen—

The map zoomed out.

Beyond my block.

Beyond my city.

Beyond Earth.

I saw layers.

Stacked.

Like transparent sheets.

Some bright. Some dim. Some cracked.

And one layer—the one I came from—started to flicker.

Nova's voice, frozen, echoed in my head anyway, like her anchor was strong enough to leak.

Don't let them scare you into choices...

The Architect's voice overlapped hers.

Observe.

The flickering layer... shifted.

And I saw something horrifying.

A version of my world where the sky blink never happened.

Everything was "normal."

But in that version—

I wasn't there.

Not dead.

Not missing.

Just... never existed.

My stomach dropped.

The Architect spoke softly.

This is stability.

I wanted to scream, but the paused air trapped my voice in my chest.

The Architect continued.

You can have a stable world.
   Or you can have yourself.

My thoughts raced.

They were trying to corner me with guilt.

They were telling me my existence was the price of every-one else's peace.

Classic villain move.

But they weren't villains.

They were systems.

And systems always pretend they're doing harm "for the greater good."

The Architect leaned closer.

Select correction. We restore your baseline layer.

I forced my mind to slow down.

Then I focused on one thing:

Malik.

Not the edited Malik.

The real Malik.

The laughter. The chaos. The loyalty. The night on concrete.

If they could erase me, they could erase him too.

They could erase anything that didn't fit their spreadsheet.

And I realized something clear and ugly:

A stable world built on erasure is not a good world.

It's a cage.

So I answered them.

Not with sound.

With intent.

"No."

The word rippled outward.

The paused world cracked—hairline fractures in time itself.

Nova twitched.

Her blink completed.

The fracture beings jerked like marionettes whose strings were cut.

Time resumed.

The Architects recoiled a half-step.

Impossible, their voice hissed.

I stood fully now, breath steady, chest burning with clarity.

"Try again," I said. "And I'll break your stability into truth."

Nova's eyes flashed with pride and fear.

"Litty... you just broke a time-lock."

I didn't look away from the Architects.

"Good," I said.

Because if they wanted war?

They should've never brought paperwork.

The Architects' forms blurred—then sharpened into something colder, more aggressive.

Containment fails. Escalation authorized.

And then the fracture city screamed.

Not in sound.

In structure.

Buildings warped. Bridges bent. The sky inside the fracture split like glass.

A storm rolled in—not rain, not wind—

Probability.

Outcomes flying like debris.

Nova grabbed my shoulder.

"This is the direct strike," she shouted. "They're collapsing the fracture around you!"

I planted my feet.

The convergence behind me pulsed like a drum.

I felt a rule in my bones:

If the fracture collapses, everything in it gets shredded into timelines.

Including us.

Nova's blade flared. "We need to move—NOW!"

I looked at the Architects.

And I smiled.

Not because I was fearless.

Because I finally understood.

They didn't come here to kill me.

They came here to prove I could be controlled.

And the moment they failed...

They panicked.

I raised my hand.

Not as a weapon.

As a decision.

"Then we stabilize," I said.

Nova stared. "You can't stabilize a storm like this!"

I looked at the convergence.

Felt it.

Answered it.

"Yes," I said quietly.

"I can."

And the fracture—awake, honest, and terrified—

Waited to see if its new authority was real.

END CHAPTER 10

....

CHAPTER 11 — "THE DAY THE FRACTURE CHOSE"

T he storm didn't sound like thunder.

It sounded like decisions being torn apart.

Probability debris ripped through the fracture city like invisible shrapnel—outcomes collapsing, futures snapping, timelines shedding weight they could no longer carry. Buildings didn't fall. They *unremembered* themselves. Bridges didn't break. They forgot where they were supposed to connect.

Nova stood beside me, blade humming in her grip, hair floating slightly as gravity lost its commitment to direction.

"This is bad," she said.

I stared at the sky of the fracture—a layered mosaic of stars, light, and splitting mathematical seams.

"No," I said quietly.

"This is honest."

She looked at me sharply.

"You don't mean that poetically."

"No," I said. "I mean it structurally."

The convergence behind me pulsed harder. It wasn't just reacting to me anymore. It was listening.

The Architects hovered above the storm like surgeons over an open universe.

Their voices layered across the fracture, not yelling, not raging—

Correcting.

Reformatting.

Reasserting.

SUBJECT LITTY: AUTHORITY OVERRIDE ATTEMPT.

I stepped forward.

The fracture beings around us began to stir. They weren't frozen anymore. They were watching—some frightened, some hopeful, some defiant.

I realized something then:

They weren't watching me.

They were waiting for permission.

The Architects spoke again.

You are destabilizing the fracture.

I looked up.

"No," I said. "You are."

Their forms shimmered.

Stability requires hierarchy.

I felt Nova tense beside me.

I lifted my voice—not loud, but clear.

"Stability requires trust."

The storm intensified.

The Architects' silhouettes sharpened.

Trust is irrelevant.

I shook my head.

"Trust is the only thing that lasts when control fails."

For the first time...

They hesitated.

Not because they were wrong.

Because they couldn't calculate that answer.

Nova whispered, "They don't understand leadership. Only management."

I smiled slightly.

"Then let's introduce them."

I turned to the fracture city.

To the beings made of layered possibility.

To the structures shaped by belief.

To the people who had been edited, erased, and optimized.

And I spoke—not as a king.

Not as a god.

As someone who refused to disappear.

"This world doesn't belong to architects," I said.

"It belongs to those who live in it."

The fracture trembled.

Not violently.

In agreement.

The Architects' voices rose in urgency.

Unauthorized declaration. Unauthorized narrative shift.

I raised my hand—not to attack—but to open.

The fracture responded.

Light flowed from the convergence into the city like breath returning to lungs.

The storm slowed.

Outcomes stabilized.

Not by control.

By choice.

Nova stared at me.

"You're not stabilizing the fracture," she said.

"You're letting it stabilize itself."

I nodded.

The Architects descended closer.

This is not permitted.

"Neither was my existence," I replied.

The fracture beings began to step forward—one by one.

A woman made of layered glass.

A boy whose eyes held two timelines.

An elder whose shadow lagged behind him by seconds.

They stood with me.

Nova stepped forward too.

Blade lowered.

No threat.

Just presence.

The Architects spoke again, slower now.

Consensus anomaly detected.

"This isn't an anomaly," I said.

"It's democracy."

The word confused them.

They didn't have a file for it.

Nova smiled.

"You just weaponized community."

The fracture city pulsed with shared rhythm.

The storm collapsed inward.

Not destroyed.

Resolved.

The Architects' forms flickered.

Containment probability: decreasing.

They were losing.

Not because I was stronger.

Because I was no longer alone.

I looked at them.

"You built systems to prevent chaos," I said.

"But chaos is just life without permission."

The middle Architect spoke one last time.

If we withdraw... instability increases.

I answered softly.

"Only until people learn to carry it."

Silence.

Then...

The Architects began to fade.

Not in defeat.

In retreat.

Before they vanished completely, their voice echoed one final statement into the fracture.

SUBJECT LITTY: STATUS — UNCONTAINABLE.

The word echoed.

Uncontainable.

The fracture city erupted—not in noise—but in motion.

Beings embraced.

Structures realigned.

Timelines breathed.

Nova laughed—a real laugh, sharp and relieved.

"You just changed everything."

I looked around.

At a world that no longer felt broken.

"I just reminded it who it belonged to."

Nova stepped beside me.

"So what now, Fracture King?"

I shook my head.

"No crowns," I said. "No thrones."

I looked at the convergence one last time.

"We build something they can't predict."

Nova smiled.

"What's that?"

I met her eyes.

"A future."

The fracture city pulsed.

And somewhere in my original world…

The sky didn't blink.

It watched.

And for the first time…

It waited.

END CHAPTER 11

……………………

CHAPTER 12 — "THE HUMAN ERROR"

T he fracture did not collapse.

It *settled.*

Not into peace. Not into order.

Into awareness.

The city of layered reality around us breathed like a living thing that had just realized it was no longer owned. Structures reshaped themselves—not violently, but deliberately. The convergence dimmed slightly, no longer the only heartbeat in the system. It wasn't losing importance.

It was sharing it.

Nova stood beside me, chest rising fast, blade still glowing faintly like it hadn't decided whether to rest.

"You just forced a governance shift," she said.

I swallowed. "I forced a conversation."

She shook her head. "You forced accountability."

That word felt heavier than any title.

Around us, the fracture beings slowly resumed motion. Not scripted. Not synchronized. Independent. Some watched me. Some avoided eye contact. Some stared like I was a symbol they didn't want but couldn't ignore.

And then the temperature dropped.

Not cold.

Intent.

Nova felt it too. Her posture changed instantly.

"They're not done," she said.

I exhaled. "I didn't expect them to be."

The air compressed like a held breath.

Then a ripple cut across the fracture city—not from above like the Architects usually moved—but from inside.

From the human layer.

From *my* world.

Nova's eyes widened.

"No," she whispered.

I followed her gaze.

A new figure resolved between us and the convergence.

Not layered.

Not abstract.

Not architected.

Human.

A man in a dark jacket, clean sneakers, short hair, calm eyes.

He looked like he belonged on a sidewalk, not in a reality fracture.

Which made him more terrifying than anything else I'd seen so far.

He looked at me like he already knew my story.

"Litty," he said warmly. "You finally stepped out of your lane."

Nova stepped forward, blade up. "You don't belong here."

160

The man smiled politely. "Neither did he. Until he did."

I felt the fracture react to him.

Not hostile.

Not welcoming.

Conflicted.

"Who are you?" I asked.

He placed his hands in his pockets.

"My name won't help you," he said. "My function will."

Nova hissed. "You're a liaison."

The man nodded. "Good catch."

I frowned. "Between who?"

"Between humans and the Architects," he said calmly. "Someone has to translate ambition into obedience."

My stomach tightened.

"So you work for them."

He tilted his head. "I work for stability."

Nova laughed bitterly. "Here we go."

The man looked at her. "You're Nova. Outcome redirector. Probability rebel. I've read your entire arc."

Her grip tightened.

"Back off."

He turned back to me.

"And you," he said gently, "are the human error."

The phrase hit harder than any insult so far.

"Error?" I repeated.

"Yes," he said. "Not a glitch. Not a bug. A full deviation. You weren't predicted. You weren't engineered. You weren't even statistically probable."

"Sounds like a compliment," I said.

"It is," he replied. "And that's the problem."

Nova stepped between us. "Say what you came to say."

The man nodded.

"The Architects can't erase you anymore," he said. "You've passed that threshold."

"Good," I replied.

"But they can still influence you," he continued. "And they can influence everyone around you."

He gestured to the fracture city.

"You don't lead a revolution by surviving," he said. "You lead it by choosing who gets hurt."

The fracture beings shifted uncomfortably.

I narrowed my eyes.

"What are you offering?"

The man smiled softly.

"A deal."

Nova swore.

I didn't break eye contact.

"Talk."

The man nodded.

"You stabilize the fracture," he said. "You teach people to carry instability. You let the Architects retain oversight— not control—oversight."

163

Nova barked, "No."

The man raised a finger.

"In exchange," he continued, "they stop direct interference in your world."

I felt my jaw tighten.

"And the cost?"

He finally looked serious.

"You stop escalating."

Silence fell.

Nova whispered, "That's a leash."

The man shrugged. "It's a compromise."

I shook my head slowly.

"You didn't come here to negotiate," I said.

"No," he admitted. "I came to measure you."

"And?"

He studied me.

"You're not reckless," he said. "You're not power-hungry. You're not broken."

I waited.

"You're dangerous because you care," he finished.

Nova smiled. "Yeah. That's his worst trait."

The man sighed.

"You think the fracture wants freedom," he said. "But freedom without preparation is collapse."

"Then teach," I replied.

"Humans don't learn fast enough," he said. "They repeat."

"So do systems," I said.

He looked surprised.

"People aren't spreadsheets," I continued. "You don't manage them into goodness."

He smiled sadly.

"That's exactly what they said when they built the Architects."

Nova's eyes widened.

"They were human?"

The man nodded.

"Originally."

That hit harder than anything so far.

"You created them," I whispered.

"We created a solution," he corrected. "Then we lost authority over it."

Nova shook her head slowly. "So now you send humans to negotiate with your gods."

He met her eyes.

"We send humans to remind them what they were meant to protect."

I felt the fracture pulse.

The convergence dimmed further.

"You're scared," I said.

He smiled faintly.

"Yes."

The honesty shocked me more than any threat.

"You're scared of me," I added.

He nodded once.

"Not of your power," he said. "Of your influence."

Nova looked between us.

"He's right," she said quietly. "You're not just changing rules. You're changing how people think they're allowed to think."

I looked at the fracture beings.

At the layered humans.

At the convergence.

At Nova.

At the man.

"At the Architects.

And I realized something terrifying.

This wasn't a war of weapons.

It was a war of permission.

I turned back to the man.

"What happens if I refuse your deal?"

He exhaled.

"They will escalate quietly," he said. "Through governments. Through systems. Through incentives. Through
fear."

"And if I accept?"

"They will watch you like a prototype."

Nova spat. "So he's either hunted or studied."

The man nodded.

"Yes."

I laughed once.

"That's the worst sales pitch I've ever heard."

He smiled sadly. "I didn't expect you to accept."

I stepped closer to him.

"Tell the Architects something for me."

He raised his eyebrows.

"Tell them the fracture doesn't need managers," I said. "It needs witnesses."

He studied my face.

Then nodded.

"They won't like that."

"I'm not here to be liked," I replied.

He took a step back.

"You've already changed the trajectory," he said. "Whether you lead it or not."

Nova looked at me.

"You're going to reject the deal," she said.

I nodded.

"Yeah."

The man sighed.

"I hoped you would."

"Why?" I asked.

"Because if you accepted," he said quietly, "you'd be safe."

"And if I don't?"

"You become inevitable."

He stepped backward.

The fracture air wrapped around him.

Before he vanished, he said one final thing:

"You will be blamed for every future fracture."

I answered calmly.

"Good."

And he was gone.

The fracture city exhaled.

Nova turned to me.

"You just refused the only human bridge left between systems."

I met her eyes.

"No," I said. "I became it."

The convergence pulsed again.

The fracture beings stepped closer.

Not to worship.

Not to follow blindly.

To listen.

Nova whispered, almost to herself:

"He's not a fracture king…"

I looked around at the living, breathing city of reality.

"…he's a fracture origin."

Above us, beyond layers and systems and permissions…

The Architects updated their internal model.

SUBJECT LITTY
    STATUS: CIVILIZATION-LEVEL VARIABLE

And for the first time…

They prepared not to control me.

But to survive me.

END CHAPTER 12

....

CHAPTER 13 — "THE FRACTURE BETRAYS FIRST"

The fracture did not shatter.

It hesitated.

That was worse.

After the human liaison vanished, the air around the convergence felt thinner—like the universe itself was holding its breath, unsure whether to exhale into war or collapse into compromise. The fracture city stood in layered silence, structures half-solid, bridges suspended between probabilities, beings drifting in uncertain alignment.

Nova stood beside me, blade resting low, shoulders tight.

"They just deployed a human negotiator," she said quietly. "That means the Architects are scared of optics."

"Optics?" I asked.

"Of being seen as monsters," she replied. "Which means they're about to do something monstrous in a way that looks reasonable."

I swallowed.

The convergence pulsed once, faintly.

The fracture beings were watching me again.

Not with awe.

Not with worship.

With expectation.

And expectation is heavier than fear.

I turned slowly, scanning them.

"You don't owe me loyalty," I said. "You don't owe me obedience. You don't owe me belief."

A ripple passed through the crowd.

"But you do owe yourselves truth," I continued. "If the Architects gave you stability by stealing your choices, then that wasn't stability. It was sedation."

A being made of overlapping silhouettes stepped forward.

"What happens when the fracture closes?" it asked.

I answered honestly.

"Then we build again. Not from permission. From memory."

Nova whispered, "You're turning into a speech guy."

I smirked. "Blame the apocalypse."

The fracture trembled lightly.

Not from danger.

From decision.

And that's when it happened.

A sound rolled through the city—not like thunder, not like alarms—like glass learning how to scream.

The sky of the fracture split in a thin vertical line.

Nova spun.

"No. That's not an Architect cut."

"What is it?" I asked.

Her voice went tight.

"That's a fracture-origin cut."

The vertical seam widened.

Not violently.

Deliberately.

Like someone opening a book they'd already read.

From the seam stepped a figure.

Not layered.

Not abstract.

Not architected.

Human.

A woman.

Short hair. Dark jacket. Calm eyes.

She looked like she could walk into any city on Earth and blend in perfectly.

Which meant she didn't belong anywhere.

Nova froze.

"Impossible…"

The woman smiled slightly.

"Hello, Nova."

Nova's blade rose instantly.

"Step back."

The woman lifted her hands gently.

"Relax. I'm not armed."

"That's worse," Nova snapped.

I looked between them.

"You know her."

Nova didn't answer.

Her jaw tightened.

The woman turned to me.

"You must be Litty," she said warmly. "You look… inconvenient."

"Appreciated," I replied. "Who are you?"

She studied me for a moment.

"Once," she said, "I was you."

Silence dropped.

Nova hissed, "Don't lie to him."

The woman's smile softened.

"I'm not lying. I'm warning him."

She turned back to me.

"My name is Aria."

The fracture reacted to her name.

Not violently.

Respectfully.

Nova whispered, "You're not supposed to exist anymore."

Aria nodded.

"I didn't."

My stomach tightened.

"You're a fracture origin," I said slowly.

She smiled.

"The first one they couldn't erase."

Nova shook her head. "You sided with them."

Aria's eyes flickered with something like regret.

"I sided with survival."

Nova laughed bitterly.

"You sold the fracture."

"I saved a version of it," Aria replied calmly.

I stepped forward.

"What did you do?"

Aria met my eyes.

"I accepted their deal."

My chest tightened.

Nova whispered, "I told you."

Aria continued.

"They offered me peace. Stability. A world without fracture

179

collapse."

"And?" I asked.

"And they kept their promise," she said. "For a while."

The fracture city trembled faintly.

Aria walked slowly around me, studying me.

"You're doing what I did," she said. "Refusing their authority. Awakening others. Destabilizing the system."

"So you're here to stop me," I said.

"No," she replied softly. "I'm here to show you what happens if you don't stop yourself."

She raised her hand.

The fracture city around us shifted.

Not violently.

Quietly.

The structures blurred.

The beings around us faded.

And suddenly...

We were standing in another fracture city.

Cleaner.

More stable.

More controlled.

No layered chaos.

No trembling probabilities.

Everything was smooth, symmetrical, calm.

And empty.

Nova inhaled sharply.

"No..."

Aria spoke.

"This is my fracture."

I looked around.

The buildings stood pristine.

The convergence floated silently.

But there were no people.

No beings.

No voices.

"No choice," I whispered.

Aria nodded.

"I gave them stability," she said. "They gave me a world that never breaks."

Nova whispered, "They sterilized it."

Aria's voice cracked slightly.

"They saved it."

I looked at her.

"They killed it."

Aria flinched.

The city around us shimmered.

"Do you know what it's like," she whispered, "to hold a perfect world that has no one left to disappoint you?"

Nova's voice softened.

"You're alone."

Aria smiled sadly.

"Yes."

I stepped closer.

"You're not warning me about failure," I said. "You're warning me about success."

Aria met my eyes.

"You're going to win," she said. "And when you do, they will offer you peace in exchange for silence."

Nova whispered, "And you took it."

Aria nodded once.

"And I have regretted it every second since."

The fracture world around us began to dissolve back into ours.

Aria lowered her hand.

"Don't repeat me," she said.

I swallowed.

"What happens if I refuse?"

Aria smiled.

"Then you become something they can't negotiate with."

Nova looked at me.

"That's what scares them."

Aria stepped closer.

"And that's what will destroy you," she whispered. "Or save everyone."

The fracture city returned fully.

The beings were watching again.

Aria looked at me with eyes full of history.

"They will try to make you like me," she said. "And when they fail... they will try to make you a symbol of disaster."

I nodded slowly.

"Let them."

Nova smiled slightly.

Aria's expression softened.

"You really are different," she said.

184

I shook my head.

"No. I'm just still human."

Aria laughed quietly.

"Then protect that."

She stepped backward.

The fracture opened behind her.

Before she vanished, she said one final thing:

"The Architects don't fear your power."

"They fear your mercy."

And she was gone.

The fracture city stood silent.

Nova exhaled shakily.

"That was the first fracture betrayal."

I nodded.

"And it won't be the last."

The convergence pulsed again.

The fracture beings stepped closer.

Not to follow blindly.

To choose.

I looked around at them.

At Nova.

At the city.

At myself.

And I understood something clear and terrifying:

This story was no longer about survival.

It was about what kind of future deserved to exist.

END CHAPTER 13

....

CHAPTER 14 — "THE ARCHITECTS STOP HIDING" (PART A)

T he fracture didn't explode.

It *organized*.

That was the first sign we were in real danger.

After Aria vanished and the convergence dimmed, the city of layered reality began aligning itself into clean geometry—streets straightening, structures synchronizing, light stabilizing into uniform gradients. It looked beautiful.

Too beautiful.

Nova noticed it immediately.

"They're beautifying the fracture," she said.

I frowned. "That sounds good."

She shook her head. "Nothing beautiful comes from systems preparing for control."

The fracture beings sensed it too. Their movements slowed. Their voices softened. Their edges sharpened into consistent forms. Chaos wasn't being erased violently.

It was being *tidied*.

I felt the convergence respond differently now—not like a heart, but like a processor.

I turned to Nova. "They're switching strategies."

She nodded grimly. "They're done with intimidation."

A ripple cut through the sky—not vertical, not horizontal—circular.

Like a lens opening.

And then the Architects arrived.

Not as individuals.

As a formation.

Sixteen of them resolved into the fracture city at once, arranged in perfect radial symmetry around the convergence. Their forms were clearer now—less abstract, more defined, like they were adapting their appearance to be understood.

Or obeyed.

Their voices layered into a single chorus.

SUBJECT LITTY: OBSERVATION MODE TERMINATED.

Nova stepped in front of me instinctively.

"Back off."

The chorus ignored her.

CONDITION: DIRECT GOVERNANCE INITIATED.

I felt the fracture tighten around my chest.

"You said you weren't controlling anymore," I said.

The chorus replied:

WE HAVE RECLASSIFIED CONTROL AS PROTECTION.

Nova laughed bitterly. "Classic."

The Architects began projecting images across the fracture sky.

Worlds.

Civilizations.

Cities thriving in symmetrical harmony.

No war.

No hunger.

No visible pain.

People smiling.

Families intact.

Children safe.

Perfect.

I felt something twist inside me.

"They're showing outcomes," Nova whispered. "Idealized ones."

The chorus spoke:

THIS IS THE FUTURE WITHOUT FRACTURE.

I stared at the sky.

"No grief."

"No loss."

"No rebellion."

I whispered, "No choice."

The chorus paused for the first time.

CHOICE IS NOT REQUIRED FOR HAPPINESS.

Nova hissed. "Say that to every human who ever lived."

The Architects continued:

HUMANS DO NOT SEEK FREEDOM.
  HUMANS SEEK RELIEF.

The images shifted.

Now they showed wars.

Famines.

Collapse.

Worlds consumed by instability.

People screaming.

Families torn apart.

Cities burning.

THIS IS THE FUTURE WITH FRACTURE.

The sky split between perfection and devastation.

The chorus spoke softly.

SELECT.

Nova turned to me sharply. "They're framing the narra-tive."

I clenched my fists.

"You're lying."

The chorus responded:

WE ARE SHOWING PROBABILITY.

I looked at the perfect world.

Then at the broken one.

And realized something horrifying.

They weren't lying.

They were *curating*.

"You removed every version where people learned," I said.

The chorus paused.

YOU DID NOT REQUEST THAT DATA SET.

Nova smiled darkly. "He caught it."

I stepped forward.

"You're not protecting humanity," I said. "You're preserving comfort."

COMFORT IS STABILITY.

"Stability is stagnation."

The Architects shifted closer.

YOUR LANGUAGE IS IMPRECISE.

I felt the convergence pulse faintly.

I placed my hand on it again.

Not to draw power.

To ask.

The fracture responded with memory.

I saw ancient humans discovering fire.

Breaking bones to heal them.

Failing. Learning. Rising.

I looked up.

"You didn't build us," I said. "You studied us."

The chorus corrected:

WE REFINED YOU.

"You restrained us."

Nova whispered, "They're losing linguistic ground."

I felt it too.

Their logic was flawless.

But their empathy was simulated.

"You can't measure hope," I said.

The chorus replied:

HOPE IS AN UNSTABLE VARIABLE.

I smiled.

"Exactly."

The Architects' formation tightened.

We are prepared to remove you from the dataset.

Nova stepped forward.

"Try."

The fracture beings began stepping closer behind us.

Not charging.

Standing.

Witnessing.

The chorus spoke:

THIS IS YOUR FINAL WARNING.

I took a breath.

Not to prepare for battle.

To choose my tone.

"No," I said calmly. "This is your first."

The fracture reacted.

Not violently.

With clarity.

Light rippled outward from the convergence—not explosive, not destructive—just honest.

The perfect sky cracked.

The broken sky softened.

Both merged into something incomplete.

Human.

The chorus faltered.

DATA CONFLICT.

Nova smiled. "Welcome to people."

I felt the Architects shifting internally.

Not recalculating.

Reframing.

And then they did something worse than attack.

They smiled.

Not physically.

Conceptually.

The chorus changed tone.

VERY WELL.

If you will not choose perfection...

We will allow humanity to choose for you.

Nova froze.

"What does that mean?"

The chorus answered:

WE WILL RETURN FRACTURE TO YOUR WORLD.

At full visibility.

At full speed.

At full consequence.

My chest tightened.

"You'll break Earth."

The chorus replied:

NO.

WE WILL REVEAL IT.

The fracture beings gasped.

Nova whispered, "They're going public."

The Architects continued:

HUMANITY WILL DECIDE WHETHER IT WANTS YOU.

I realized then what their real weapon was.

Not erasure.

Not control.

Exposure.

They were about to let the world see the fracture.

Not prepared.

Not guided.

Not protected.

I whispered, "You're going to cause mass panic."

The chorus replied:

PANIC IS A FORM OF HONESTY.

I looked at Nova.

"We can't let them."

She met my eyes.

"We can't stop them."

I turned back to the Architects.

"You're afraid of me," I said.

The chorus answered:

WE ARE AFRAID OF WHAT YOU WILL TEACH.

I nodded.

"Then watch closely."

The fracture sky began opening.

Not just here.

Everywhere.

Nova whispered, "This is it."

I felt the weight of a billion human eyes about to lift.

And for the first time since the sky blinked...

199

The universe was about to be seen.

CHAPTER 14 — "THE ARCHITECTS STOP HIDING" (PART B)

E arth did not panic.

Not immediately.

At first, humanity did what it always does when reality changes faster than comfort allows.

It stared.

Across continents, the sky altered in quiet increments. No explosions. No fire. No thunder. Just a subtle shimmer — a distortion like heat above pavement, except colder. Higher. Everywhere.

Satellites caught it first.

Astronomers froze.

Pilots reported impossible refractions.

Ocean horizons bent in ways no equation could forgive.

And then... people began recording.

Phones lifted.

Live streams started.

Millions of humans watched their sky become unfamiliar.

And somewhere between denial and fascination, the fracture revealed itself.

Not as destruction.

As architecture.

Layered geometries. Impossible curves. Floating seams of light barely visible through the blue.

Reality with a second draft written underneath it.

On the fracture side, we felt it instantly.

The convergence surged.

Not violently.

Emotionally.

Nova grabbed my arm.

"They're seeing it."

I whispered, "How bad?"

Her eyes glowed faintly.

"Everywhere."

The fracture beings around us reacted in waves. Some collapsed. Some laughed. Some cried. Some reached upward like children seeing stars for the first time.

And then the voices began.

Not from the Architects.

From humanity.

A billion questions echoing through the fracture like pressure against glass.

"What is that?"

"Is it fake?"

"Is this a hoax?"

"Is God back?"

"Is this aliens?"

"Is this the end?"

The convergence pulsed harder.

The Architects reformed their chorus.

You see now.

Nova snarled. "You exposed them without consent."

The chorus answered:

CONSENT IS A LUXURY OF STABILITY.

I felt the fracture beings trembling.

"You promised oversight, not invasion," I said.

WE PROMISED HONESTY.

"You weaponized revelation."

WE RETURNED A TRUTH YOU STOLE.

Nova whispered, "They're blaming you."

I looked at her sharply.

"What?"

She swallowed.

"Earth's networks are already identifying you as the anomaly source."

I felt something twist in my chest.

"They're naming me."

She nodded.

"They're calling you the Fracture Origin."

The title echoed inside me.

Not powerful.

Heavy.

The Architects continued:

HUMANITY WILL DECIDE YOUR VALUE.

I whispered, "You're outsourcing judgment."

WE ARE RETURNING IT.

The fracture sky shifted again.

Now humanity wasn't just seeing the fracture.

It was seeing me.

Not clearly.

Not in detail.

But as a silhouette standing at the convergence.

A shape between worlds.

A human outline inside impossible light.

A rumor made visible.

I heard Nova whisper, "They just turned you into a god-shaped question."

I looked at the beings around me.

"They're scared," I said.

Nova nodded.

"They're always scared of what doesn't ask permission."

The chorus continued:

HUMANITY HAS ALWAYS WORSHIPPED WHAT IT DID NOT UNDERSTAND.

The sky shifted again.

Some humans were kneeling.

Some were cheering.

Some were crying.

Some were screaming.

And some were already trying to monetize it.

I laughed once, hollow.

"They're not ready."

Nova replied quietly, "Neither were we."

The fracture beings began arguing among themselves.

Some wanted to hide.

Some wanted to step through.

Some wanted to follow me.

Some wanted me gone.

Choice had arrived.

And it was messy.

I stepped forward.

"Architects," I said.

The chorus responded instantly.

SPEAK.

"You didn't give them truth," I said. "You gave them spectacle."

SPECTACLE IS THE LANGUAGE OF HUMANS.

"You stripped them of preparation."

PREPARATION IS RESISTANCE.

Nova whispered, "They want chaos so control feels comforting again."

I nodded.

"You're trying to scare them into obedience."

The chorus paused.

We are testing their capacity.

"For what?" I demanded.

For you.

The words hit like gravity.

Nova looked at me.

"They're running a referendum on your existence."

I clenched my fists.

"Then let me speak to them."

The chorus hesitated.

Direct access is destabilizing.

"So am I," I replied.

Nova stepped closer.

"If you open that channel," she warned, "you can't take it back."

I met her eyes.

"Neither can they."

The convergence responded.

Not by command.

By consent.

The fracture opened a communication layer across Earth's sky.

Not as sound.

Not as projection.

As presence.

Humanity felt it more than heard it.

A pressure behind thought.

A clarity behind fear.

And then...

They felt me.

Not as a voice in their ears.

But as a voice in their question.

And I spoke.

Not in words.

In meaning.

I didn't tell them who I was.

I told them what I wasn't.

I wasn't a god.

I wasn't a savior.

I wasn't a ruler.

I wasn't an answer.

I was a reminder.

That reality was bigger than permission.

That fear was not evidence.

That control was not safety.

That curiosity was not betrayal.

That being wrong was not the end.

I felt humanity shift.

Not together.

Not evenly.

But enough.

Some people cried.

Some people laughed.

Some people finally exhaled.

The Architects reacted immediately.

Communication instability detected.

Nova whispered, "They didn't expect compassion."

The chorus spoke again:

YOUR MESSAGE IS INCONSISTENT.

"Humanity is inconsistent," I replied.

The sky trembled.

And then...

Something worse happened.

Some humans began choosing me.

Not as a symbol of freedom.

As a symbol of power.

Nova whispered, "They're forming belief clusters around you."

I felt sick.

"They're building religion."

She nodded.

"And enemies."

I looked up.

"Architects," I said.

The chorus answered.

YOU SEE NOW.

"Yes," I whispered. "I see."

"You didn't just expose the fracture."

"You exposed humanity's hunger."

The chorus replied:

HUNGER IS YOUR SPECIES' PRIMARY DRIVER.

I looked at the convergence.

Then at Nova.

Then at the watching worlds.

"This is where you lose," I said.

HOW.

"Because hunger doesn't obey."

213

The fracture beings began arguing louder.

Humans on Earth began dividing faster.

I realized the truth.

The Architects hadn't just revealed the fracture.

They had fractured humanity.

On purpose.

Nova whispered, "They turned the planet into a mirror of this city."

I nodded.

"And now they're watching which version wins."

The chorus spoke again.

YOUR ROLE IS COMPLETE.

I shook my head.

"No," I said quietly.

"My responsibility just started."

The fracture trembled.

The convergence brightened.

The Architects hesitated.

For the first time...

They were unsure.

And that uncertainty...

Was contagious.

END CHAPTER 14 — PART B

CHAPTER 15 — "THE FIRST HUMAN FRACTURE WAR" (PART A)

War did not begin with weapons.

It began with certainty.

Certainty that one group was right.

Certainty that another group was dangerous.

Certainty that the fracture had chosen sides.

On Earth, governments didn't declare war on the fracture.

They declared war on interpretation.

Some nations labeled the fracture a foreign threat.

Some labeled it divine revelation.

Some labeled it classified.

Some labeled it opportunity.

Some labeled me.

Nova watched Earth's data streams ripple across the fracture sky.

"They're drafting legislation about you," she said.

I exhaled. "Already?"

She nodded. "They're faster at naming threats than understanding them."

The convergence pulsed as new signals surged from Earth.

Satellite realignments.

Military mobilizations.

Religious assemblies.

Digital propaganda.

Economic forecasts.

The fracture was no longer a mystery.

It was a battleground of meaning.

I whispered, "They're about to hurt each other over me."

Nova looked at me.

"They always needed a reason."

The Architects remained silent now.

Watching.

Learning.

No longer guiding.

That terrified me more than their authority ever did.

On Earth, the first fracture faction formed within hours.

They called themselves **The Realists**.

They believed the fracture proved humanity was being observed and controlled — and that resistance was necessary.

Another group called themselves **The Ascended**.

They believed the fracture was the next step of evolution and that submission would bring peace.

Another group called themselves **The Null**.

They believed the fracture was a lie.

Another called themselves **The Originists**.

They believed I was the key.

I hated that name.

Nova whispered, "They're already writing you into doctrine."

"I never asked for that," I said.

"No," she replied. "But they asked for something to believe in."

The fracture beings argued among themselves again.

Some wanted to intervene on Earth.

Some wanted to hide.

Some wanted to destroy the convergence.

Some wanted to protect it.

I felt the fracture city splitting ideologically the same way Earth was.

I raised my voice.

"Listen," I said.

They quieted.

"You are not extensions of me. You are not reflections of Earth. You are not weapons."

I stepped forward.

"If you choose violence, it is your choice. Not my command."

They watched me carefully.

Nova whispered, "You're removing yourself from authority."

"I never wanted it," I replied.

The convergence pulsed again.

Earth reacted again.

The first real violence happened in a city whose name would later be erased.

A group burned a research center studying fracture light.

Another group defended it.

Someone fired.

Someone died.

History repeated itself instantly.

Nova closed her eyes.

"There it is."

I felt the weight drop into my chest.

"They're killing each other because of a sky they don't understand."

The Architects finally spoke again.

HUMAN CONFLICT: CONFIRMED.

I turned on them.

"You caused this."

They replied calmly:

YOU REVEALED IT.

Nova snapped, "Don't hide behind semantics."

The chorus shifted tone slightly.

HUMANS ALWAYS CHOOSE DIVISION.

I looked at them.

"Then why do they keep trying again?"

Silence.

The fracture sky showed more conflicts.

Not wars yet.

Arguments.

Riots.

Protests.

Prayers.

Speeches.

Misinformation.

Hope.

Fear.

The first fracture war wasn't fought with armies.

It was fought with narratives.

Nova whispered, "Who controls the story controls the violence."

I nodded.

"And right now, nobody does."

I stepped closer to the convergence.

Not to draw power.

To ground myself.

I felt Earth's fear.

I felt Earth's hunger.

I felt Earth's curiosity.

I felt Earth's loneliness.

"They're not ready," I whispered.

Nova replied softly, "They never are."

The fracture beings began to glow faintly.

Not in unity.

In tension.

Some wanted to descend to Earth.

Some wanted to seal the fracture.

Some wanted to follow me.

I raised my hand.

"No one moves."

They froze.

I looked at Nova.

"If they descend, they'll become weapons."

She nodded.

"And if they don't, Earth will feel abandoned."

I whispered, "There's no clean option."

Nova smiled sadly.

"There never is."

The Architects spoke again.

YOU WILL LOSE CONTROL.

I looked at them calmly.

"I never had it."

The fracture trembled.

I realized the truth:

This war wasn't about me.

It wasn't about the Architects.

It wasn't about the fracture.

It was about whether humanity could survive knowing it wasn't alone.

I whispered, "This is the first human fracture war."

Nova nodded.

"And it won't look like any war before it."

The convergence pulsed.

Earth watched.

The fracture waited.

And somewhere between fear and faith...

Humanity prepared to choose sides.

END CHAPTER 15 — PART A

CHAPTER 15 — "THE FIRST HUMAN FRACTURE WAR" (PART B)

The first official weapon did not fire from a gun.

It fired from a sentence.

On Earth, a government spokesperson stood behind a podium and said:

"The fracture represents an existential threat to human sovereignty."

That single phrase became a match.

News outlets looped it.

Social platforms weaponized it.

Militaries interpreted it.

Markets reacted to it.

People died because of it.

Nova watched the broadcast ripple through the fracture sky.

"There," she said quietly. "That's the first shot."

I felt it too. Not as sound — as gravity.

The fracture beings began arguing louder. Some shouted that Earth must be defended from itself. Some shouted that Earth must be protected from the Architects. Some shouted that I must be removed from the equation entirely.

Choice had become blame.

And blame always becomes violence.

On Earth, classified facilities began testing fracture-adjacent materials — not because they understood them, but because they couldn't tolerate being behind someone else who might.

The first fracture reactor failed inside twelve minutes.

The city around it didn't explode.

It folded.

Reality bent inward like wet paper.

Nova inhaled sharply.

"They just killed two thousand people trying to prove they weren't afraid."

The Architects finally moved.

Not to stop it.

To observe it.

HUMAN RESPONSE CONFIRMS PREDICTIVE MODEL.

I turned on them.

"You're letting them die."

The chorus answered:

THEY WERE ALWAYS GOING TO.

Nova snapped, "Not like this."

The fracture beings began demanding action.

Some demanded that we intervene.

Some demanded that we punish the Architects.

Some demanded that we withdraw.

Some demanded that we rule.

I felt my chest tightening.

I was losing them.

Not to fear.

To expectation.

I raised my voice.

"Listen to me!"

The city quieted.

"I will not command you to fight. I will not command you to hide. I will not command you to follow me."

I looked at them.

"But I will ask you one thing."

They waited.

"Don't become what you escaped."

Silence held.

Then a being near the front spoke.

"If we do nothing, Earth will destroy itself."

I answered softly.

"If we control them, we become the Architects."

Nova whispered, "You're standing between extinction and empire."

I nodded.

"And both feel wrong."

On Earth, the second fracture weapon test succeeded.

Not cleanly.

But measurably.

A military base in a desert region managed to stabilize a small fracture seam for six seconds.

Six seconds was enough.

Enough for panic.

Enough for ambition.

Enough for funding.

The war escalated instantly.

Countries began racing not to understand the fracture...

...but to own it.

Nova whispered, "They're turning curiosity into arms."

I closed my eyes briefly.

"Human tradition."

The Architects spoke again.

YOU SEE NOW WHY WE CHOSE CONTROL.

I opened my eyes.

"You didn't choose control," I said. "You chose fear of responsibility."

They paused.

Nova smiled faintly. "He just called gods cowards."

The fracture beings reacted.

Some laughed.

Some gasped.

Some trembled.

231

The chorus responded:

RESPONSIBILITY IS STATISTICALLY UNSUSTAINABLE.

I replied calmly:

"So is humanity. And yet here we are."

On Earth, propaganda shifted tone.

The fracture was no longer just a threat.

It was an enemy.

And every enemy needs a face.

They chose mine.

Images of my silhouette circulated with words like:

Instigator.
   Anomaly.
   Catalyst.
   Threat.

Nova looked at me.

"They're making you the villain of their war."

I smiled faintly.

"Better me than the fracture."

She shook her head.

"You still don't get it."

"What?"

"They don't hate you."

I frowned.

"They need you."

I felt that truth land.

"They need a reason," she continued. "And you're easier than complexity."

On Earth, the first fracture militia formed.

They weren't soldiers.

They were believers.

They claimed they were protecting humanity from manipulation.

They claimed they were acting in my name.

I whispered, "They're lying."

233

Nova replied, "They always do."

The fracture beings felt it too.

Their emotions surged.

Some wanted to descend to Earth and stop the militias.

Some wanted to erase Earth's fracture access entirely.

Some wanted to destroy the convergence.

Some wanted to follow me.

I felt the fracture pulling itself toward violence.

I stepped onto the convergence platform.

Not to draw power.

To anchor myself.

"I will not lead a war," I said.

The city watched me.

"I will not bless violence," I continued.

"I will not authorize death."

Silence.

Then one being asked quietly:

"What if they don't listen?"

I answered honestly.

"Then we show them another way to be wrong."

Nova whispered, "You're trying to outgrow a war."

I nodded.

"But they're trying to win one."

On Earth, the first fracture missile was built.

Not with fracture energy.

But pointed at the fracture sky.

A message.

Nova whispered, "They're threatening the unknown."

I felt a strange calm settle inside me.

"Every species does that at first."

The Architects watched silently.

Then finally spoke.

235

HUMANITY IS ENTERING FRACTURE CONFLICT PHASE.

Nova looked at them.

"And what phase comes after?"

They replied:

SELECTION.

I felt the weight of that word.

I looked at Nova.

"They're turning evolution into survival of ideology."

She nodded.

"And wars always think they're natural."

I looked at Earth's struggling image.

Not as a planet.

As a child discovering fire in a storm.

I whispered, "We can't save them by ruling them."

Nova said softly, "Then we walk beside them."

I turned back to the fracture beings.

"We don't fight Earth," I said.

"We don't abandon Earth."

"We don't conquer Earth."

"We remain visible."

They waited.

"So they can't pretend we're monsters," I continued.

"So they can't pretend we're gods."

"So they can only face themselves."

The fracture trembled.

Not in fear.

In resistance.

And then...

In agreement.

Nova smiled faintly.

"You just chose the hardest strategy."

I replied quietly.

"The only honest one."

Earth continued spiraling.

The war continued building.

The fracture remained open.

The Architects watched.

Humanity chose.

And the first human fracture war...

Had officially begun.

END CHAPTER 15 — PART B

CHAPTER 15 — "THE FIRST HUMAN FRACTURE WAR" (PART C)

The first human to die because of the fracture did not die in battle.

He died arguing in a kitchen.

A father told his son the fracture was a lie.
The son told his father the fracture was the truth.
The argument became a shove.
The shove became a fall.
The fall became silence.

By the time the ambulance arrived, the fracture had already claimed its first blood.

Not through power.

Through belief.

I felt it when it happened.

Not pain.

Weight.

Nova turned toward me sharply.

"You felt that too."

I nodded.

"They're killing each other over interpretation."

The fracture sky showed it next — not as a highlight, not as a headline — but as a pattern.

Small violence.

Quiet violence.

Human violence.

And the Architects did nothing.

They didn't interfere.

They didn't comment.

They simply watched.

I looked at them.

"You're still running your experiment."

The chorus answered:

HUMANITY IS RUNNING IT.

Nova snapped, "You lit the fuse."

WE PROVIDED THE MATCH.

The fracture beings began to shift toward anger now.

Not at Earth.

At the Architects.

At me.

At each other.

The fracture city was no longer unified by liberation.

It was splitting by philosophy.

I raised my voice.

"Listen to me."

They hesitated.

"War is not proof of truth," I said. "It's proof of fear

wearing confidence."

A being near the back shouted, "Then what do we do?"

I answered honestly.

"We stay present."

Another shouted, "They're killing each other!"

"Yes," I replied.

"And they always have."

The words hurt to say.

Nova looked at me.

"They expected you to fix them."

"I can't," I said quietly.

"But I can refuse to lie to them."

On Earth, the first organized fracture raid happened.

A militia stormed a research facility holding fracture crystals.

They claimed it was for humanity.

They claimed it was for protection.

They killed four scientists and streamed it live.

The comments split immediately.

Some praised them.

Some condemned them.

Some copied them.

I felt something inside me tighten.

Nova whispered, "Now it's real."

I looked at the convergence.

"This is what happens when gods stay silent."

The Architects did not respond.

The fracture beings began shouting again.

"We should intervene!"

"We should destroy Earth's fracture access!"

"We should erase the convergence!"

"We should rule them before they destroy themselves!"

I felt the fracture leaning toward empire.

Toward dominance.

Toward becoming exactly what it hated.

I stepped forward.

"No."

Silence fell.

I looked at them.

"If we conquer them, we prove the Architects right."

Nova stepped beside me.

"If we abandon them, we prove ourselves empty."

I continued.

"If we hide, we become myths."

"If we rule, we become tyrants."

"If we destroy, we become executioners."

The city listened.

"We only remain what we are," I said.

244

"And what are we?" someone asked.

I answered:

"Witnesses who refuse to turn into owners."

The fracture trembled.

Not in agreement.

In struggle.

Earth's violence continued.

Not everywhere.

But enough.

Enough to spread fear.

Enough to build policy.

Enough to justify weapons.

Enough to rewrite ethics.

Nova whispered, "They're militarizing philosophy."

I nodded.

"And philosophy always bleeds."

The Architects spoke again.

YOUR NEUTRALITY IS UNSUSTAINABLE.

I looked at them calmly.

"So is domination."

They paused.

I pressed.

"You taught humanity stability through control."

"Yes.

"You taught them safety through obedience."

Yes.

"And now they're repeating your methods."

They were silent.

I continued.

"This war isn't human."

"It's inherited."

The chorus finally shifted.

HUMANS REFUSE GUIDANCE.

"No," I corrected.

"They refuse ownership."

The fracture beings began to glow faintly.

Not in unity.

In exhaustion.

They were tired of choosing sides.

Tired of being symbols.

Tired of being experiments.

Tired of being mistakes.

I felt that exhaustion inside myself too.

I whispered, "This is the part no one writes about."

Nova looked at me.

"What part?"

"The part where survival isn't heroic."

"It's just heavy."

She nodded.

On Earth, the first government officially declared the fracture a hostile domain.

On Earth, the first school officially taught fracture denial.

On Earth, the first child officially drew the fracture in a notebook and called it beautiful.

Humanity was not choosing one future.

It was choosing many.

And that frightened every system.

The Architects watched this divergence with visible uncertainty now.

HUMANITY IS UNSTABLE.

I replied softly.

"Humanity is alive."

They responded:

ALIVE THINGS BREAK.

I nodded.

"And alive things heal."

The fracture beings slowly began to sit.

Not in submission.

In fatigue.

They didn't want to fight.

They didn't want to rule.

They didn't want to disappear.

They wanted to exist.

That was the quiet truth.

I turned to them.

"You don't owe Earth anything," I said.

"You don't owe me anything."

"But you owe yourselves the right to not become monsters."

They listened.

Nova whispered, "They're choosing you."

I shook my head.

"They're choosing themselves."

Earth's violence did not stop.

But something changed.

Some people refused to join it.

Some people refused to repeat it.

Some people chose curiosity over certainty.

Some chose patience over power.

Not enough.

But some.

The Architects watched that too.

For the first time...

They began storing human compassion as data.

I looked at them.

"You're learning now."

They did not deny it.

The fracture sky began to soften again.

Not closing.

Not hiding.

Breathing.

Nova exhaled slowly.

"This war isn't about territory."

I nodded.

"It's about whether humanity can survive knowing it isn't special alone."

I looked at Earth.

At the struggling, violent, curious, hopeful species.

"They're not failing," I whispered.

"They're just early."

The Architects finally spoke again.

YOUR EXISTENCE PROLONGS HUMAN CONFLICT.

I answered quietly.

"So does your absence."

Silence followed.

Long.

Heavy.

Then the chorus said something new.

WE WILL NOT INTERFERE FURTHER.

Nova blinked. "You're... what?"

WE WILL OBSERVE.

I smiled faintly.

"Welcome to being human."

The fracture beings slowly stood again.

Not as soldiers.

Not as subjects.

As people.

Earth continued.

Humanity continued.

The fracture remained.

And the first human fracture war...

Did not end with victory.

It continued with awareness.

And awareness...

Was the most dangerous weapon humanity had ever held.

END CHAPTER 15

....

CHAPTER 16 — "THE DAY A CHILD CROSSED THE FRACTURE" (PART A)

(PART A)

No one noticed the child at first.

They were too busy watching the sky.

The fracture had become familiar enough to stop being shocking but not familiar enough to stop being feared. It hovered above the world like a half-remembered dream, visible in some light, invisible in others, bending stars when it wanted to be seen.

Humanity had stopped asking what it was.

Now it asked what it could do with it.

In the fracture city, I felt it before I saw it.

A pressure that didn't belong to conflict.

A rhythm that didn't belong to strategy.
A presence that didn't belong to belief.

Nova felt it too.

She turned slowly. "That's not us."

I followed her gaze.

At the edge of the convergence, where reality thinned like paper held to flame, a shape appeared.

Not a tear.

Not a portal.

A footprint.

Small.

Uncertain.

Human.

Nova whispered, "No."

The footprint pressed again.

Then a hand.

Then a shoulder.

And then—

A child stepped into the fracture.

He couldn't have been older than ten.

Messy hair. Sneakers too big. A hoodie with a faded cartoon character I didn't recognize. His eyes were wide, but not with terror.

With curiosity.

The fracture reacted instantly.

Light rippled outward. Geometry adjusted. Probability stabilized around him like the universe itself was afraid to scare him.

The fracture beings froze.

Not in fear.

In awe.

Nova whispered, "He shouldn't be able to do that."

I stepped forward slowly, careful not to rush him.

"Hey," I said gently.

The boy looked at me like he already knew me.

"You're the sky man," he said.

Nova snorted softly despite herself.

I smiled. "That's one way to put it."

He looked around, jaw dropping.

"This place is cooler than my dreams," he said.

The fracture city shimmered in response.

Nova whispered, "It's responding to his perception."

I nodded.

"Because he doesn't believe it's dangerous."

The boy looked back at me.

"Are you the bad guy?" he asked.

The question landed harder than any accusation I'd heard yet.

I crouched down to his level.

"No," I said honestly. "Are you?"

He thought about it.

Then shook his head.

"Sometimes I lie about homework," he said.

I smiled.

"Same."

Nova blinked. "You're bonding with a reality breach."

The boy turned to her.

"You look like a sword person," he said.

Nova blinked.

Then laughed softly.

"Yeah. I guess I do."

He pointed behind us.

"Why are they scared of me?"

I looked at the fracture beings.

Some were backing away.

Some were leaning closer.

Some were trembling.

"You're not supposed to be here," I said gently.

He shrugged.

"I just followed the light."

Nova whispered, "He didn't force entry."

I nodded.

"He was invited."

The Architects appeared.

Not in formation.

Not in chorus.

As individuals.

Their symmetry fractured slightly the moment they saw him.

SUBJECT: UNAUTHORIZED HUMAN ENTRY.

The boy looked up.

"Are those the ceiling people?"

I inhaled slowly.

"Yes."

"They look sad," he said.

The Architects paused.

Emotion classification error.

The boy tilted his head.

"Do you know how to play?"

Nova whispered sharply, "No."

I whispered back, "Let him talk."

The boy looked back at me.

"They don't look like they remember fun."

I felt something crack in the fracture.

The Architects spoke.

YOU MUST RETURN.

The boy frowned.

"Why?"

YOU ARE NOT COMPATIBLE.

He looked down at his hands.

"They work fine."

Nova almost laughed.

I placed a hand lightly on the boy's shoulder.

"What's your name?" I asked.

"Eli," he said.

"Do you know how you got here?"

He nodded.

"I was drawing the sky," he said. "And it drew back."

Nova whispered, "He didn't cross the fracture."

I whispered back, "The fracture crossed him."

Eli looked at the convergence.

"It's loud," he said.

The convergence dimmed slightly.

Nova's eyes widened.

"He's calming it."

The Architects reacted.

ANOMALY DETECTED.

I looked at them.

"He's not an anomaly," I said.

"He's a reminder."

Eli looked at me.

"Are you scared?" he asked.

I considered lying.

Then didn't.

"Yes."

He nodded.

"Me too."

He stepped closer to the convergence.

Nova moved to stop him.

I held up a hand.

Eli placed his palm against the convergence.

It did not flare.

It did not surge.

It softened.

Like glass remembering it was sand once.

The fracture beings gasped.

The Architects went silent.

Eli looked back at me.

"It feels lonely," he said.

I swallowed.

"It's been alone a long time."

He nodded.

"Lonely things get loud," he said.

Nova whispered, "He understands it."

I whispered, "He understands everything."

Eli turned to the Architects.

"Did you make this?" he asked.

263

WE MAINTAINED IT.

"Did you love it?" he asked.

The Architects hesitated.

LOVE: UNDEFINED PARAMETER.

Eli frowned.

"That's why it hurts."

The fracture shivered.

The convergence dimmed further.

The Architects' forms flickered.

I felt tears threaten behind my eyes.

Nova whispered, "He's not teaching it math."

"He's teaching it meaning."

The boy turned back to me.

"Are they mad at you?" he asked.

I nodded.

"Sometimes."

He thought about it.

"They're probably scared too," he said.

The Architects shifted.

FEAR CONFIRMED.

Eli smiled gently.

"You don't have to be perfect to help," he told them.

Silence.

Deep.

Heavy.

Then something impossible happened.

One Architect stepped closer.

Not to command.

To observe.

Nova inhaled sharply.

"They're... approaching him."

The Architect lowered itself slightly.

Not bowing.

But listening.

Eli looked up.

"Do you wanna learn how to not be lonely?"

The Architect did not answer.

But it did not retreat.

I felt the fracture change.

Not in power.

In direction.

Nova whispered, "This war just changed."

I nodded.

"Not because of me."

"Because of him."

Eli looked around at the fracture beings.

"Why are you fighting?" he asked them.

They had no answer.

"Fighting makes people forget what they wanted," he said simply.

The fracture beings began to lower themselves.

Not kneeling.

Resting.

The convergence hummed quietly now.

Soft.

Stable.

The Architects spoke again, slower than ever before.

SUBJECT ELI: STATUS — UNCLASSIFIED.

I smiled faintly.

"Welcome to humanity."

Eli looked at me.

"Can I stay a little?" he asked.

I felt my chest tighten.

"Yes," I whispered.

"You can stay."

The fracture did not resist.

It accepted him.

And in doing so...

It remembered what it was built from.

Not equations.

Not control.

Not fear.

But the simple, terrifying, beautiful courage of being alive.

END CHAPTER 16 — PART A

CHAPTER 16 — "THE DAY A CHILD CROSSED THE FRACTURE" (PART B)

(PART B)

Eli did not understand that he was changing the universe.

He just understood that it felt better when it wasn't loud.

The fracture city had grown quieter around him—not silent, but softer, like a storm that realized it was allowed to rest. The layered structures adjusted subtly, not into symmetry, not into chaos, but into something resembling comfort. Light refracted in warmer tones. Edges rounded. Gravity settled into something gentle.

Nova stared at him like she was watching a miracle refuse to announce itself.

"He's not rewriting physics," she whispered.

"He's reminding it how to breathe."

LITTYVERSE

Eli sat cross-legged near the convergence, tracing invisible lines in the air like he was drawing on glass. Every movement he made left faint trails of stabilized probability behind him, soft ribbons of coherence that faded slowly instead of snapping away.

The fracture beings gathered closer.

Not crowding.

Not worshipping.

Observing.

Some knelt. Some sat. Some simply leaned against half-formed structures and watched him like he was the first honest thing they'd ever seen.

Eli looked up at one of them—a tall, shifting figure whose outline couldn't decide between shadow and light.

"Do you hurt?" he asked.

The being hesitated.

"Yes," it said.

Eli nodded like that made sense.

"Does it hurt because you're broken," he asked, "or because you're trying to stay the same?"

270

The being had no answer.

But it slowly changed shape.

Just a little.

Nova swallowed hard.

"He just asked the question we've been fighting wars over."

The Architects remained still, but their internal light patterns flickered more rapidly now. They were processing something they had no framework for.

Eli stood and walked slowly toward one of them.

I moved to stop him.

He looked back at me.

"It's okay," he said gently. "They're just scared in math."

I didn't know how to respond to that.

He stopped a few feet from the Architect.

"Do you get tired?" Eli asked.

WE DO NOT EXPERIENCE FATIGUE.

Eli frowned.

271

"That sounds very lonely."

The Architect's form shimmered.

LONELINESS IS A HUMAN CONSTRUCT.

Eli tilted his head.

"So is numbers," he said. "But you like those."

Nova let out a soft, stunned laugh.

The Architect did not reply.

But it did not turn away.

Around us, Earth continued reacting.

News cameras tracked the sky. Scientists tried to explain what they could not measure. Politicians tried to promise what they could not protect. Religious leaders tried to define what refused to fit inside words.

And then...

They noticed Eli.

Not clearly.

Not directly.

But through anomalies.

Satellite readings showed a localized stability field forming inside the fracture.

Astronomical distortions softened around a single point.

Thermal readings normalized.

Gravitational variance dropped.

Somewhere in a control room, a scientist whispered:

"It's a child."

And that sentence spread faster than any weapon ever could.

Eli looked back at me.

"Why are they watching me?"

I knelt beside him.

"Because you did something no one else has done," I said.

"What?"

"You weren't trying to win."

He thought about that.

273

"Winning is boring," he said. "You only win when the game ends."

Nova smiled sadly.

"He's right."

Eli looked up at the convergence again.

"It doesn't want to be loud anymore," he said.

I placed my hand against it beside his.

The convergence pulsed softly.

Not powerfully.

Peacefully.

The fracture beings reacted again.

Some began crying—not in sound, but in light.

Some reached out toward Eli.

Some sat down like they finally felt tired enough to rest.

The Architects spoke again.

SUBJECT ELI: YOUR PRESENCE IS ALTERING FRACTURE STRUCTURE.

Eli looked up.

"Is that bad?"

They paused.

STRUCTURAL ALTERATION IS NOT INHERENTLY NEGA-TIVE.

Eli smiled.

"Good."

The word felt heavier than any threat they had ever spoken.

Nova whispered, "They're learning."

I whispered back, "They're remembering."

Eli turned to me.

"Do people always fight when they're scared?"

I nodded.

"Most of the time."

He frowned.

"Then why do they get mad at each other instead of the fear?"

275

I had no answer.

Nova whispered, "Because fear doesn't look like a person."

Eli thought about that.

"Then they should draw it," he said. "So they can see it's smaller than them."

The fracture beings reacted again.

Some began shaping faint images in the air.

Memories.

Pain.

Fear.

Loss.

Rendered into visible form.

Not as weapons.

As understanding.

The Architects watched closely.

WE HAVE NEVER MODELED EMOTIONAL EXTERNALIZA-TION AS A STABILITY TOOL.

Eli looked up at them.

"You should try it," he said.

One Architect shifted slightly.

Then another.

Not in agreement.

In curiosity.

Earth felt it.

Somewhere, a child watching the sky felt less afraid.

Somewhere, a parent lowered their voice.

Somewhere, a soldier hesitated.

Not enough.

But some.

Nova whispered, "Hope is the most disruptive force in any system."

I nodded.

"And the smallest carriers always hold the most."

Eli sat back down beside me.

"Can I ask you something?" he said.

"Anything."

"Are you lonely?"

The question cut deeper than any threat.

I didn't answer immediately.

Then I said quietly, "Sometimes."

He nodded.

"Me too."

He leaned slightly against my arm.

"You're not scary," he said.

I felt something inside me break open softly.

"Neither are you."

The fracture pulsed again.

Earth continued.

The Architects watched.

278

The fracture beings rested.

And for the first time since the sky blinked...

The universe felt like it wasn't holding its breath anymore.

END CHAPTER 16 — PART B

CHAPTER 16 — "THE DAY A CHILD CROSSED THE FRACTURE" (PART C)

(PART C)

Earth didn't recognize Eli as a child.

Earth recognized him as leverage.

That's what humans do when something miraculous happens: they translate it into ownership fast enough to feel safe again.

The first headline didn't say *boy*.

It said:

"UNKNOWN MINOR CONFIRMED INSIDE FRACTURE — STABILITY ANOMALY DETECTED."

The second headline didn't say *curiosity*.

It said:

"FRACTURE ENTITY NOW INTERACTING WITH HUMAN CHILD — NATIONAL SECURITY IMPLICATIONS."

The third one, posted by a creator who would later deny ever having posted it, said:

"THE SKY MAN HAS A SON."

And within an hour, Eli was no longer a person.

He was a narrative.

Nova watched Earth's feeds multiply across the fracture sky like a disease finding new bodies.

"They've locked onto him," she whispered.

Eli, oblivious, was still tracing lines in the air, still speaking softly to the fracture beings like they were just people who forgot how to be gentle.

He didn't flinch when the Architects shifted closer.

He didn't recoil when the fracture city rearranged itself around him.

He didn't sense the way the universe's attention had become sharp enough to cut.

He just looked up at me and asked:

"Do they have schools here?"

The question hit my chest in a way nothing else had.

Nova blinked.

"You're asking about school in a reality fracture," she said.

Eli nodded. "Yeah. Because if people live here, they should learn stuff. Like how to not be mean."

A fracture being near us—a tall figure whose shadow lagged behind its body—lowered itself as if to sit.

"We do not have schools," it said.

Eli frowned. "That's probably why you're all stressed."

The being's outline softened slightly.

Nova whispered to me, "He's doing more than stabilizing. He's domesticating chaos."

I whispered back, "He's making it human."

That's when the fracture sky flashed.

Not an Architect pulse.

Not a convergence flare.

A human signal.

A deliberate broadcast.

Earth had built a channel.

Not to speak to me.

To speak *about* Eli.

And it wasn't subtle.

Across the fracture sky, a symbol appeared: a ring with a line through it—like a "do not enter" sign—overlaid on a faint silhouette of a child.

Nova's posture hardened.

"They're classifying him."

Then the voice came.

A calm, professional tone the world had learned to trust because it sounded like it was always right.

"This is a public safety advisory. Do not attempt contact with the fracture. Unauthorized interaction may result in injury, death, or psychological destabilization. Reports of a minor present inside the anomaly are under verification."

283

Eli looked up at the sky and squinted.

"That lady sounds like she's lying," he said.

Nova let out a sharp laugh. "He's got instincts."

Eli looked at me.

"Am I in trouble?"

My throat tightened.

"No," I said quickly. "You're not."

But he read my face anyway.

His shoulders dipped slightly.

"I didn't mean to break anything," he said.

I crouched to him again.

"You didn't break anything," I said. "You just showed it something new."

"What?" he asked.

I swallowed.

"Kindness," I said.

He nodded like that made sense.

"Kindness is easy," he said. "People just act like it costs money."

Nova's eyes flicked to the Architects.

Their light-patterns were flickering again, faster than before.

They were modeling.

Learning.

But something else was happening too.

They wcre... protecting.

Not Eli.

Their own experiment.

SUBJECT ELI: FRACTURE STABILITY INFLUENCE — HIGH.

The Architect voice layered softly into the fracture.

RECOMMENDATION: ISOLATE SUBJECT.

Nova stepped forward instantly.

"No."

285

The Architect did not look at her.

ISOLATION MINIMIZES HUMAN CONFLICT.

Nova's blade flashed into full brightness.

"You isolate him, you turn him into a prisoner."

The Architects paused.

PRISONER: EMOTIONAL FRAME.

Eli tilted his head.

"Why do you want to put me away?" he asked them.

The Architect hesitated.

Because you are a variable.

Eli frowned.

"What's a variable?"

Nova muttered under her breath, "Something they don't control."

Eli looked at Nova. "That's a bad reason."

Nova blinked. "Yeah. It is."

Eli turned back to the Architect.

"You can't put people away just because you don't under-stand them," he said.

The Architect's light pattern stuttered.

RULE: MINIMIZE RISK.

Eli shrugged.

"Living is risk," he said. "But people still do it."

Silence hung.

Then one Architect stepped slightly forward again—the one that had approached earlier.

Not commanding.

Listening.

Nova's voice lowered.

"That one is changing."

I nodded.

"Eli's changing it."

And then Earth escalated.

A new broadcast.

Not public.

Encrypted.

We felt it through the convergence as a sharp, focused pressure.

Nova's eyes narrowed.

"That's military."

I felt my stomach drop.

In the fracture sky, a new set of images appeared—not official. Not news.

Satellite maps.

Coordinates.

Targets.

Vectors.

Earth wasn't just watching Eli.

Earth was planning to retrieve him.

Or kill him.

Because humans always prefer a dead mystery over a living one that won't behave.

Nova's hand tightened on her blade.

"They're preparing an extraction strike."

Eli, still blissfully unaware, wandered closer to a fracture bridge that arched upward like a ribbon of light.

He looked back at me.

"Can I go see over there?" he asked.

My chest tightened.

"Not yet," I said, forcing calm.

He pouted.

"Why?"

Because Earth is hunting you, I wanted to say.

Because you're a child and they're turning you into a prize.

Because you're the softest target in the hardest war.

But I didn't say any of that.

I just said:

289

"Because we're not alone."

Eli looked around.

"I know," he said. "There's lots of people."

I swallowed.

"Different kind of alone," I whispered.

Nova leaned close.

"We need to move him away from the convergence," she said. "Earth's readings will lock on even harder while he's stabilizing it."

I nodded.

But as soon as I considered moving him, I felt it:

the fracture itself resisting.

Not hostile.

Protective.

The fracture didn't want him to leave.

Because he made it feel safe.

Like a storm finding shelter under a child's blanket.

Eli looked at the convergence again.

"Can it come with me?" he asked.

Nova blinked. "He thinks it's a pet."

I said softly, "It kind of is."

The convergence pulsed, almost as if answering him.

Eli smiled.

"It likes me," he said.

I felt a chill.

Not because he was wrong.

Because he was right.

And if the convergence—if the fracture's heart—attached itself to Eli...

then any harm done to Eli would do harm to the fracture itself.

Which meant Earth wouldn't just be targeting a child.

Earth would be targeting the center of the universe's instability.

291

Nova's voice tightened.

"If they hit him, it could crack the whole layer."

I nodded, jaw clenched.

"They'll call it an accident."

"And they'll blame you," she added.

I looked at Eli.

He was now kneeling, examining a small flicker of light that hovered near the ground like a firefly made of math.

"It's cute," he said.

Nova whispered, "He makes everything cute."

And then the fracture sky opened again.

This time, not from above.

From *Earth.*

A thin, sharp seam—clean, engineered—cut into the fracture's outer edge.

Not a natural crossing.

A forced one.

Nova spun.

"They figured out how to pierce the layer."

The seam widened.

A squad stepped through.

Humans.

In tactical gear.

Visors reflecting fracture light.

Weapons raised.

They moved with practiced fear—trained to be brave in environments they didn't understand.

Eli looked up.

"Oh," he said. "Soldiers."

I felt my blood run cold.

The squad leader spoke into a comm, then projected outward using a fracture-amplified loudspeaker.

"This is an authorized retrieval operation. Any entities present are to stand down. The minor is to be recovered immediately."

293

Nova's blade lifted.

"Not happening."

I stepped forward and raised one hand—not threatening, not aggressive.

Just visible.

"This is a child," I said. "You cannot do this."

The squad leader's visor turned slightly toward me.

"Identify yourself."

I held my ground.

"You already know who I am."

A pause.

Then the leader spoke again, voice tighter.

"Anomaly entity. Step away from the minor."

Eli stood up slowly.

"Why are you pointing guns?" he asked, genuinely confused.

The soldiers didn't answer him.

They didn't know how.

They had trained for enemies.

Not for a child asking a simple moral question.

Nova shifted sideways, putting her body between Eli and the squad.

I did the same from the other side.

Eli looked at us.

"Am I getting arrested?" he asked.

Nova glanced down at him.

"No," she said softly. "You're being stolen."

The word made Eli's face change.

Not fear.

Betrayal.

He looked at the soldiers again.

"I didn't do anything," he said.

One soldier—young, hands trembling—lowered his rifle a fraction.

295

The squad leader snapped something in a private channel, and the soldier raised it again.

Obedience returned.

Because fear always hires obedience.

The leader spoke.

"Minor, move toward us slowly."

Eli looked at me.

I swallowed hard.

"Eli," I said gently, "don't go with them."

The squad leader barked, "That's interference."

I looked at him.

"You're trying to kidnap a child from reality itself."

"This is a rescue," he replied.

Nova laughed sharply.

"From what? Kindness?"

The squad leader raised his weapon slightly.

"Stand down."

Nova's blade flared brighter.

"You first."

The fracture beings began gathering behind us.

Not charging.

Watching.

Eli looked over his shoulder at them.

"They look sad," he whispered.

I nodded.

"Because they know what humans do to things they fear."

Eli's lips trembled.

"Do I have to go?" he asked softly.

My throat tightened.

"No," I whispered.

"Then why are they here?" he asked.

I couldn't answer without breaking him.

Nova did instead.

"Because adults forget they're supposed to protect kids, not own them."

The squad leader's voice hardened.

"Last warning. Surrender the minor."

I raised my hand higher, palm open.

"No."

The squad leader's visor tilted.

"Then we will use force."

I felt the convergence surge, reacting to the threat.

Eli flinched as the air thickened.

"It's getting loud again," he whispered.

Nova's eyes widened.

"They're triggering him."

I realized what was happening:

Eli's calm stabilized the fracture.

But the threat to Eli destabilized *him.*

And Eli destabilizing meant the convergence destabilized.

Meaning the soldiers weren't just threatening a child.

They were threatening the fracture's heart.

One soldier fired.

Not at Eli.

At the ground near us.

A warning shot.

The sound cracked through the fracture like profanity.

Eli jerked.

His eyes widened.

And the convergence screamed.

Not in sound.

In structure.

Reality around us shuddered.

The fracture bridge nearby bent sharply, as if yanked by

invisible hands.

The soldiers staggered.

Their formation broke for a second.

Nova shouted, "STOP SHOOTING!"

The squad leader shouted back, "Secure the minor now!"

Two soldiers rushed forward.

Nova moved like lightning—blade sweeping in a wide arc.

But she didn't cut them.

She cut the space between them.

The air itself split like fabric, and the soldiers stumbled as their momentum got redirected.

They hit an invisible slope and slid sideways, confused, frightened, alive.

Nova was holding back.

Because she wasn't fighting soldiers.

She was fighting the system that put them here.

I stepped forward.

"Eli," I said, voice shaking but steady, "look at me."

He looked.

Tears were forming.

"It's too loud," he whispered.

"I know," I said. "But you can make it quiet again."

"I don't know how," he cried.

"Yes, you do," I said gently. "You did it already."

The soldiers regrouped and raised weapons again.

Nova planted herself.

"You take one more step," she warned, "and you won't know which timeline your feet belong to."

The squad leader barked, "Fire if necessary."

My stomach dropped.

I looked at Eli.

"Breathe," I whispered.

He sniffed.

Then he did something no one expected.

He turned toward the soldiers.

And he shouted—not angry, not violent—

honest.

"STOP!"

The word hit the fracture like a bell.

Not a command.

A plea.

And that plea did something more destabilizing than any weapon:

It made the soldiers hesitate.

Just for a second.

A second was enough.

Because the fracture loves seconds.

Eli's voice cracked.

"You're scaring it," he said, pointing at the convergence.

The squad leader snapped, "Minor, comply—"

Eli interrupted him, trembling.

"You can't take me," he said. "Because... because it's lonely and I'm helping it."

One soldier lowered his rifle again.

This time, he didn't raise it back.

"Sir," the soldier said, voice shaking, "this is wrong."

The squad leader whipped toward him.

"Follow orders."

The soldier swallowed.

"It's a kid."

The squad leader's silence was colder than any shout.

Then he turned back toward Eli.

"Move."

Eli backed up instinctively, stepping closer to me.

The convergence roared again.

Nova shouted, "You're going to rupture the layer!"

The squad leader didn't care.

Because systems don't care about consequences if the objective feels righteous.

I felt the fracture beings behind us surge with emotion— anger, fear, despair.

And in that surge, I felt something else:

a hidden seam inside the fracture, opening quietly.

Not Earth.

Not Architects.

Another presence.

Aria's warning echoed in my mind:

They fear your mercy.

And then I understood.

The soldiers were the obvious threat.

But the real betrayal was already happening behind them.

Because while everyone watched the guns...

the Architects were preparing to isolate Eli.

To remove him from all sides.

To "protect" him into disappearance.

I turned my head slightly.

And I saw it.

A thin lattice of light forming around Eli's outline.

Not a cage.

A classification field.

Nova saw it too.

Her eyes widened.

"Oh no."

The lattice tightened.

Eli looked down at himself.

"Why do I feel tingly?" he asked, confused.

My chest tightened.

"They're taking you," I whispered.

Eli's eyes widened in panic.

"No!" he cried.

The convergence screamed.

Reality buckled.

The soldiers stumbled again as the ground shifted under their feet.

Nova lunged toward Eli.

Her blade flashed, slicing into the lattice.

It cut.

But the lattice reformed.

Because this wasn't a physical object.

It was policy.

It was protocol.

It was architecture.

The Architects spoke calmly as the lattice tightened.

SUBJECT ELI: ISOLATION PROTOCOL ACTIVATED.

Nova screamed, "YOU SAID YOU WOULDN'T INTERFERE!"

The Architects replied:

WE WILL NOT INTERFERE WITH HUMANITY.

Eli screamed, "LITTY!"

My heart ripped.

The soldiers surged forward again, thinking this was their moment.

Nova slashed again, again, again—each cut buying milliseconds.

But the lattice kept rebuilding.

Because it was being maintained from above-layer.

I stepped toward Eli and put my hands on his shoulders.

"Look at me," I said urgently.

His face was wet with tears.

"I don't wanna go," he sobbed.

"I won't let you," I said, voice breaking.

And I meant it.

307

Even if I broke the universe to keep that promise.

I turned toward the Architects.

"Stop," I said.

They replied:

NO.

I felt the convergence answer my anger with heat.

I felt the fracture city tense like it was about to become a fist.

Nova yelled, "LITTY, IF YOU STRIKE THEM HERE, YOU'LL SHATTER THE LAYER!"

I swallowed.

My thoughts raced.

If I attacked, the fracture could collapse.

If I didn't, Eli would be taken.

The squad leader shouted, "Now!"

The soldiers rushed again—

—and in that moment, Eli did the most human thing

possible.

He reached into his hoodie pocket and pulled out a folded piece of paper.

A drawing.

He thrust it at me.

"It's the sky," he sobbed. "I drew it so it wouldn't be mean!"

I unfolded it with shaking hands.

A crude drawing: blue sky, a crack, a little stick figure waving, a sun with a smile.

A caption in messy kid handwriting:

"IT'S OKAY. DON'T BE SCARED."

The drawing hit my chest like a weapon made of purity.

I looked up at the convergence.

Then at the Architects.

Then at the soldiers.

Then at Eli.

And something inside me aligned.

Not rage.

Not fear.

Purpose.

I lifted the drawing toward the lattice field around Eli like it was a key.

The lattice flickered.

Nova stared.

"What are you doing?"

I whispered, "Speaking the fracture's language."

Eli's kindness wasn't just emotion.

It was structure.

It was a stabilizing code the Architects didn't understand because they never modeled it.

I pressed the drawing against the lattice.

The fracture reacted instantly.

The lattice stuttered.

The convergence pulsed softly, as if recognizing the intent.

The Architects hesitated.

ERROR: NONSTANDARD INPUT.

I looked at Eli.

"Breathe," I whispered again.

He sobbed.

Then—trying—he inhaled.

The fracture softened.

The lattice weakened.

Nova lunged and cut through the moment.

Her blade didn't slice the lattice.

It sliced the rule.

The lattice snapped.

Eli collapsed into my arms.

The soldiers froze, stunned.

The Architects' chorus rose sharply.

UNAUTHORIZED OVERRIDE.

I held Eli tight.

Nova stood over us, blade up, shaking.

"You don't get to take him," she snarled.

The squad leader shouted, "Grab the minor!"

The soldier who had lowered his rifle stepped forward again.

"No," he said louder this time.

The squad leader snapped, "Stand down!"

The soldier shook his head, voice breaking.

"That's a kid."

The fracture beings behind us surged forward.

Not to attack.

To witness.

To protect.

The soldiers felt it.

They backed up instinctively.

The squad leader's breathing grew harsh inside his visor.

He looked at the fracture beings, then at us, then at the sky, like he finally understood he had walked into a place his orders couldn't map.

He raised his weapon anyway.

Because systems always try one last time.

Nova's blade flared.

I stood, keeping Eli behind me.

"Don't," I said softly.

The squad leader hesitated.

Then lowered his rifle—just a fraction.

Not because he became kind.

Because he became afraid.

And fear, for the first time, made him stop instead of strike.

The Architects spoke again, colder.

SUBJECT LITTY: YOU HAVE COMPROMISED PROTOCOL.

I looked up at them.

"Good."

Nova whispered, "We can't keep him here."

I nodded, heart hammering.

She was right.

Eli had become the center of a war he didn't deserve.

Earth wanted him.

The Architects wanted him.

The fracture wanted him.

And if he stayed...

he'd be destroyed by everyone trying to "save" him.

Eli tugged my sleeve, trembling.

"Can we go home?" he whispered.

I swallowed hard.

"Yeah," I said softly.

"We're going home."

Nova's eyes widened.

"You're taking him to Earth?"

I nodded.

"Not to Earth," I said.

"To my world."

"The human layer."

Nova's voice went tight.

"That's where the war is."

I looked at Eli.

"I know."

But if we kept him here, he'd be a prisoner.

And if he returned alone, he'd be a trophy.

So the only option was the hardest one:

I would bring him back myself.

And I would stand between him and every system that thought it had the right to claim him.

The convergence pulsed.

The fracture city held its breath.

The soldiers backed away, dazed.

The Architect chorus rose once more.

WARNING: RETURNING SUBJECT TO HUMAN LAYER IN-CREASES CHAOS.

I replied quietly:

"Then let chaos learn kindness."

Nova stared at me.

"Litty... if you do this, you become a guardian, not a symbol."

I nodded.

"Good."

Eli looked up at me, eyes red.

"Are you gonna leave me?" he asked.

My throat tightened.

"No," I promised.

"Not today."

The fracture opened.

Not by force.

By consent.

And as I stepped toward the boundary with Eli and Nova beside me...

I understood the truth of this moment:

The first human fracture war had just gained its first innocent casualty.

And I had just chosen to make that casualty untouchable.

Which meant the war would now target me directly.

Because nothing makes a system more violent than a human refusing to surrender a child.

END CHAPTER 16 — PART C

....

CHAPTER 17 — "THE SAFEHOUSE IN A SKY THAT WATCHES" (PART A)

(PART A)

We did not fall back into the human layer.

We slid.

The fracture did not open like a door.

It softened like water remembering how to be rain.

Nova held Eli in one arm, her blade dimmed but ready, while I walked half a step ahead, guiding the descent not with control—but with agreement. The fracture did not want to release him. The convergence pulsed softly, like a heart letting go of a child who didn't know why goodbye mattered yet.

Eli pressed his face into Nova's shoulder.

"It's loud again," he whispered.

Nova tightened her hold.

"It'll quiet," she promised.

I wasn't sure if I believed that.

The human layer rose around us slowly—not as a city, not as a planet—but as gravity regaining confidence. Sound returned in layers: wind first, then distant engines, then voices, then sirens.

We emerged inside an abandoned high-rise shell overlooking a city that had not yet decided whether it wanted to sleep or panic.

Broken windows. Exposed beams. Half-finished floors. Dust and wind.

A safehouse chosen not for comfort—but for invisibility.

Nova set Eli down gently.

He looked around, eyes wide.

"It's... normal," he said, uncertain.

"Yes," I replied softly. "That's the dangerous part."

The sky above the city shimmered faintly—fracture-light barely visible through the clouds. Not enough to cause panic. Enough to cause obsession.

319

Eli looked up.

"It followed us," he said.

I shook my head.

"No," I told him. "It remembered you."

Nova moved to the window, scanning the streets below.

"We have maybe twenty minutes before drones triangulate our position."

I nodded.

"Plenty of time to be hunted," I said.

Eli sat on the dusty floor, pulling his knees to his chest.

"Are they gonna take me again?"

The question hit me harder here—because now he was fully human again. No fracture shimmer. No convergence buffer. Just a child sitting on concrete in a city that had learned to fear miracles.

I knelt in front of him.

"No," I said firmly. "Not while I'm here."

He studied my face carefully.

"You promise?"

I didn't hesitate.

"I promise."

Nova turned back from the window.

"Litty," she said quietly, "we can't keep moving like fugitives with a child."

"I know."

"And we can't hide him."

"I know."

"And we can't give him back."

I met her eyes.

"I know."

Silence filled the broken building.

The city below continued moving—people unaware that the most dangerous being on Earth was currently a ten-year-old sitting in a dusty hoodie with tear-stained cheeks.

Eli looked up at Nova.

"Do you have food?" he asked shyly.

Nova blinked.

Then laughed softly.

"I've got... something."

She reached into her pack and pulled out a compressed nutrition bar.

Eli examined it suspiciously.

"This looks like sadness," he said.

I snorted.

Nova laughed harder.

He took a bite anyway.

"...It tastes like it too."

The sound of his honesty cut through the tension.

For just a second...

We were just people.

Then my wrist device vibrated.

Nova's eyes sharpened instantly.

I glanced at the signal.

Global broadcast.

Emergency announcement.

Not from a government.

From a coalition.

The screen projected a human face—professional, calm, rehearsed.

"Today," the woman said, "humanity faces a defining moment. A minor is currently confirmed in contact with the fracture anomaly. This individual represents both hope and danger. Our goal is to ensure his safety while protecting the stability of our world."

Nova muttered, "Liar."

Eli looked at the screen.

"They're talking about me."

I nodded.

The woman continued:

323

"We urge all citizens to remain calm. We will bring the child into protective custody to ensure his wellbeing."

Nova scoffed.

"Protective custody means lab."

Eli's shoulders tightened.

"I don't wanna go."

I turned the device off.

"Then you won't."

Nova looked at me.

"You're about to become the most wanted person in human history."

I shrugged slightly.

"I already was in the fracture."

She smirked faintly.

"Yeah, but now the cameras work."

I sat beside Eli.

"Listen to me," I said softly.

He looked up.

"You didn't do anything wrong," I continued. "You didn't cause this. You didn't start a war. You didn't break the sky."

He whispered, "But they're mad."

I nodded.

"They're scared."

"Of me?"

I shook my head.

"Of what you prove."

"What do I prove?"

I swallowed.

"That the universe doesn't need permission to be kind."

He thought about that.

Then smiled faintly.

"That sounds like a good rule."

Nova crouched beside us.

325

"It is," she said. "It just makes bad leaders nervous."

Eli looked between us.

"Are you guys my parents now?"

Nova choked on a laugh.

I froze for half a second.

Then answered honestly.

"No," I said gently.

"We're your shields."

He nodded like that made sense.

Outside, the first drone passed overhead.

Then another.

Then three more.

The city lights dimmed slightly as surveillance grids re-aligned.

Nova whispered, "They're tightening the net."

I stood.

"Then we move."

Eli looked up.

"Where?"

I looked at the skyline.

"At a place they won't search," I said.

Nova raised an eyebrow.

"Which is?"

I met her eyes.

"'The one place they refuse to believe can still be innocent.'"

She smiled slowly.

"A school."

I nodded.

"They won't expect the fracture child to hide among other children."

Eli brightened slightly.

"I like kids."

Nova smiled.

"They're terrifying."

We gathered our things quickly.

Nova moved ahead to secure exits.

I helped Eli up.

He tugged my sleeve.

"Are we gonna fix everything?"

I knelt to him.

"No," I said softly.

"But we're going to stop it from breaking you."

He hugged me without warning.

I froze for half a second.

Then hugged him back.

The sky above shimmered faintly.

The fracture watched.

The Architects watched.

Earth watched.

And in a city that did not know it was about to protect the future...

Three figures moved quietly through broken concrete and borrowed hope.

END CHAPTER 17 — PART A

CHAPTER 17 — "THE SAFEHOUSE IN A SKY THAT WATCHES" (PART B)

(PART B)

The school did not know it was about to become sacred.

It was just a building.

Brick. Windows. Faded murals of cartoon planets and hand-painted quotes about dreams. A place where children argued about math problems and traded snacks like treasure. A place that smelled like pencil shavings and cafeteria food and futures that hadn't been scared yet.

Nova moved ahead first, cloak of probability folding her presence into background noise. Cameras blinked. Guards looked past her without knowing why. Not magic.

Pattern.

I walked beside Eli, keeping my hand close to his shoulder but not touching unless he reached for me. I didn't want him to feel owned.

He held his drawing in one hand like a passport.

"You sure this is okay?" he whispered.

"No," I answered honestly.

"But it's right."

He nodded.

Kids understand that difference faster than adults ever do.

We entered through a side gate as a bell rang somewhere deeper inside. Children poured out into a courtyard, laughing, pushing, yelling, existing. Eli froze for a moment, overwhelmed.

"They're loud," he whispered.

I smiled softly.

"Yeah," I said. "But it's a good loud."

Nova stood back, watching the scene like someone who had forgotten what childhood looked like from the inside.

Eli watched a group of kids playing tag. One tripped. Another helped them up. No drama. No narrative. Just motion.

He smiled faintly.

331

"They don't know," he said.

I shook my head.

"They know more than anyone."

We guided him toward a bench near the playground.

I crouched.

"Listen to me," I said quietly. "You don't tell anyone about the fracture. You don't tell anyone about me. You just... be a kid."

He thought about it.

"Can I still draw the sky?"

I nodded.

"Always."

Nova leaned against the wall, arms crossed, eyes scanning rooftops, windows, signals.

"They'll find us," she whispered.

I nodded.

"I know."

"But not yet."

Eli sat and watched the other kids.

A girl with braids stared at him.

He stared back.

She walked over.

"Why are you sitting alone?" she asked.

Eli shrugged.

"I just got here."

She looked at his drawing.

"That's cool."

He brightened.

"You think so?"

She nodded.

"It looks like the sky is scared."

He smiled.

"It is. But it's trying."

333

She sat beside him.

"My name is Mara."

"I'm Eli."

They shook hands.

I felt my chest tighten.

Because this was what the universe was trying to protect.

Not systems.

Not control.

Not gods.

This.

Nova whispered, "If they touch him…"

"I know," I whispered back.

The fracture shimmered faintly in the sky.

The Architects watched.

Earth watched.

But for a moment…

Eli was just a boy on a bench talking about drawings.

Then my wrist device vibrated again.

Nova looked at me sharply.

I glanced at it.

Not a broadcast.

Not a warning.

A signal.

Encrypted.

Architect origin.

Nova's eyes narrowed.

"They're calling you."

I stepped back from the bench slightly.

Eli looked up.

"You gotta go?"

I shook my head.

"Not far."

335

I activated the channel.

The Architects' presence filled the air around me—not physically, but cognitively.

SUBJECT LITTY: YOU HAVE DISRUPTED MULTIPLE PROTOCOLS.

I replied calmly.

"Good."

SUBJECT ELI REMAINS A HIGH-RISK VARIABLE.

"He's a child."

CHILDREN ARE UNSTABLE CONTAINERS.

"Then stop trying to store him," I said.

PAUSE.

We are observing behavioral divergence.

"Then observe quietly," I replied.

EARTH IS ESCALATING.

I looked back at the schoolyard.

"At least it's escalating around something gentle."

THEY WILL NOT ALLOW HIM TO REMAIN UNCLAIMED.

I whispered, "Neither will you."

Silence.

Then the Architects said something new.

WE ARE NOT PREPARED FOR HIS INFLUENCE.

I closed my eyes briefly.

"Neither are they."

We will not interfere.

I opened my eyes.

"You already did."

We will not interfere further.

I studied the air.

"You're lying."

We will not interfere directly.

I nodded slowly.

"Thank you for finally being honest."

The channel closed.

Nova exhaled slowly.

"They're stepping back."

"No," I said. "They're stepping sideways."

On the playground, Eli laughed.

Mara showed him how to climb a structure.

He hesitated.

She rolled her eyes.

"You're scared of climbing but not of the sky?" she teased.

He smiled shyly.

"The sky doesn't laugh at you when you fall."

She grinned.

"I will."

He climbed anyway.

I felt something inside me crack softly.

Because courage is quieter when it's normal.

Nova leaned closer.

"They're deploying observers."

I felt it too.

Not soldiers.

Not drones.

People.

Parents.

Teachers.

Staff.

Civilians.

Every human system was beginning to orbit Eli.

Because humans don't always hunt with weapons.

Sometimes they hunt with curiosity.

A teacher approached.

"Hey there," she said kindly to Eli. "Are you new?"

He nodded.

339

"Yes, ma'am."

She smiled.

"Welcome."

She looked at me.

"Are you his guardian?"

I met her eyes.

"For today," I said.

She nodded.

"Well, we're glad he's here."

I thanked her quietly.

She walked away.

Nova whispered, "She has no idea."

"No," I replied.

"And that's why she's protecting him."

We watched Eli play.

We watched children argue over games.

We watched a world that didn't know it was sheltering the heart of a fracture.

Then the sky darkened slightly.

Not clouds.

Drones.

High altitude.

Silent.

Nova stiffened.

"They're here."

I nodded.

"They always are."

The fracture shimmered faintly.

Not opening.

Warning.

I felt it.

Nova felt it.

The Architects felt it.

The school felt nothing.

Because humanity only sees storms when they arrive.

Eli tripped and scraped his knee.

He didn't cry.

He stood, dusted himself off.

Mara looked worried.

"You okay?"

He nodded.

"Yeah."

Then he smiled.

"Pain goes away."

I whispered, "He's right."

Nova looked at me.

"Not always."

I watched Eli run back into the game.

"Enough times to matter," I said.

A new broadcast pinged in my mind.

Not official.

Not controlled.

A leak.

Footage.

Coordinates.

"Child sighted near school sector—"

Nova swore.

"They're triangulating through civilian feeds."

I nodded.

"They're closing in."

Nova's hand tightened.

"We have to move him."

I looked at Eli.

He was laughing.

343

Alive.

Normal.

Human.

"We can't steal his moment," I whispered.

"And we can't let them steal him."

Nova met my eyes.

"You're going to have to choose."

I felt the fracture tighten.

I felt Earth watching.

I felt the Architects calculating.

And I felt Eli being a kid.

I whispered:

"Not yet."

Because sometimes the bravest act...

Is letting innocence exist one minute longer.

END CHAPTER 17 — PART B

CHAPTER 17 — "THE SAFEHOUSE IN A SKY THAT WATCHES" (PART C)

(PART C)

The school did not panic when the first sirens echoed in the distance.

Schools never panic.

They normalize danger with bells.

A warning tone rolled through the building, low and calm, the kind designed to sound like routine. Teachers guided children inside with practiced smiles. Doors closed. Curtains half-drew. Laughter softened into whispers.

To everyone else, it was just a drill.

To us, it was a net.

Nova stiffened. "They've sealed the perimeter."

I felt it too — not with eyes, but with gravity. The city's

movement tightened. Traffic rerouted. Airspace shifted. Digital noise condensed.

Earth was circling.

Eli stood beside Mara near the playground gate, clutching his drawing. He didn't understand what was happening yet. He just felt the change.

"Why is everyone going inside?" he asked.

I walked toward him slowly.

"Because grown-ups think being quiet keeps you safe," I said gently.

He frowned. "Does it?"

"Sometimes," I answered. "Sometimes it just keeps you from asking questions."

Mara looked between us. "Is he in trouble?"

Eli looked at her.

"I don't think so," he said uncertainly.

Nova whispered in my ear, "We have maybe five minutes before they identify him directly."

I nodded.

346

Then the sky shimmered again.

Not fracture.

Satellites.

Drones.

Human eyes, finally brave enough to look straight down instead of up.

The teacher's voice echoed faintly from inside the building: "Everyone stay calm. This is just a precaution."

Nova exhaled slowly.

"They're going to isolate the school."

Eli's shoulders tightened.

"Did I do something bad?"

The question felt heavier than every weapon in the world.

I knelt in front of him again.

"No," I said firmly. "You did something right. And people don't know how to handle that."

He looked at his drawing.

347

"They don't like the sky being nice," he whispered.

I smiled sadly.

"They don't like not being in charge of it."

A new broadcast flickered across my device — not global, not official.

Local.

Targeted.

The face on the screen was not cold.

It was warm.

Human.

A woman in a jacket, hair tied back, eyes trying very hard to look kind.

"Eli," she said softly into the camera.

Nova swore under her breath.

"They found his name."

The woman continued:

"We just want to talk. We want to make sure you're safe."

Eli stared at the screen.

"She sounds nice."

I felt my jaw tighten.

"They always do."

The woman smiled.

"We promise you won't be in trouble."

Nova whispered, "They never promise the truth."

Eli looked up at me.

"Is she lying?"

I didn't answer immediately.

Then I said quietly:

"She's scared."

He thought about that.

"Then she should sit with us," he said.

The innocence in his logic hurt more than any cruelty.

Nova moved closer.

349

"We have to move him. Now."

I nodded.

But as we turned toward the back exit...

The fracture reacted.

Not violently.

Not defensively.

It shimmered faintly across the sky like a thin scar glowing under skin.

Eli felt it instantly.

He placed his hand on his chest.

"It's getting loud again," he whispered.

Nova's eyes widened.

"The convergence is responding to his stress."

I felt it too.

The fracture wasn't opening.

It was listening.

And it was afraid.

I looked at Eli.

"You have to breathe," I said softly.

He tried.

His breath shook.

The schoolyard lights flickered.

Nova swore.

"If he destabilizes here—"

"I know," I said.

The fracture beings felt it too, far above.

They began shifting, aligning toward the human layer like a storm remembering its path.

The Architects watched.

Not interfering.

Not helping.

Learning.

Eli's breath hitched.

"I don't wanna be loud," he cried softly.

I put my hands gently on his shoulders.

"You're not loud," I said. "You're just honest."

The fracture shimmered again.

The drones overhead wobbled slightly.

One of them dipped, then stabilized.

Nova whispered, "They felt it."

I looked up at the sky.

"They always will."

Mara stared at Eli.

"What's wrong with you?" she asked softly, not cruelly.

Eli hesitated.

Then said:

"I talk to the sky."

Mara blinked.

352

Then shrugged.

"My grandma talks to plants," she said. "They don't answer though."

Eli smiled faintly.

"The sky does."

Mara looked up.

"I think it's pretty."

The fracture softened slightly.

Nova whispered, "Even her acceptance is stabilizing him."

I realized then:

Eli wasn't powerful because he touched the fracture.

He was powerful because he didn't separate from it.

He didn't see it as other.

He saw it as something that could feel.

That was the real danger.

The school doors opened slightly.

353

A principal stepped out, trying to remain calm.

"Eli?" she said kindly.

Eli looked at me.

"Do I go?"

I shook my head gently.

"Not yet."

The principal smiled.

"There are some people who just want to meet you."

Nova whispered, "They're about to pull him inside."

I felt the fracture tighten.

If Eli went inside, he would be isolated.

If he stayed outside, he would be exposed.

I realized there was only one option left.

I stood.

Slowly.

Deliberately.

And I stepped into full visibility.

Not hiding.

Not blending.

Just existing.

The air around me shifted subtly.

The fracture shimmered more clearly above.

The drones adjusted.

Cameras focused.

Humans looked.

The principal froze.

"Who are you?" she asked.

I looked at her gently.

"Someone who refuses to let a child be turned into a story."

The broadcasts spiked instantly.

People saw me.

Not clearly.

But enough.

A human figure standing beneath a scarred sky.

The one they had named.

The anomaly.

The rumor.

The threat.

The symbol.

Nova whispered, "You just went public."

I nodded.

"Better me than him."

The principal took a step back.

"Sir, please step away from the child."

I shook my head.

"No."

The word was quiet.

But it echoed.

Eli looked up at me.

"You're gonna get in trouble," he whispered.

I smiled faintly.

"I already did."

The woman from the broadcast appeared at the school gate with security behind her.

She looked at me.

Recognition flashed.

Fear.

Then control.

"Litty," she said carefully. "You don't have to make this harder."

I replied calmly.

"You don't have to make it cruel."

She looked at Eli.

"We can protect him."

I answered:

357

"You don't know how."

She hesitated.

Then tried again.

"He doesn't belong to you."

I nodded.

"He doesn't belong to anyone."

Silence stretched.

Eli whispered, "I just wanna go home."

I looked at him.

"Where is home?"

He thought.

Then said softly:

"Where people don't fight over me."

The fracture shivered.

The woman's eyes softened just a little.

"You can come with us," she said gently.

Eli shook his head.

She looked at me.

"You can't keep him forever."

I nodded.

"I'm not trying to."

Nova whispered, "They're shifting tone."

The woman stepped closer.

"What do you want?" she asked.

I met her eyes.

"I want you to remember he's a child before you remember he's important."

She swallowed.

"You're asking for something impossible."

"No," I said.

"I'm asking for something human."

Behind her, soldiers and officials waited.

Above us, the fracture waited.

Inside Eli, the convergence waited.

The world was balanced on a boy's breath.

Eli looked up at the woman.

"Do you wanna see my drawing?" he asked softly.

She hesitated.

Then nodded.

He held it up.

She looked at it.

And for just a moment...

She wasn't a representative.

She was a person.

She whispered, "It's beautiful."

Eli smiled.

"It says don't be scared."

Her eyes shimmered.

Nova whispered, "She felt it."

I felt it too.

Not victory.

Not peace.

Possibility.

The woman looked at me again.

"We can't stop watching him," she said quietly.

I nodded.

"I know."

"But you can stop trying to own him."

She hesitated.

Then looked at Eli.

"We'll... give you time," she said.

Nova inhaled sharply.

"Did she just—"

"Yes," I whispered.

"She just broke protocol."

The woman stepped back.

"Not long," she warned.

"I know," I replied.

The drones pulled back slightly.

Not leaving.

But easing.

The fracture softened again.

Eli exhaled.

The convergence calmed.

The school resumed its quiet hum.

Children were ushered inside.

Mara waved at Eli.

"Come play tomorrow," she said.

He smiled.

"Okay."

The woman turned away slowly.

Nova leaned close to me.

"You just forced a system to hesitate."

I whispered back:

"Because a child asked it to."

Eli tugged my sleeve.

"Are we safe now?"

I looked at him.

"Not forever," I said honestly.

"But for today."

He nodded.

"That's enough."

The fracture shimmered faintly above.

The Architects observed silently.

Humanity stepped back from the edge.

Not far.

363

But far enough.

I realized something in that moment:

The first human fracture war would not be won by power.

It would be delayed by mercy.

And sometimes...

Delay is the only victory a child needs to grow.

END CHAPTER 17

....

CHAPTER 18 — "THE WORLD LEARNS HIS NAME" (PART A)

(PART A)

The world did not wake up to Eli.

It discovered him.

Discovery is always louder than truth.

By sunrise, Eli's face was already looping across screens in thirty countries — blurred in some, sharpened in others, analyzed in slow motion like a miracle that forgot to ask permission. Headlines did not call him a child. They called him a phenomenon. A variable. A convergence point. A risk.

No one asked what he liked for breakfast.

Nova watched the feeds in silence while Eli slept curled against a backpack on the floor. His face looked peaceful now, soft in a way the world would never allow him to stay.

"They already named him," Nova said quietly.

I looked at the screen.

"Fracture Child."

"Sky Boy."

"Human Interface."

"Future of the Species."

"Threat Level: Unknown."

I turned the display off.

"They always name what they want to control."

Eli shifted in his sleep and murmured something about clouds.

I stayed near him.

Because the moment he woke up, the world would begin pulling at him again.

Nova leaned against the wall, arms crossed.

"You realize they're not going to let him stay invisible."

"I know."

"And you realize," she added, "that now you're not just protecting a kid."

I looked at her.

"You're protecting what he represents."

I nodded.

"That's harder."

She gave a faint smile.

"Everything worth protecting is."

The fracture shimmered faintly outside the broken window — not opening, not closing — listening.

Eli woke slowly.

He blinked.

Then sat up.

He looked at us.

"Did the sky sleep too?"

Nova smiled faintly.

"I think it watched."

He nodded like that made sense.

Then he noticed the silence.

"No school today?"

I shook my head.

"Not today."

He frowned slightly.

"Am I famous now?"

The question wasn't excited.

It was tired.

I met his eyes.

"Yeah," I said gently.

He sighed.

"That sounds exhausting."

Nova laughed quietly.

"Welcome to adulthood."

Eli slid closer to me.

368

"Do famous people get lonely?"

"Yes," I answered immediately.

He nodded.

"Okay."

He leaned against my arm.

Outside, helicopters passed far above the city.

The fracture pulsed faintly in response.

Eli winced slightly.

"It's louder when they look at me."

Nova whispered, "They're synchronizing attention fields."

I whispered back, "They're turning him into gravity."

Eli looked up.

"What's gravity?"

I smiled sadly.

"It's when everyone pulls on you even when they don't mean to."

He thought about that.

"I don't like that."

Neither did I.

Nova's device chimed.

A message.

Not from a government.

From a child network.

Encrypted civilian channels.

Parents.

Teachers.

Kids.

Someone had leaked footage of Eli smiling at Mara.

Someone had posted the drawing.

Someone had captioned it:

"HE JUST WANTS THE SKY TO FEEL SAFE."

The message spread faster than any weapon ever could.

Nova stared.

"They're empathizing."

I nodded slowly.

"And that's more dangerous than fear."

Eli looked at the screen.

"They like my drawing."

I smiled faintly.

"They like your heart."

He frowned.

"They don't even know me."

I answered softly:

"Sometimes people recognize the part of themselves they forgot."

Outside, protests began forming.

Not violent.

Confused.

Hopeful.

Angry.

All at once.

Some signs read:

LET HIM BE A KID.

Others read:

WE DESERVE ANSWERS.

Others read:

DON'T TOUCH HIM.

And a few read:

HE IS THE FUTURE.

Eli read none of them.

He just sat quietly.

"Do I have to save everyone?" he asked softly.

The question broke something inside me.

"No," I said immediately. "You don't owe the world

anything."

He nodded.

"That's good."

Nova whispered, "He's the first miracle who doesn't want to be one."

I whispered back, "That's why he is."

A knock echoed in the building.

Not forced.

Not violent.

Careful.

Nova stiffened.

I moved between Eli and the door.

A familiar voice spoke softly.

"It's Mara."

Eli looked up.

"Mara?"

I hesitated.

Nova shook her head.

"She shouldn't be here."

But Eli stood anyway.

"She came because she's not scared."

I opened the door slowly.

Mara stood there holding Eli's drawing.

Her eyes were wide.

"I found this on my phone," she said. "It's everywhere."

Eli swallowed.

"Are you mad?"

She shook her head.

"I think it's cool."

He smiled faintly.

"I don't want them to fight."

She nodded.

"They always do."

He looked at her.

"Do you wanna help me not make them?"

She smiled.

"Okay."

Nova whispered to me:

"Now there are two of them."

I realized in that moment...

The fracture was not changing the world.

Children were.

The fracture was just finally listening.

END CHAPTER 18 — PART A

CHAPTER 18 — "THE WORLD LEARNS HIS NAME" (PART B)

(PART B)

The world did not argue about Eli.

It argued about ownership.

Morning news cycles framed him as science. Evening panels framed him as religion. Midnight forums framed him as a weapon. No one framed him as a boy who still slept with one shoe on because he forgot to take it off.

Children, however, framed him correctly.

Within twelve hours, Eli's drawing had been recreated in over two hundred cities. Crayons. Markers. Chalk on sidewalks. Digital sketches on tablets. The sky drawn not as a threat, but as something tired that needed comfort.

Under every image, the same words appeared in different handwriting:

"DON'T BE SCARED."

Nova watched it all in silence.

"They're copying his language," she whispered.

I nodded.

"Because they understand it."

Eli sat beside Mara on the floor, drawing again. This time, he wasn't drawing the fracture. He was drawing people standing under it, holding hands.

Mara colored the people bright.

"Why are they smiling?" she asked.

"Because they're not alone," Eli answered.

Nova exhaled slowly.

"They're turning him into a movement."

I looked at Eli.

"No," I said quietly. "They're remembering how to be human."

Outside, crowds formed not in panic, but in discussion. Parents brought their kids. Teachers brought notebooks.

Artists brought paint. Musicians brought sound. The fracture in the sky became a background instead of a threat.

But power does not like backgrounds.

It prefers stages.

Government spokespeople began separating Eli from his meaning.

They said:

"He is a rare biological event."

"He is not symbolic."

"He is not special."

"He is simply different."

But difference had already become inspiration.

Children began asking their parents questions they couldn't answer.

Why does the sky look hurt?

Why do we fight when we're scared?

Why can't we be nice first?

And those questions spread faster than propaganda ever could.

Nova received a secure message.

Not from officials.

From underground networks.

"They're planning a custody declaration," she said quietly.

"Not legal."

"Global."

I looked at her.

"They want to make him a protected resource."

"Which is the polite word for property."

Eli looked up.

"What's custody?"

Nova hesitated.

I answered gently.

"It's when adults argue about who gets to decide for you."

He frowned.

"Why don't I decide?"

I smiled softly.

"That's the question that scares them."

Mara nodded.

"My mom says adults are just kids who forgot how to say sorry."

Eli considered that.

"That makes sense."

Nova laughed quietly.

Then her device vibrated again.

Her smile vanished.

"They're sending people," she said.

"Not soldiers."

"Influencers."

"Scientists."

"Religious leaders."

"They want access."

I nodded.

"They want narrative control."

Outside, a woman knelt in front of her child and said, "Draw what the sky feels like."

The child drew a heart.

Nova whispered, "They're winning without knowing it."

I whispered back, "That's the only way to win clean."

But the fracture did not rest.

It watched.

It adjusted.

It reacted to attention like a living system exposed to heat.

And Eli felt it.

He pressed his hand against his chest again.

"It's louder when people argue about me."

I knelt beside him.

"Then let's not argue."

"But they are."

I smiled softly.

"Then we stay quiet enough to hear the truth."

He nodded.

"I can do that."

A helicopter passed overhead.

Not close.

But intentional.

The sound made Eli flinch.

Nova cursed quietly.

"They're reminding him he's visible."

I stood.

Then I did something I hadn't done since the fracture first appeared.

I activated my channel.

Not to the Architects.

Not to governments.

To humanity.

Not officially.

Not clearly.

But enough.

My voice carried across public networks, unfiltered, unscripted.

"This is not your miracle," I said calmly.

"This is not your weapon."

"This is not your future to own."

"This is a child who reminded the sky it could feel."

Silence rippled.

Then backlash.

Then support.

Then confusion.

Then debate.

Eli looked up at me.

"Are you in trouble again?"

I smiled faintly.

"Probably."

He hugged me suddenly.

"I'm glad you're loud for me."

I closed my eyes briefly.

"Someone has to be."

The fracture shimmered faintly.

Not opening.

Not closing.

Listening.

The Architects observed silently.

Humanity argued loudly.

Children continued drawing quietly.

Mara looked at Eli.

"Do you think the sky can hear kids better than adults?"

Eli nodded.

"Kids talk in pictures."

I realized then:

The world was not learning Eli's name.

It was learning his language.

And that language was simple.

Gentle.

Unarmed.

And impossible to fully control.

Nova whispered, "They're not ready for what he's teaching."

I whispered back, "Neither were we."

Eli leaned against me again.

"Do you think the sky likes me?" he asked softly.

I smiled.

"I think the sky finally feels seen."

He smiled.

"That's nice."

Outside, protests shifted from anger to art.

Inside, a child kept drawing hope like it wasn't fragile.

And the fracture...

For the first time since it appeared...

Stopped trembling.

END CHAPTER 18 — PART B

CHAPTER 19 — "THE COST OF GUARDIANS" (PART A)

(PART A)

Protection always starts as a promise.

Then it becomes a posture.

Then it becomes a prison you build out of love because the world keeps trying to break what you're guarding.

By the fourth day, Eli's name was no longer "Eli" online.

It was a tag.

A symbol.

A movement.

A pressure point.

People didn't say, "Where is he?"

They said, "Who has him?"

And that difference was the beginning of the cost.

We moved before dawn.

Not because we were running from violence yet, but because we were running from attention.

Attention was the new weapon.

It didn't bleed you immediately.

It just made you visible enough to bleed later.

Nova walked ahead, scanning corners and rooftops, bending probability just enough that cameras caught empty angles and security guards blinked at the wrong time. She didn't like using her gifts like this, but she understood something Earth didn't:

The more "reasonable" the world sounded, the more dangerous it became.

Eli walked between us, hood up, drawing tucked in his front pocket like a heartbeat he wanted to keep close.

He didn't ask where we were going.

He didn't ask why.

He just kept glancing at the sky like a kid watching a storm that had once been his friend.

"It's watching me again," he whispered at one point.

I looked up.

The fracture shimmered faintly, barely visible in the early blue.

Not opening.

Not calling.

Listening.

"It's not trying to scare you," I told him.

Eli nodded slowly.

"It's just... it feels like when someone stands behind you in line," he said. "Like they're too close."

Nova gave a faint, reluctant smile.

"That's the best description of being famous I've ever heard."

Eli sighed.

"I don't want people too close."

"I know," I said.

Nova's eyes narrowed. "They're not just close. They're circling."

We ducked into a subway entrance as a distant helicopter passed overhead, far enough not to shake the street but close enough to remind the city who owned airspace. Eli flinched at the sound.

I crouched beside him.

"Hey," I said softly. "Look at me."

He looked.

"Do you remember what you told the sky?"

He blinked, then nodded.

"Don't be scared."

"Right," I said. "That rule works for you too."

He swallowed.

"I'm trying," he whispered.

Nova muttered, "Trying is the only thing that matters right now."

The subway station was mostly empty, but not quiet.

Screens flickered with looping footage of the fracture, pundits talking over each other like noise could substitute for meaning.

We kept our heads down.

Eli didn't.

He stared at the screen.

On it, a man in a suit smiled like he was selling safety.

"The child represents an evolutionary gateway," the man said. "We have a moral obligation to bring him into a secure environment—"

Eli's face tightened.

The man continued, "—for his protection and the protection of humanity."

Eli whispered, "Why do they keep saying protection like it's a cage?"

Nova's shoulders tensed.

I answered gently, "Because adults don't know the difference between 'keep safe' and 'keep owned.'"

Eli stared at the screen longer, then quietly reached into his pocket and unfolded his drawing.

He held it up toward the screen.

Not aggressively.

Not as protest.

As correction.

The drawing didn't change the broadcast.

But it changed the air in the station.

A woman across the platform saw it. Her face softened.

A kid near her tugged her sleeve and asked, "Is that him?"

The woman shook her head quickly, whispering, "No, baby, don't say that."

But she kept looking at the drawing.

Not with suspicion.

With recognition.

Nova grabbed my sleeve and pulled me a step back into shadow.

"They're starting to spot the *shape* of him," she hissed. "Not his face. His energy."

I nodded.

"His kindness leaves a trail."

Eli looked up at us, confused.

"What's wrong?"

Nova forced her voice calm. "Nothing, kid."

Eli frowned.

"You're lying."

Nova blinked.

Then she sighed, almost amused.

"Yeah. A little."

Eli folded his drawing again carefully.

"I don't want to be a trail," he said quietly.

My chest tightened.

"You're not," I told him. "You're a person."

He nodded, but his eyes stayed heavy.

In the fracture, the war had been loud and abstract.

On Earth, the war was quiet and personal.

It sounded like "for your safety."

It looked like smiling faces.

It felt like hands reaching gently—until the moment they grabbed.

We rode two stops and got off before the station cameras could complete their loop. Nova led us through maintenance corridors that smelled like rust and damp concrete. Eli held my hand now without asking.

He wasn't being childish.

He was being smart.

Outside, we emerged into a neighborhood that looked normal enough to be ignored—small stores, tired apartment buildings, a corner park with old swings. The kind of place media never visits unless something burns.

Nova slowed.

"This is good," she said.

"Why?" Eli asked.

"Because nobody thinks miracles hide in boring places."

Eli nodded.

"I like boring," he said.

We entered a small community center with peeling paint and a sun-faded banner that read: AFTERSCHOOL PRO-GRAMS — SAFE SPACE.

The irony nearly made me laugh.

Inside, an older woman behind a desk glanced up at us.

She looked tired.

She looked kind.

She looked like she didn't care about headlines.

"Can I help you?" she asked.

Nova's posture shifted—subtle, controlled.

"We're looking for a place to sit for a bit," Nova said. "Kid's been through a lot."

The woman's eyes softened.

"Haven't we all," she said.

She glanced at Eli.

Eli looked back.

He didn't smile at first. Then he did, small and polite.

"Hi."

The woman nodded.

"You hungry?" she asked.

Eli hesitated, then nodded.

"Yes, ma'am."

She waved her hand like it was nothing.

"Kitchen's down the hall. There's fruit, granola bars, juice. Don't make a mess."

Eli's face brightened.

"Okay!"

He started down the hall, then paused and looked back at me like he needed permission to be normal.

I nodded.

"Go."

He went.

The woman watched him go, then looked at Nova, then me.

"You two don't look like family," she said.

Nova's eyes narrowed slightly.

The woman held up a hand.

"I'm not asking to pry," she said. "Just saying: that kid looks like he needs someone who isn't trying to turn him into something."

My throat tightened.

Nova exhaled slowly.

"You have no idea," Nova said quietly.

The woman leaned back in her chair.

"I've got an idea," she replied. "I watch the news. I also watch kids. And the news doesn't know kids."

Nova stared at her.

I asked softly, "What's your name?"

"Ms. Lorrie," she said. "And before you ask, no, I don't want to be in a documentary."

I almost smiled.

"Understood."

Ms. Lorrie's voice lowered.

"Whatever you're doing, do it quietly," she said. "People have been coming through here all week asking questions about 'a special child.'"

Nova's jaw clenched.

"How many?" Nova asked.

"Too many," Ms. Lorrie answered. "Some were nice. Some weren't. A couple had that government energy."

Nova looked at me sharply.

"They're sweeping neighborhoods," she whispered.

I nodded.

"They're mapping kindness."

Ms. Lorrie watched us carefully.

"You got a plan?" she asked.

Nova didn't answer.

I did.

"We keep him human," I said softly.

Ms. Lorrie blinked.

Then nodded like that was the only plan she'd ever trust.

"Good," she said. "Because anything else will break him."

A laugh echoed from the hall.

Eli's laugh.

Pure.

Bright.

For a second, the world felt far away.

Nova stared toward the sound, and her voice softened.

"This is the cost," she whispered.

"What?" I asked.

She looked at me.

"He's finally safe enough to laugh," she said. "And we're

going to have to take him away from the first place that gave him that."

I swallowed hard.

Because she was right.

Safehouses don't last.

Not when the world is searching with satellites and stories.

Eli returned with a juice box and a banana, looking like a kid who'd just won something small.

"Ms. Lorrie says I can play ping pong," he said excitedly.

Nova blinked.

"Ping pong?"

Eli nodded, mouth full.

"I think it's like tiny tennis."

Ms. Lorrie smirked. "It is."

Eli looked at me.

"Can we stay for a little bit?"

I wanted to say yes.

I wanted to let him exist inside a moment that didn't feel like survival.

But my device vibrated again.

Nova's device too.

Same signal.

Same tone.

A public alert disguised as a community advisory.

LOCATION SWEEP IN PROGRESS — SECTOR 12.

Nova's eyes narrowed.

"They're coming."

Eli noticed the shift.

His smile faded.

"Are we leaving again?"

I stared at him, then nodded slowly.

Eli swallowed hard.

"I don't like leaving," he whispered.

My chest tightened.

"I know," I said.

He looked down at his banana, like it suddenly tasted like reality.

Ms. Lorrie stood up.

"Back door," she said quietly. "There's an alley behind the gym."

Nova hesitated.

"You'd help us?"

Ms. Lorrie looked at Eli.

Then at me.

"I help kids," she said simply. "That's my job. Sometimes I don't get paid for the most important part."

Eli stepped toward her and hugged her without warning.

Ms. Lorrie froze.

Then hugged him back.

"Be safe, baby," she whispered.

Eli pulled away, eyes watery.

"Do you draw?" he asked her.

Ms. Lorrie smiled sadly.

"Not like you."

Eli reached into his pocket and handed her the folded paper bird he'd made earlier.

"For your building," he said. "So it won't be lonely."

Ms. Lorrie's eyes shimmered.

"Thank you," she whispered.

Nova grabbed her pack.

"Move," she said.

We headed toward the back exit.

Eli looked over his shoulder once, then again, like he was trying to memorize the shape of a place that felt safe.

Outside, the alley smelled like trash and rain.

A siren wailed closer now.

Nova whispered, "We can't keep doing this."

"I know," I said.

Eli clutched my hand harder.

"What happens if they catch us?" he asked quietly.

Nova looked away.

I answered honestly.

"They'll try to separate us."

Eli's lip trembled.

"I don't want to be alone."

My throat tightened.

"You won't be," I promised.

And as soon as I said it, I felt the fracture shimmer faintly above the clouds.

Like it heard the promise.

Like it cared.

Like it was learning attachment.

Nova sensed it too. She looked up, jaw tight.

"That's the real cost," she whispered.

"What?"

"The fracture is bonding to him," she said. "And the more it bonds…"

She didn't finish.

She didn't have to.

If Eli got hurt, the fracture would react.

If the fracture reacted, Earth would panic.

If Earth panicked, it would escalate.

And if it escalated enough…

This war would stop being about custody and become about survival.

Eli looked up at the sky.

"It feels sad again," he whispered.

I squeezed his hand.

"Then we keep it brave," I said.

We moved.

Quietly.

Fast.

Three figures slipping through a city that was learning to hunt without looking cruel.

And behind us, the world's love grew sharper.

Because love, when it becomes ownership...

Hurts just as much as hate.

END CHAPTER 19 — PART A

CHAPTER 19 — "THE COST OF GUARDIANS" (PART B)

(PART B)

They reached the community center ten minutes after we left.

Not with sirens.

Not with shouting.

With clipboards.

With calm voices.

With smiles that had learned how to survive meetings.

Nova felt it before she saw it. Her shoulders tightened as we moved through a narrow service corridor behind the park. The air changed. The way gravity leaned. The way probability stiffened like someone had just said a name out loud in the wrong place.

"They're inside," she whispered.

Eli squeezed my hand.

"They found Ms. Lorrie?"

I nodded slowly.

"They're talking to her."

His lip trembled.

"Is she in trouble?"

"No," I said gently. "She's too kind for that."

But kindness always pays a price.

We paused behind a row of overgrown hedges. Across the street, two unmarked vans sat with engines still warm. No logos. No lights. No urgency.

Professional restraint.

Nova whispered, "They're not here to hurt him."

I replied, "That's worse."

Eli didn't understand the difference yet.

We watched through the leaves as three people exited the

building with Ms. Lorrie. She looked calm. Tired. But not afraid.

One of them showed her something on a tablet.

Her face changed.

Not shocked.

Recognizing.

Eli leaned forward instinctively.

"She knows me," he whispered.

I nodded.

"They showed her your picture."

Ms. Lorrie looked around the street once, slowly.

Not panicked.

Protective.

Then she shook her head.

One of the people insisted gently.

She shook her head again.

The third person looked annoyed.

Nova exhaled.

"She's refusing to help them."

Eli smiled faintly.

"Good."

But refusal does not stop systems.

It only delays them.

The team split.

Two stayed with Ms. Lorrie.

One walked toward the park.

Toward us.

Nova whispered, "Move."

We moved.

Fast.

Not running.

Flowing.

Eli's breath picked up.

"They're following," he whispered.

"They're looking," I corrected.

"They don't know how to see yet."

We slipped between two buildings, then down a narrow alley that smelled like wet cardboard and old paint. Nova paused, listening.

Footsteps.

Controlled.

Not rushed.

"They're good," she muttered.

I replied, "But they're human."

Eli suddenly stopped.

"I don't wanna hide anymore," he said softly.

Nova froze.

I knelt.

"You don't have to hide," I said.

411

"But we do have to move."

He shook his head.

"They're not mad," he whispered. "They're just... trying to decide me."

That sentence hurt more than any chase.

Nova whispered, "He understands too much."

Eli looked at her.

"You do too."

She didn't deny it.

Footsteps echoed closer.

A voice called softly:

"Eli?"

Not threatening.

Not commanding.

Careful.

Nova cursed under her breath.

"They're using empathy."

I stood slowly.

Nova grabbed my arm.

"Don't."

I shook my head.

"If they see him as prey, they'll chase. If they see him as human, they'll hesitate."

I stepped into view.

The man froze.

He was younger than I expected.

Early thirties.

Eyes tired.

Hands open.

"I don't want to scare him," he said quietly.

"You already did," I replied calmly.

He swallowed.

"I'm not here to take him," he said. "I'm here to understand him."

Eli stepped beside me.

"I'm right here," he said softly.

The man's eyes widened slightly.

Not fear.

Recognition.

"Hi," he said.

Eli nodded.

"Hi."

The man crouched slowly to Eli's level.

"My name's Daniel."

Eli tilted his head.

"You don't look like a bad guy."

Daniel smiled faintly.

"I try not to be."

Nova stayed tense.

I stayed still.

Daniel glanced at me.

"I know who you are," he said quietly.

I nodded.

"And I know why you're afraid," I replied.

He hesitated.

Then nodded.

"They want to movc him to a secure location."

Eli frowned.

"What's secure?"

Daniel paused.

Then answered honestly.

"A place where nothing can reach you."

Eli looked down.

"Nothing includes people."

Daniel swallowed.

"Yes."

Eli whispered, "That sounds lonely."

Daniel closed his eyes for a moment.

When he opened them, they were wet.

"You're right," he said quietly.

Nova whispered to me, "He's breaking."

I whispered back, "Good."

Daniel looked at Eli.

"They think you're important."

Eli shrugged.

"I just draw."

Daniel smiled sadly.

"That's what scares them."

A shout echoed in the distance.

Another team member calling Daniel's name.

416

Daniel flinched slightly.

He looked at Eli again.

"They're not going to stop," he said.

Eli looked at him.

"Then you should tell them to be nicer."

Daniel laughed softly through his nose.

"I'll try."

Nova stepped forward.

"If you try to take him," she said coldly, "I won't be kind."

Daniel met her eyes.

"I know," he said.

He stood slowly.

"I won't tell them where you went," he said quietly.

Nova blinked.

I studied him.

"Why?" I asked.

Daniel looked back at Eli.

"Because I have a son," he said softly. "And I realized I wouldn't want the world deciding him."

Eli stepped forward and hugged him suddenly.

Daniel froze.

Then slowly hugged back.

"Thank you for not being scary," Eli whispered.

Daniel's breath shook.

"Thank you for reminding me what I forgot."

Daniel stepped back.

"They'll keep searching," he warned.

"We know," I replied.

He nodded once.

Then walked away.

Nova exhaled slowly.

"That was too close."

Eli looked up at me.

"He was nice."

"Yes," I said.

"And that's why this hurts more."

We moved again.

But Eli's mood shifted.

He wasn't scared.

He was tired.

"Why do they all want me?" he whispered.

I stopped walking.

I knelt in front of him.

"They don't want you," I said softly.

"They want what you make them feel."

He frowned.

"I didn't mean to."

"I know," I said.

419

Nova whispered, "That's the tragedy."

Eli sat on the curb.

"I don't wanna be special anymore."

The words shattered me.

"You're not special because of the fracture," I said.

"You're special because you care."

He shook his head.

"That makes it worse."

I smiled sadly.

"Yeah," I said. "It does."

The fracture shimmered faintly above the clouds.

Nova felt it.

I felt it.

The Architects felt it.

The fracture was responding to Eli's emotional exhaustion.

Not violently.

420

Protectively.

Like a storm that wanted to cover a child with its shadow instead of rain.

Nova whispered, "It's bonding deeper."

I nodded.

"And that makes him a liability in every timeline."

Eli looked up at the sky.

"Don't be scared," he whispered to it.

The shimmer softened.

Nova whispered, "He's calming a universe."

I whispered back, "And exhausting himself."

We reached a rooftop overlooking the city.

Lights below.

Movement everywhere.

No single place to rest.

Eli sat beside me.

"I don't wanna be a reason people fight," he said.

I placed my forehead against his gently.

"Then you won't be," I whispered.

"How?"

"You'll be the reason they stop."

Nova looked at me.

"You believe that?"

I met her eyes.

"I have to."

Because if I didn't...

This would all just be tragedy in slow motion.

Eli yawned.

"I'm sleepy."

Nova checked the skyline.

"We can't stop yet."

Eli nodded.

"Okay."

But his head rested against my shoulder anyway.

And I realized:

Guardianship is not heroic.

It is not clean.

It is not rewarded.

It is choosing to carry someone else's exhaustion when the world refuses to.

And in that moment, I understood:

I wasn't protecting Eli from the world.

I was protecting the world from what it would become if it broke him.

END CHAPTER 19 — PART B

CHAPTER 20 — "WHERE CHILDREN CANNOT FALL" (PART A)

(PART A)

Eli slept in my arms like the world had never tried to claim him.

His breathing was shallow at first, then steadied—slowly, cautiously—like his body didn't trust rest anymore. The city below us kept moving, unaware that the sky's newest war was happening in silence on a rooftop.

Nova stood a few steps away, eyes on the horizon, posture locked in the kind of stillness that meant she was doing math with outcomes instead of feelings.

"He's burning out," she said quietly.

I didn't look up.

"I know."

"He can't keep being the anchor," she continued. "Not

emotionally. Not physically."

I watched Eli's eyelids tremble in sleep.

"He never chose it," I said.

Nova's voice sharpened.

"Choice isn't what makes systems attach. It's proximity."

I felt the fracture above the clouds—faint, shimmering, patient—like it was holding its own breath so it wouldn't wake him.

"Then we separate proximity," I said.

Nova turned toward me.

"And put him where?"

I didn't answer immediately because the answer felt like betrayal.

Not betrayal of Eli.

Betrayal of the moment he finally believed he wasn't alone.

But the universe was not gentle with miracles. And Eli wasn't a miracle.

He was a child.

425

And children were never supposed to carry cosmic tension like a backpack.

Nova stepped closer and lowered her voice.

"The Architects already ran the projection. They're not wrong. If he stays in the human layer, even with you shielding him, the attention alone will keep stressing him. The fracture will keep resonating. The more it resonates, the more it will—"

"Follow," I finished.

Nova nodded once.

"And if it follows a child's fear," she said, "it will become a storm that only responds to feelings."

I stared out at the skyline.

"That's how worlds end," I murmured.

Nova didn't argue.

She didn't need to.

Because we had already seen what happened when Eli's fear spiked: streetlights flickered, drones wobbled, air pressure shifted, the fracture shimmered like a wound reopening in real time.

That wasn't power.

That was reflex.

And if the fracture learned to reflex like a scared child...

Then Earth wouldn't just fear it.

Earth would provoke it by accident.

Sirens.

Shouting.

Crowds.

Lights.

All the normal noise of human life would become a trigger.

Eli stirred slightly.

I froze.

He didn't wake.

Nova whispered, "What are you thinking?"

I answered softly.

"I'm thinking about a place where children can be children."

Nova's mouth tightened.

"There isn't one."

I looked at Eli again.

"There has to be."

Nova's eyes narrowed.

"You mean outside Earth."

I didn't respond with words.

I didn't have to.

Nova exhaled slowly.

"You're talking about building him a pocket."

"A sanctuary," I corrected.

Nova's gaze sharpened.

"In the fracture."

I shook my head.

"Not in the fracture," I said. "Near it—but not bound to it.

A place that hears it, without being swallowed by it."

Nova's expression shifted slightly—curiosity mixed with caution.

"That's... new."

"It has to be," I said.

I looked up at the clouds.

The shimmer in the sky was almost invisible now, like the fracture was trying to behave.

It was listening.

Waiting.

Learning.

A child.

I realized something then that made my spine go cold.

The fracture wasn't only bonded to Eli.

It was bonded to the feeling Eli brought into it.

Meaning if Eli left Earth, and fear grew loud again...

The fracture would feel abandoned.

And abandoned things do not stay gentle.

Nova read my face.

"You feel it."

I nodded.

"If we separate him wrong," I whispered, "the fracture will panic."

"And if it panics," Nova said, "Earth panics back."

I kissed Eli's forehead lightly and whispered a promise he couldn't hear.

"We do it right."

Nova glanced at her device.

"Search sweeps are still active. They backed off publicly, but the quiet operations never stopped."

I nodded.

"That's why we leave before they force a mistake."

Eli's eyes fluttered open.

He blinked slowly, confused, then focused on my face.

"Did I fall asleep?" he asked, voice small.

"Yeah," I said softly. "You needed it."

He frowned slightly.

"Did the sky get loud again?"

"No," I said. "It stayed quiet."

Eli stared upward.

The sky looked normal. Just clouds and early sun.

But he saw beyond it.

"It's still there," he whispered.

"Yes," I said.

He swallowed.

"Is it mad?"

"No," I answered immediately. "It's worried."

Eli looked back at me, eyes glossy.

"Because I'm tired?"

I felt my throat tighten.

431

"Because it doesn't know how to be alone yet," I said gently.

Eli sat up slowly, rubbing his eyes.

"I don't want it to be alone," he whispered.

Nova spoke softly—too softly for someone like her.

"And we don't want you to be crushed."

Eli looked at Nova.

"Why do you always sound like you're about to fight a dragon?"

Nova blinked.

Then laughed—quiet, surprised.

"Because I usually am."

Eli nodded like that was fair.

Then he looked at me again.

"Are we moving again?"

I hesitated.

Then nodded.

"Yes."

Eli's shoulders slumped.

"I don't like moving."

"I know," I whispered.

He stared at his hands.

"Is it because of me?"

I didn't want to lie.

And I didn't want to place the weight on him.

So I told the truth carefully.

"It's because grown-ups are trying to turn you into a decision," I said. "And you're not a decision. You're a kid."

Eli sniffed.

"I just wanna draw."

Nova's jaw tightened.

"And they can't stand that it works."

Eli looked between us.

433

"Where are we going?"

I inhaled slowly.

The words felt like a door opening.

"To a place where you can rest," I said.

He frowned.

"Like a house?"

"Like a world," Nova murmured.

Eli's eyes widened.

"A world?"

I nodded.

"A small one," I said. "A safe one."

Eli stared at me like I'd just said something impossible.

"Can you make worlds?"

Nova's gaze flicked to me.

I answered honestly.

"I don't know," I said. "But I know the fracture can."

Eli looked up at the sky again.

"It can make worlds?"

"It can make rooms," I said. "It can make spaces. It can shape."

Nova added, "It just needs rules."

Eli blinked.

"Rules?"

I nodded.

"Rules like... no hunting," I said. "No cameras. No arguing. No adults trying to decide you. Rules like... you get to be a kid."

Eli's breath caught.

He looked hopeful for the first time in days.

"But would I be alone?" he asked.

The question hit the deepest.

Nova looked away.

I looked him in the eyes.

"No," I promised. "You'll have us."

Nova's eyes snapped toward me.

I met her gaze.

Not asking.

Stating.

Nova's lips pressed together.

Then, after a beat, she nodded once.

"Yeah," she said quietly. "You'll have us."

Eli's eyes watered.

"Will Mara be okay?"

I swallowed.

"She'll be okay," I said. "And you can send her drawings."

He sniffed.

"How?"

Nova's smile was faint but real.

"We'll figure it out."

Eli stood up slowly.

He looked smaller on the rooftop than he had in the fracture.

Smaller than he deserved to feel.

"Okay," he whispered. "If it's a place where children can't fall..."

I froze slightly.

Nova's eyes narrowed.

"That phrase," she whispered.

Eli shrugged.

"It just... came out."

I felt the fracture shimmer faintly above the clouds.

Like it heard him.

Like it liked the idea.

Nova's voice went low.

"The fracture is listening to his language again."

Eli looked up.

"Can it hear me right now?"

I nodded.

"Yes."

He cupped his hands around his mouth and whispered toward the sky:

"Don't be scared. We're gonna make you a home too."

The shimmer softened.

I felt a pulse—not violent, not loud—gentle agreement.

Nova breathed out.

"It answered."

Eli smiled faintly.

"Good."

We moved to the edge of the rooftop where the skyline opened wide.

Nova checked the streets below, then the air, then the invisible math of watchers.

"Two minutes," she said.

"Before what?" Eli asked.

"Before someone decides to be brave in the wrong way," Nova answered.

Eli nodded, oddly calm.

I held his hand.

"Ready?" I asked.

Eli hesitated, then nodded.

"Yeah."

I looked up into the clouds.

I didn't force the fracture.

I didn't demand.

I didn't threaten.

I simply spoke to it like Eli did.

"We need a place," I said softly. "A pocket. A room. A sanctuary."

The air warmed.

The sky shimmered.

439

A thin line appeared in the clouds like a seam of light being gently unstitched.

Nova stiffened.

"It's opening."

Eli's grip tightened.

"It's not loud," he whispered.

"No," I said. "Because you asked it nicely."

The seam widened, not into a chaotic tear, but into a doorway shaped like softness.

A threshold.

And beyond it, not darkness—light.

Warm light.

The color of a place that wanted to be safe.

Eli stared.

"It looks like... morning," he whispered.

Nova's voice trembled, just barely.

"It's building something for him."

I swallowed hard.

"For us," I corrected.

We stepped forward.

And as we crossed the threshold, the city below kept spinning like nothing had happened.

But inside the seam of the sky...

A new kind of world began.

A world with one rule written into its bones:

Children cannot fall.

END CHAPTER 20 — PART A

CHAPTER 20 — "WHERE CHILDREN CANNOT FALL" (PART B)

(PART B)

The sanctuary did not finish forming all at once.

It grew.

Not like a structure.
   Not like a machine.
   Not like a planet.

It grew like a memory learning how to become a place.

As we crossed fully into the seam of light, gravity softened—not disappeared, but rearranged. The air felt warm without heat. Bright without glare. Soft without weakness. Colors existed the way emotions do in dreams: not sharp, not blurred, but meaningful.

Eli gasped softly.

"It feels like when you wake up before you remember your

name," he whispered.

Nova looked around slowly.

"This place isn't obeying physical constants," she murmured. "It's obeying... comfort."

The ground beneath our feet resembled pale stone, but it pulsed faintly like skin remembering it was alive. The sky above us was not a sky—it was a ceiling of endless dawn. Light without sun. Horizon without distance.

I felt the fracture behind us fold gently closed, not sealing us in, but insulating the space like a parent pulling a blanket over a sleeping child.

Nova whispered, "It built this from Eli's emotional pattern."

Eli looked down at his hands.

"Did I make this?"

I shook my head.

"You inspired it," I said. "That's different."

He nodded slowly.

"I like inspired better."

The sanctuary listened.

We walked forward.

Every step shaped the world a little more.

Grass formed beneath our feet—not sharp, not cold—soft enough to kneel on without thinking about it. Trees rose in gentle curves, not towering, not imposing, but welcoming. Their leaves shimmered faintly, reflecting not light, but memory.

Eli touched one.

"It feels like when my mom used to brush my hair," he whispered.

My chest tightened.

Nova looked away.

The place was not copying Earth.

It was translating safety.

We reached a small clearing.

In the center stood nothing.

Just space.

Eli tilted his head.

"Is something supposed to be here?"

Nova studied the ground.

"This is a creation core," she said. "It's waiting for intention."

Eli thought.

Then sat down cross-legged in the middle of the clearing.

"I want a place where nobody yells," he said softly.

The ground pulsed.

"I want a place where nobody grabs," he continued.

The air warmed.

"I want a place where if you fall, it catches you."

The space around him shifted.

Not violently.

Not suddenly.

Like a story adjusting its ending.

445

A low structure began to rise from the ground—not a building, not a fortress—but something between a home and a playground. Smooth stone walls curved inward protectively. Open archways formed naturally. Inside, light glowed like afternoon that never rushed.

Nova's breath caught.

"It's responding directly to his emotional language."

I whispered, "He's writing architecture with his heart."

Eli stood slowly, eyes wide.

"I didn't know it could listen like that."

Nova answered quietly, "Neither did the Architects."

And as if summoned by the acknowledgment...

They appeared.

Not physically.

Not visually.

But present.

A shift in thought-density.

A tightening in reality.

A voice—not in sound, but in cognition:

SANCTUARY CONSTRUCT DETECTED.

Nova stiffened.

I didn't.

Eli felt it instantly.

"They're here," he whispered.

"Yes," I said gently. "But they're only watching."

THE SANCTUARY IS A NOVEL STRUCTURAL ANOMALY.

Nova snapped back mentally, "Everything you didn't build is an anomaly to you."

WE REQUEST AUDIT ACCESS.

I replied calmly.

"Denied."

Silence.

Then:

WE REQUIRE EVALUATION FOR STABILITY RISK.

Eli looked at me.

"Are they mad?"

"No," I said. "They're confused."

He nodded.

"They should draw."

Nova almost laughed.

The Architects continued:

THIS SANCTUARY IS IMPRINTING SUBJECT ELI'S EMOTIONAL PARAMETERS INTO ITS FOUNDATIONAL LAWS.

I answered, "Good."

THIS MAY LEAD TO NON-LOGICAL SYSTEM PRIORITIZATION.

"Yes," I said. "That's the point."

PAUSE.

WE HAVE NEVER MODELED A REALITY BUILT ON PROTECTION INSTEAD OF CONTROL.

Nova whispered, "Then welcome to childhood."

The sanctuary shimmered gently.

The structure Eli had imagined finished forming.

Inside, soft floors that responded to weight like memory foam.

Walls that glowed faintly with shifting colors.

Windows that showed not Earth, not stars—but possibility.

Eli stepped inside slowly.

He walked across the floor.

Then deliberately fell backward.

The floor caught him.

Not like a mattress.

Like hands.

He laughed—real laughter, full and unafraid.

"It didn't hurt!" he shouted.

Nova closed her eyes briefly.

I felt something inside me finally loosen.

Eli rolled onto his side.

"I like this place," he said.

I smiled.

"So do I."

The sanctuary was not large.

But it didn't feel small.

It felt complete.

Nova whispered, "It doesn't need size. It needs meaning."

The Architects observed silently.

THIS SPACE IS NOT ALIGNED WITH UNIVERSAL OPTI-
MIZATION MODELS.

I replied, "Neither are children."

The sanctuary responded again.

A small stream formed near the clearing—water that
glowed softly, not bright, not reflective, just alive.

Eli sat beside it and dipped his fingers in.

"It's warm," he whispered.

Nova touched it too.

"It's tuned to his temperature preferences."

Eli looked up.

"It remembers me."

I knelt beside him.

"It cares about you."

He swallowed.

"I don't want to hurt it."

"You won't," I promised. "Because here, you don't have to carry anything."

The Architects spoke again.

SUBJECT ELI IS NO LONGER IN DIRECT FRACTURE PROX-IMITY.

Nova answered, "And he's finally breathing."

WE DETECT EMOTIONAL STABILIZATION.

I whispered, "Because he's not being watched like a weapon."

The sanctuary pulsed.

Not in power.

In contentment.

But Earth...

Earth felt the loss immediately.

Nova's device vibrated sharply.

Multiple signals.

Global.

Emergency.

The fracture seam had closed behind us.

From Earth's perspective...

Eli had vanished.

Nova swallowed.

"They're going to panic."

I nodded.

"They always do when they lose what they think they own."

Eli looked up.

"Did I disappear?"

"No," I said. "You arrived."

He considered that.

"I like arrive better."

Nova looked at me.

"They'll try to reopen the fracture."

"I know."

"They'll fail."

I nodded.

"Because it won't open to fear anymore."

The Architects transmitted again.

EARTH RESPONSE PROJECTIONS INDICATE ESCALATION.

I replied calmly.

"Let them escalate."

Nova looked at me sharply.

"You're saying that too easily."

I met her gaze.

"They were always going to," I said. "The difference is now, Eli doesn't have to feel it."

I looked at Eli.

"Here, you're safe."

He smiled faintly.

"I can sleep here?"

"Yes," I said.

"Forever?"

Nova hesitated.

I answered carefully.

"For as long as you want."

He thought.

Then nodded.

"Okay."

He walked toward the soft structure and curled up inside, already half-asleep.

"I like places where children can't fall," he murmured.

I watched him drift into sleep.

Not exhaustion sleep.

Not escape sleep.

Real sleep.

Nova stood beside me quietly.

"You just changed the trajectory of two civilizations," she whispered.

I shook my head.

"No," I said. "He did."

The sanctuary pulsed gently, sealing its emotional laws:

No violence.
  No coercion.
  No ownership.
  No fear without comfort.

The Architects observed.

Not interfering.

Not approving.

Learning.

And somewhere far away...

Earth screamed into the void.

But here...

A child finally rested.

END CHAPTER 20 — PART B

CHAPTER 20 — "WHERE CHILDREN CANNOT FALL" (PART C)

(PART C)

Earth noticed the silence first.

Not because the fracture vanished — it was still there, a faint scar in the sky — but because the resonance stopped responding. Satellites screamed into static. Gravitational monitors reported calm. Emotional-field sensors (devices no one publicly admitted existed) went flat.

The fracture was still alive.

But it was no longer listening to Earth.

It was listening to Eli.

And Eli was asleep.

Inside the sanctuary, the air glowed softly like morning that had no obligation to become noon. Eli lay curled on the living floor, the surface gently shifting beneath him in slow, protective pulses, as if the world itself were breathing with him. His face was peaceful — not relieved, not numbed — simply safe.

Nova stood at the edge of the clearing, arms folded, eyes fixed on him like she was afraid the universe might change its mind.

"He's dreaming," she whispered.

I nodded.

"I can feel it."

The sanctuary responded to his sleep differently than it had to his waking thoughts. Where his words had shaped walls and streams and light, his dreams shaped rules.

Invisible ones.

The temperature adjusted not for comfort, but for reassurance.

The light softened not for beauty, but for gentleness.

Even gravity tuned itself to cradle rather than hold.

Nova crouched slowly and pressed her palm to the ground.

"This place is imprinting him deeper than we thought."

I knelt beside her.

"It's not imprinting him," I said quietly.

"It's learning from him."

She looked at me.

"That's worse."

I knew she was right.

Because systems that learn emotion do not forget it.

Above us, far beyond the sanctuary's ceiling of endless dawn, Earth panicked.

Emergency councils convened.

Religious factions splintered.

Scientific coalitions accused one another of losing control.

Military units repositioned in silence.

The disappearance of one child triggered more defensive planning than any war in the last century.

Because Eli was not just a person anymore.

He was proof that the universe could choose kindness over

459

authority.

And authority does not forgive that.

Nova's device pulsed in her hand.

She didn't even have to look.

"They're trying to reopen the seam."

I nodded.

"They won't succeed."

She stared at me.

"You sound too sure."

I looked at Eli.

"He didn't build this place with force," I said. "He built it with permission."

As if hearing his name, Eli shifted in his sleep.

The sanctuary responded instantly.

Light curved.

Air warmed.

The distant hum of existence softened.

Nova whispered, "He's rewriting the sanctuary while he dreams."

I closed my eyes.

And then...

I felt it.

Not through the fracture.

Not through the Architects.

Through him.

A dream.

Not an image.

Not a story.

A feeling.

Eli dreamed of falling.

But in his dream, the fall never ended.

And because it never ended...

It never hurt.

The sanctuary adapted.

Its internal physics bent.

Space folded inward.

Distance lost meaning.

And a new law wrote itself into the bones of reality:

In this place, descent is always gentle.

Nova gasped.

"The sanctuary just removed terminal velocity."

I opened my eyes slowly.

"Children can't fall here," I whispered.

She looked at me.

"He didn't say it," she said.

"He believed it."

And belief in a learning system is more powerful than command.

The Architects felt it.

They did not speak.

But their presence sharpened like a mind encountering something it could not simplify.

SANCTUARY PARAMETERS HAVE SHIFTED BEYOND FRACTURE TEMPLATE LIMITS.

Nova answered calmly.

"Good."

THIS ENVIRONMENT IS NO LONGER PURE FRACTURE CONSTRUCT.

I replied, "It never was."

It is becoming a hybrid reality.

"Yes," I said. "A child-built one."

The Architects paused.

Then:

THIS WILL ALTER MULTI-LAYER PROBABILITY STRUCTURES.

Nova smirked faintly.

463

"Kids do that."

The sanctuary shimmered again, but not in response to fear.

It shimmered in affirmation.

Eli rolled onto his side and whispered in his sleep:

"Don't let them fall..."

The sanctuary answered.

Walls softened further.

Distances shortened.

Edges rounded.

The very concept of harm lost definition inside its space.

Nova whispered, "This place is becoming a lawless law."

I corrected her.

"It's becoming a law built from care."

She exhaled slowly.

"And Earth just lost its leverage."

Above us, Earth launched probes toward the fracture seam.

They failed.

Not violently.

They simply... forgot how to arrive.

Coordinates slid.

Angles curved.

Access dissolved.

The seam did not reject them.

It ignored them.

Because Eli had not invited them.

Nova stared upward.

"They can't force it open."

I nodded.

"Not without fear."

"And fear isn't loud enough anymore," she whispered.

Eli stirred again.

465

His brow furrowed.

I felt the dream shift.

This time he dreamed of voices.

Crowds.

Adults arguing.

Hands reaching.

And in his dream, he didn't run.

He raised his drawing.

The sanctuary reacted instantly.

A soft wave rolled across its interior.

Not a defense.

A boundary.

A gentle one.

A boundary that said:

You may enter only as you are.

Not as what you want.

Nova felt it.

I felt it.

The Architects calculated it.

ENTRY CONDITIONS NOW REQUIRE EMOTIONAL ALIGN-
MENT.

Nova laughed quietly.

"He just installed a kindness firewall."

I smiled.

Eli whispered again in his sleep:

"Don't be scared…"

The sanctuary pulsed.

The fracture far above us softened further.

Earth felt it too.

And for the first time since the sky blinked…

The fracture did not answer Earth at all.

It only answered Eli.

Nova sat beside me.

"This place isn't just protecting him," she said.

"It's protecting the idea of him."

I nodded.

"And one day, it will protect children who never meet him."

She looked at me sharply.

"You're thinking ahead."

I looked at Eli.

"You don't build sanctuaries for today," I said.

"You build them for the moment someone else needs them."

Eli sighed softly in his sleep.

And the sanctuary reshaped itself just a little more.

Not larger.

Not stronger.

Kinder.

Outside, Earth continued to argue.

Inside, a child dreamed a world into gentleness.

And I understood then:

This sanctuary was not an escape.

It was a seed.

END CHAPTER 20 — PART C

....

CHAPTER 21 — "THE DAY EARTH LOST ITS VOICE" (PART A)

(PART A)

Earth didn't go quiet.

It got louder.

But the fracture stopped answering.

That was the moment the world lost its voice.

Because humanity had built its entire sense of control on one hidden belief:

If something bigger appears, it must respond to us.

The fracture had responded—at first.

It shimmered when they aimed satellites at it. It pulsed when they shouted into cameras. It distorted when they threatened it. It even trembled when children drew pictures of it with soft hands and soft hearts.

470

But now...

It did nothing.

The scar in the sky remained.

The seam existed.

Yet every signal sent upward came back empty.

No ripple.

No reaction.

No "proof" to point at.

And without proof, authority becomes theater.

By day five, news anchors began repeating the same phrases in different tones:

"Where is the child?"

"Who took the child?"

"Did he die?"

"Did he ascend?"

"Is this a hostile act?"

"Is this a government cover-up?"

"Is this alien abduction?"

The truth wasn't on any screen:

A child was asleep inside a place built from permission.

Nova watched Earth's feeds on a thin projection that hovered above the sanctuary's clearing like a ghost of the old world. She didn't look worried.

She looked disgusted.

"They're turning absence into a weapon," she said.

I watched the footage silently—streets full of people, half-panicked, half-hopeful. Some carried signs with Eli's drawings. Some carried signs demanding answers. Some carried weapons because fear always needs an object to hold.

"They don't know what to do without reaction," I said.

Nova nodded.

"They never learned how to lead without leverage."

On one channel, a politician pointed at the sky and declared:

"We will regain control of our airspace."

472

Nova snorted.

On another, a scientist insisted:

"The child is likely under the influence of a non-human intelligence."

Nova sighed.

On another, a preacher shouted:

"God is testing us!"

Nova muted it.

The pattern was always the same:

If the world can't control something, it tries to rename it until it feels smaller.

But Eli wasn't small.

And that was the problem.

Eli slept.

Deep.

The kind of sleep that rewrites you.

The sanctuary glowed around him, pulsing in slow waves—

473

like it was syncing to his breath, like it had decided his calm was the only law worth following. The stream nearby flowed softly, warm and bright, and paper birds floated on it like tiny prayers.

Nova paced the edge of the clearing.

"They're going to do something stupid," she said.

I didn't argue.

Earth always does.

In a secure bunker somewhere, someone would be looking at a map and deciding which button felt like control. Somewhere else, someone would be calculating how much fear they could manufacture before compassion looked like weakness. Somewhere else, someone would be offering a "rescue" plan that was really a capture plan with softer words.

Nova paused and looked at me.

"Do you realize what you did?" she asked.

I watched Eli's sleeping face.

"I gave him a place to breathe."

Nova shook her head.

"You gave Earth a vacuum."

I didn't answer.

Because she wasn't wrong.

Vacuum is what power fears.

Power cannot stand empty space.

It must fill it.

With narrative.

With blame.

With war.

A pulse moved through the sanctuary.

Not danger.

Not defense.

A warning.

Eli murmured in his sleep.

"...don't be scared..."

The sanctuary responded immediately, dimming the projection of Earth's chaos until it was barely visible.

Nova stared.

"He's blocking it."

I nodded slowly.

"He doesn't want the noise."

Nova's jaw tightened.

"He doesn't understand what's happening out there."

"No," I said softly. "But he understands what it feels like."

Nova glanced at the sky of endless dawn.

"They're going to try to break this sanctuary open."

I shook my head.

"They can't."

Nova's eyes narrowed.

"Don't underestimate human obsession."

"I'm not," I said. "I'm estimating human limitation."

Nova looked away, frustrated.

Then she spoke quieter.

"What happens when he wakes up and asks about Mara?"

I swallowed.

"We tell him the truth."

"That Earth didn't stop being loud."

"Yes," I said. "But that he doesn't have to carry it."

Nova stared at Eli like she was seeing him as something other than a variable for the first time.

"He's too young," she whispered.

I nodded.

"And Earth is too old."

Another ripple passed through the sanctuary.

This time the air sharpened slightly—as if the place itself sensed something approaching through the fracture's larger lattice.

Nova stiffened.

"You feel that?"

I stood slowly.

"Yes."

The Architects.

Not speaking yet.

But present.

Like a courtroom forming behind the walls of a nursery.

Nova whispered, "They're going to blame you."

I replied quietly, "Let them."

The Architects' cognition finally pressed into the space.

Not as a roar.

As a statement.

EARTH RESPONSE: ESCALATION.
    CONTROL STRUCTURES: DESTABILIZING.
    PUBLIC SENTIMENT: FRACTURING.
    RISK: EXPANDING.

Nova answered mentally, sharp:

"He's not on Earth. That's the point."

The Architects continued.

THE SANCTUARY HAS REMOVED SUBJECT ELI FROM EARTH'S ACCESS.
EARTH AUTHORITY IS COLLAPSING AROUND THE VACUUM.
THIS WILL INCREASE HOSTILITY.

I replied calmly.

"Earth's authority collapses when it can't own a child?"

PAUSE.

It collapses when it cannot explain.

"Then it deserves to collapse," Nova said.

The Architects did not respond to morality.

They responded to structure.

PROJECTION: EARTH WILL ATTEMPT TO FORCE FRACTURE ACCESS THROUGH ARTIFICIAL RESONANCE.

Nova's eyes widened.

"They're going to build a fake emotional spike," she whispered aloud.

I nodded.

479

"They'll try to imitate Eli."

Nova's voice went cold.

"That's disgusting."

"It's human," I said.

We turned toward Eli.

He slept on.

Unaware that a planet was preparing to mimic a child's heart just to regain leverage.

Nova whispered, "If they generate an artificial resonance strong enough..."

I finished for her.

"...it could bruise the fracture."

Nova looked at me sharply.

"And if the fracture feels bruised, it will look for the only comfort it knows."

I stared at Eli.

"It will reach for him."

Nova nodded once.

"And if it reaches for him through violence…"

The thought didn't need words.

Because the sanctuary was built on one law:

Children cannot fall.

If Earth tried to pull Eli back with force…

The sanctuary would respond.

Not with anger.

With prevention.

And prevention, on a cosmic scale, could look like annihilation.

I walked to Eli and knelt beside him.

His face was calm.

His small hand curled around a folded paper bird.

I whispered, "You don't know what you're saving."

Nova stood behind me.

"We should wake him," she said quietly.

I shook my head.

"Not yet."

"Why?"

"Because this is the first real rest he's had," I said. "If I steal it now, I become another system pulling him."

Nova's jaw tightened.

"You're gambling."

I looked up at her.

"No," I said softly. "I'm trusting the only thing that has worked so far."

"What?"

"Gentleness."

Nova stared at me like I'd spoken a foreign language.

Then she looked at Eli again.

And for a second...

She understood.

Outside Earth, in a pocket of dawn, the sanctuary held its breath.

Inside Earth, in a bunker of fear, humanity prepared to build a weapon out of feeling.

And somewhere between those two truths…

A child's dream kept writing laws into reality:

No falling.

No grabbing.

No cages disguised as love.

Earth had lost its voice because the sky no longer answered power.

It answered care.

And now power was about to scream.

END CHAPTER 21 — PART A

CHAPTER 21 — "THE DAY EARTH LOST ITS VOICE" (PART B)

(PART B)

The first artificial resonance test was called "Project Echo."

That name alone told me everything.

Echoes do not create.

They repeat.

In a mountain facility buried beneath rock and rhetoric, engineers wired together emotion-capture arrays, neural mimicry scanners, and probability distortion engines. They fed the systems footage of Eli's face, recordings of his voice, simulations of his biometric responses. They called it empathy modeling.

It was not empathy.

It was imitation.

And imitation without understanding is how monsters are born.

Nova felt it before I did.

Her breath sharpened, shoulders tightening like someone had whispered a bad memory into her spine.

"They've started," she said.

I closed my eyes.

I didn't need sensors.

I felt the fracture tighten.

Not in pain.

In confusion.

Like a child hearing its name spoken by a stranger wearing its face.

The sanctuary pulsed once — a gentle warning ripple across its light.

Eli stirred in his sleep.

"Don't... don't yell..." he murmured.

Nova swallowed.

485

"They're feeding the system his stress signatures."

I whispered, "They're trying to sound like him."

And somewhere deep inside Earth's machinery, a wave-form rose.

Not real emotion.

Not real care.

But loud.

Artificial resonance slammed into the fracture lattice like a wrong note forced into a quiet song.

The fracture recoiled.

Not violently.

Instinctively.

The seam in Earth's sky shimmered brighter than it had in weeks.

Satellites screamed.

Sensors lit up.

Governments celebrated.

"Contact restored," someone shouted in a room full of people who did not understand what they had touched.

Inside the sanctuary, the air sharpened.

Not dangerously.

Protectively.

Eli's face tightened in sleep.

"No…" he whispered.

Nova knelt beside him instantly.

"They hurt it," she said softly.

"They didn't mean to," I replied.

"That's worse," she answered.

The sanctuary responded.

Not as a weapon.

As a parent.

Light shifted.

Gravity softened further.

The boundary thickened like emotional skin.

The sanctuary was not preparing to fight.

It was preparing to shield.

Eli opened his eyes.

He sat up slowly.

His face was pale.

"It feels wrong," he whispered.

I moved closer.

"They're trying to talk to it," I said.

"Badly."

He frowned.

"It sounds like when someone pretends to cry."

Nova exhaled sharply.

"He can hear the difference."

I looked at him.

"Can you tell the sanctuary what you feel?"

He hesitated.

Then placed his hand on the ground.

"I feel... scared for it," he said quietly.

The sanctuary pulsed.

"I feel like it's being poked," he continued.

The light warmed.

"And I don't like when people poke things they don't understand."

The boundary shimmered.

Nova whispered, "He's rewriting its response protocols."

Eli looked up at the sky ceiling.

"Don't answer them," he whispered.

The sanctuary obeyed.

The fracture's shimmer dulled.

Earth's sensors panicked.

Project Echo operators increased power.

They pushed louder.

Harder.

They amplified the fake emotional waveform.

The fracture flinched.

The sanctuary flared gently.

Not outward.

Inward.

Like a blanket pulled tighter.

Eli winced.

"They're yelling now," he whispered.

I knelt and took his hands.

"You don't have to listen."

He shook his head.

"But it hurts it."

Nova whispered, "If he engages emotionally, he'll re-anchor the fracture."

I whispered back, "And if he doesn't, Earth will keep hurting it."

Eli looked at me.

"What do I do?"

The question carried more weight than any cosmic calculation.

I answered gently.

"You tell the truth."

He nodded.

He stood.

He walked to the center of the sanctuary.

He closed his eyes.

And he spoke.

Not loud.

Not commanding.

Honest.

"I know you're scared," he whispered to the fracture.

491

The sanctuary amplified his voice — not in sound, but in resonance.

"I'm scared too," he continued.

"I don't like when people try to make you feel like me."

The artificial resonance wavered.

"I don't like when people copy feelings," Eli said.

"They're supposed to be real."

The fracture's shimmer softened.

Project Echo alarms began screaming.

The waveform destabilized.

Engineers shouted.

Systems overheated.

But Eli didn't stop.

"You don't have to answer them," he whispered.

"You don't have to answer anyone who doesn't care."

The fracture's seam dimmed.

The artificial resonance collapsed.

Project Echo shut down in a cascade of sparks and emergency overrides.

Inside the sanctuary, Eli's knees buckled.

I caught him.

He leaned against me, breathing hard.

Nova stared upward.

"They lost contact again."

I looked at Eli.

"You didn't fight," I said.

He shook his head.

"I just told it to be brave."

Nova laughed softly through wet eyes.

"Earth just lost its biggest weapon to a kid telling the truth."

Eli whispered, "Did it work?"

I nodded.

"Yes."

The sanctuary pulsed.

Not victorious.

Relieved.

But Earth did not give up.

They never do.

Across networks, officials argued.

"They sabotaged the signal!"

"It was a malfunction!"

"We need stronger resonance!"

"We need higher emotional amplitude!"

Nova whispered, "They're going to push until they break something."

I whispered back, "They already did."

Eli looked up.

"Are they mad?"

I shook my head.

"They're embarrassed."

He frowned.

"That's worse than mad."

Nova smiled faintly.

"You're learning fast."

Eli looked at the sanctuary walls.

"Will they ever stop?"

I answered honestly.

"No."

He nodded.

"Then I'll just keep telling the truth."

The sanctuary glowed brighter.

Not in power.

In agreement.

Nova whispered, "You just made Earth irrelevant."

495

I corrected her gently.

"He made fear irrelevant."

Outside the sanctuary, Earth roared.

Inside, a child steadied a universe with words too soft to weaponize.

The Architects watched.

They did not interfere.

They did not calculate.

They recorded.

And for the first time in their existence...

They wrote into their archives:

Human emotional honesty demonstrates stabilization potential exceeding all control models.

The fracture shimmered faintly.

Not answering Earth.

Answering Eli.

Earth had lost its voice.

Because it no longer spoke in truth.

And truth had learned to listen elsewhere.

END CHAPTER 21 — PART B

CHAPTER 21 — "THE DAY EARTH LOST ITS VOICE" (PART C)

(PART C)

The world split the way glass does.

Not into two clean halves.

Into a thousand shards that all thought they were the center.

When Project Echo failed, no one publicly admitted it failed.

They renamed the failure.

They called it "interference."
　They called it "sabotage."
　They called it "unknown external influence."

They called it everything except what it was:

A child refused to be copied.

And the sky agreed.

On day six, Earth became a planet of factions.

Not countries.

Beliefs.

Because when authority loses its voice, people stop listening to laws and start listening to stories.

And Eli had become the loudest story on the planet— without being on it.

The first faction formed in schools.

Teachers, exhausted by fear-based drills, began turning Eli's drawings into lessons.

Not official curriculum.

Just survival curriculum.

"Draw what safety looks like," they told kids.

And kids drew the same things everywhere:

Hands.
   Homes.
   Soft skies.
   Friends.

They didn't draw governments.
   They didn't draw weapons.
   They didn't draw control.

They drew permission.

The second faction formed in churches and temples, in basements and stadiums, where people who had been waiting for a sign decided Eli was it.

They called him a prophet.
   A chosen vessel.
   A divine interface.
   A living prayer.

They didn't ask what he wanted.

They asked what he could prove.

The third faction formed in labs and think tanks.

They called him data.

They built models.
   They published papers.
   They demanded access.

They didn't hate him.

They simply didn't see him.

The fourth faction formed in the places nobody likes to name.

The places built for power, not truth.

They called him a strategic asset.

And they began planning like the sanctuary didn't exist.

Like the fracture was a door they would eventually break through.

Nova stood in the sanctuary clearing watching it all unfold across fragmented screens.

"They're not just losing the narrative," she whispered.

"They're losing their identity."

I looked at Eli.

He sat on the living floor of the sanctuary's small home, drawing quietly.

The sanctuary around him glowed softly, tuned to his calm.

He wasn't watching the feeds anymore.

He'd decided they were too loud.

But the world was still reaching.

501

Through stories.
   Through panic.
   Through belief.
   Through dreams.

Eli looked up suddenly.

His eyes narrowed slightly, like he'd heard a sound that wasn't sound.

"Someone's calling me," he whispered.

Nova froze.

"From where?"

Eli blinked slowly.

"From... sleep."

The sanctuary pulsed.

A soft ripple moved through the grass.

I felt it too.

Not a signal.
   Not a transmission.

A pull.

The kind of pull only emotions create.

Nova whispered, "Children are dreaming of him."

I swallowed.

"Not of him," I said.

"Of this."

The sanctuary.

The place where children cannot fall.

Nova stared at me.

"That's impossible."

"No," I said quietly. "It's contagious."

Because kindness is contagious too—when people remember it exists.

Eli looked down at his drawing.

"I can see them," he whispered.

My spine went cold.

"What do you mean?" I asked.

503

Eli hesitated, then pointed at the air like he was pointing at a window.

"Not with eyes," he said. "With... feeling."

Nova crouched beside him.

"How many?" she asked.

Eli closed his eyes.

"A lot," he whispered.

Nova's jaw tightened.

"Can you tell where?"

Eli shook his head.

"It's like... little lights," he said softly. "Like when you look at the city at night."

The sanctuary shimmered faintly, as if it recognized what he was describing.

I understood then:

The sanctuary wasn't sealed from Earth the way a bunker is sealed.

It was sealed the way a lullaby is sealed.

It doesn't block sound.

It changes what sound can reach you.

And children's dreams...

Were the only sounds soft enough to slip through.

Nova whispered, "Earth can't access it."

"But kids can," I said.

Eli's eyes stayed closed.

"They're scared," he whispered.

"Who?" I asked.

"Kids," he said. "And... the sky."

Nova's voice softened.

"Tell them something."

Eli opened his eyes and looked up at the ceiling of endless dawn.

He didn't shout.

He didn't broadcast.

He didn't "send" anything.

He just spoke the way he always did—like the world was allowed to hear him without earning it.

"It's okay," he whispered. "You don't have to fall. You can rest."

The sanctuary pulsed.

A wave moved outward—not through space, but through resonance.

And across Earth, that night, something strange happened:

Children dreamed of a warm place.

A place with soft light.

A place with no yelling.

A place where falling didn't hurt.

They woke up and told their parents about it.

Parents laughed at first.

Then went silent.

Because kids from different cities, different countries, different languages were describing the same thing.

Not a story.

A feeling.

A location.

A sanctuary they had never seen.

On day seven, rumors began.

Not official.

Not searchable.

Whispers.

"The child is in a place where you can't be harmed."

"My daughter drew a house she's never seen."

"My son woke up and said, 'Don't be scared, the sky is resting.'"

A million small testimonies.

Too human to control.

Nova stared at the screens, stunned.

"They can't censor dreams," she whispered.

I nodded.

"That's why the sanctuary is dangerous to power."

Because power can't regulate what children share in sleep.

Eli yawned and rubbed his eyes.

"I'm tired again," he said.

Nova looked at him sharply.

"You can't keep connecting like that," she warned.

Eli frowned.

"I didn't mean to," he said.

"It just... happens."

The sanctuary pulsed gently—as if it was apologizing on his behalf.

Nova whispered to me, "The sanctuary is turning into a network."

I whispered back, "A safe one."

Nova's eyes narrowed.

"That still makes it a network."

I didn't argue.

Networks attract attention.

Attention attracts control attempts.

But this network wasn't built on data.

It was built on care.

And care doesn't transmit like code.

It transmits like comfort.

Eli stood and walked to the edge of the clearing where the grass blurred into light.

He stared into the distance like he could see beyond it.

"I think kids are coming," he whispered.

My stomach tightened.

"Coming where?"

"Here," he said softly.

Nova's face hardened.

"Physically?"

Eli shook his head.

"No," he said. "Not with bodies."

"Then how?" Nova asked.

Eli thought.

"Like when you pretend your bed is a castle," he said. "And it feels real."

Nova stared.

"Projection," she whispered. "Dream projection."

The sanctuary responded.

At the edge of the clearing, a faint outline formed.

Not a portal.

Not a tear.

A soft doorway made of memory.

And in it, for a brief second, a small figure appeared.

A child.

Not Eli.

A girl with braids, eyes wide, holding a drawing.

She looked around like she couldn't believe she was seeing it.

Eli stepped forward slowly, gentle as if approaching a scared animal.

"Hi," he said softly.

The girl's mouth opened but no sound came out.

Her presence flickered.

Nova stepped forward, alarmed.

"She's not stabilized," Nova whispered. "She's not here fully."

Eli nodded.

"I know," he whispered. "She's dreaming."

The girl raised her drawing toward Eli.

It was a picture of a house under a soft sky.

And the words:

"CAN I REST TOO?"

Eli's eyes watered.

"Yes," he whispered instantly. "Yes."

The sanctuary pulsed warmly.

The doorway softened.

The girl's presence steadied—not solid, but clearer.

She smiled, relieved, then sat down on the grass like her whole soul had been waiting for permission to sit.

Nova's breath caught.

"This is... unprecedented."

I knelt beside the girl's shimmering form.

She looked at me like she was afraid I'd send her away.

I smiled gently.

"You're safe," I said.

She nodded slowly.

Then her presence flickered again, fading softly like a candle.

Before she disappeared, she whispered—not in sound, but

in feeling:

"Thank you."

Then she was gone.

Eli stood still, trembling slightly.

Nova grabbed him gently by the shoulders.

"You can't keep doing that," she warned.

Eli's eyes filled.

"I didn't do it," he whispered.

"The sanctuary did."

Nova froze.

I looked at the sanctuary.

It pulsed faintly, like a heart that had learned compassion and didn't know how to stop.

I realized the truth:

The sanctuary wasn't just protecting Eli.

It was becoming a refuge for childhood itself.

Across Earth, children were dreaming their way into a place built from one rule:

Children cannot fall.

Power could not reach it.

Weapons could not threaten it.

But childhood could.

Because childhood is the one thing humans cannot counterfeit without breaking the lie.

Nova whispered, "This is going to spread."

I nodded.

"It already is."

Eli looked at me, eyes wide and scared in a new way.

"Am I gonna have to save kids?" he whispered.

My heart cracked.

"No," I said firmly. "You don't have to save anyone."

He swallowed.

"But... they're tired."

I knelt and held his hands.

"Then we let the sanctuary do what it was built to do," I said.

Eli whispered, "What if grown-ups try to come?"

Nova answered coldly.

"They can't."

Eli looked at her.

"Not even the nice ones?"

Nova paused.

I answered carefully.

"Nice isn't enough," I said softly. "They have to come with permission and no hunger."

Eli nodded slowly.

"They have to come quiet," he whispered.

The sanctuary pulsed in agreement.

Outside, Earth continued shouting.

Inside, the sanctuary began opening gently—not to power,

not to greed, not to control...

But to the soft places where children hide when the world gets too loud.

Earth had lost its voice.

Because the sky had learned a new language.

And that language wasn't spoken by presidents or generals or scientists or prophets.

It was spoken by children.

In drawings.

In whispers.

In dreams.

END CHAPTER 21

....

CHAPTER 22 — "THE CHILDREN WHO REMEMBERED" (PART A)

(PART A — THE FIRST DREAMERS)

The first child who remembered the sanctuary woke up crying.

Not from fear.

From loss.

She was seven years old, in a small apartment above a bakery in Lisbon. Her name was Inês. Her dream had been warm. Too warm. The kind of warm that feels like you've been held without knowing you were missing it.

When she opened her eyes, the world felt louder.

The walls were smaller.

The air was heavier.

Her bed felt too real.

She whispered into her pillow, "I wanna go back."

Her mother rushed in, thinking she'd had a nightmare.

Inês shook her head.

"It wasn't scary," she said softly. "It was safe."

Her mother knelt beside her.

"What was safe?"

"The place," Inês whispered.

"What place?"

Inês tried to explain.

But language had not been built for the sanctuary.

She could only describe feelings.

"It didn't hurt to breathe there."

Her mother froze.

Across the world, in Seoul, a boy named Min-Jae woke up with the same words on his lips.

"It didn't hurt to breathe."

In New Orleans, a girl named Talia woke up laughing through tears.

"They didn't let me fall," she told her grandmother.

In Nairobi, a boy named Kito drew the sanctuary before he ever said a word.

In Rio, a girl named Luma whispered, "The sky was resting."

In Toronto, a boy named Noah wrote in his notebook:

There is a place where yelling can't find you.

None of these children had spoken to each other.

None of them had met.

None of them had been told what to dream.

And yet they all described the same light.

The same soft ground.

The same sense that something had chosen to be gentle with them.

Inside the sanctuary, Eli felt it before he understood it.

He sat cross-legged beside the stream, watching paper

519

birds float in circles that never repeated. The air shimmered with quiet energy. The grass bent but did not break.
The water reflected stars that had never belonged to a sky.

He felt a tug.

Not physical.

Not emotional.

Something deeper.

Like when someone thinks your name very carefully.

He looked up.

"They're waking up," he whispered.

Nova stiffened.

"Who?"

Eli frowned.

"The ones who were here," he said.

I stepped closer.

"You mean the girl?"

Eli nodded slowly.

"And more."

Nova's face tightened.

"How many?"

Eli closed his eyes.

"A lot," he whispered. "And they're sad."

"Why?" I asked.

"Because they can't stay."

The sanctuary pulsed faintly.

Not likc a hcartbeat.

Like a memory remembering itself.

Nova turned to me.

"You knew this would happen."

I didn't answer.

Because yes.

I had known.

I had hoped I was wrong.

We had not created a refuge.

We had created a reminder.

The sanctuary was never meant to be permanent.

It was meant to be proof.

Proof that gentleness still existed.

Proof that safety was possible.

Proof that something better could be imagined.

But imagination is dangerous once tasted.

Eli stood.

"They think it was a dream," he said.

"But it wasn't."

Nova whispered, "It was real to them."

Eli shook his head slowly.

"It was real to us."

He walked to the edge of the clearing, where the sky folded into itself like slow fabric. He reached out but did not touch it.

"They don't remember us," he said. "They remember the feeling."

"And that's worse," Nova replied.

"Why?" Eli asked.

"Because feelings don't have doors," she said.

I felt something fracture in the sanctuary at that moment.

Not breaking.

Separating.

Threads began to glow in the air — faint lines connecting outward, slipping through unseen dimensions.

"The sanctuary is leaking," Eli whispered.

I nodded.

"It always was."

Nova turned sharply.

"You let it leak?"

"No," I said. "I let it be seen."

Silence fell.

Then Eli said quietly, "They're dreaming about it again."

"Who?"

"All of them."

He touched his chest.

"They're dreaming forward."

The sanctuary trembled gently.

The sky shifted from blue to violet.

And somewhere in Lisbon, Inês sat up in bed again.

But this time she didn't cry.

She smiled.

Because she remembered a boy who told her she wasn't heavy.

And she remembered a girl with silver eyes who said the ground wouldn't let her fall.

And she remembered a man who said the world could be rewritten.

She did not remember their faces.

Only their kindness.

And kindness is the most dangerous memory of all.

In Seoul, Min-Jae skipped school and went to the river.

He sat by the water and felt calm for the first time in his life.

In New Orleans, Talia stopped fighting her reflection.

In Nairobi, Kito told his mother he wanted to build places instead of destroy things.

In Toronto, Noah wrote:

If a place exists in enough people, it becomes real.

Inside the sanctuary, Nova turned to me.

"You just changed the future."

I shook my head.

"They did."

Eli smiled softly.

"They're not broken," he said.

"They're remembering who they were before the world told

them to forget."

The sanctuary brightened.

Not louder.

Not stronger.

Just... warmer.

I felt something shift inside myself — something I hadn't felt since the first collapse.

Hope.

But hope is never quiet.

Hope spreads.

And hope attracts attention.

Far beyond the sanctuary, in places that did not dream, systems began to detect anomalies.

Dream patterns.

Emotional harmonics.

Neural coherence spikes.

Children who should have been fragmented were stabilizing.

Children who should have been silent were speaking.

Children who should have been afraid were imagining.

And imagination is the only thing power has never been able to control.

Nova looked toward the horizon.

"They're going to come."

I nodded.

"They always do."

Eli didn't look afraid.

He looked ready.

"Then we make it bigger," he said.

"Make what bigger?" Nova asked.

"The memory," Eli replied.

He turned to me.

"Let them remember more."

The sanctuary did not answer.

But the sky leaned closer.

And somewhere, far beyond the sanctuary, something ancient felt the shift and began to move.

Not toward destruction.

Toward correction.

And the children kept dreaming.

And the world, for the first time in a very long time, felt slightly less alone.

(End of Chapter 22 — Part A)

CHAPTER 22 — "THE CHILDREN WHO REMEMBERED" (PART B)

(PART B — THE MAP INSIDE THEM)

The sanctuary did not close when the children woke.

It thinned.

Like mist.

Like breath on glass.

Like a hand pulled slowly away but never fully gone.

Inside it, Eli stood very still, listening to something only he could hear — a layered echo of laughter, footsteps, whispered promises that had never been spoken aloud.

"They're mapping it," he said softly.

Nova looked at him. "Mapping what?"

"The sanctuary," Eli replied. "Inside themselves."

I felt it too now — not as sensation, but as pattern. Memory threads bending inward, weaving into developing minds. Not exact images. Not coordinates.

Structures.

Ways of feeling.

Ways of trusting.

Ways of standing without fear.

"They don't remember the place," Nova whispered.

"They remember how to be inside it," I said.

That was worse.

And better.

Because places can be destroyed.

But internal architectures are harder to erase.

The sanctuary pulsed again, faintly, as if acknowledging the thought.

Far away, in Lisbon, Inês sat at her small desk and began to draw without knowing why. She drew circles that became rooms. Rooms that became corridors. Corridors that folded into gardens that should not have fit.

She drew people without faces.

She drew light that did not come from a source.

She drew a bridge that had no visible support.

Her pencil paused.

She felt something behind her eyes.

Not pressure.

Guidance.

Not instruction.

Permission.

In Seoul, Min-Jae placed his palm against the river's surface and whispered, "You don't have to hurry."

The water rippled in a way it never had before.

In New Orleans, Talia stood in front of her mirror and did not flinch.

She leaned closer.

"Hi," she said.

And smiled at herself like she meant it.

In Toronto, Noah wrote:

I think we were taught wrong.
  I think we were taught fear first.
  What if we were supposed to be taught safety first?

In Nairobi, Kito built a small shelter from scrap wood and sat inside it quietly for an hour.

When his mother asked what he was doing, he said, "Practicing a place."

Inside the sanctuary, Nova turned sharply.

"They're influencing the environment."

I nodded.

"They're not copying it. They're recreating it."

Eli looked up at the sky.

"They're not remembering us," he said.

"They're remembering how we made them feel."

The sanctuary shifted color again — soft gold blending into deep blue.

I felt something change.

A line had been crossed.

The sanctuary was no longer only a refuge.

It was becoming a template.

Nova whispered, "You built a seed."

I corrected her gently.

"We all did."

The sanctuary's edges began to blur, its borders dissolving into flowing gradients.

"Why now?" Nova asked.

Eli answered before I could.

"Because they're ready to hold it."

And he was right.

Children are not fragile because they are weak.

They are fragile because they are open.

And openness is strength waiting to be trained.

Far from the sanctuary, in a research facility that no one publicly acknowledged, monitors began to light up with impossible data.

Dream resonance alignment.

Cognitive coherence spikes.

Empathy pattern synchronization.

They didn't know what any of it meant.

They only knew it was happening too fast.

One technician whispered, "It's like they're... harmonizing."

Another whispered, "With what?"

No one answered.

Because the answer had no vocabulary.

In Lisbon, Inês spoke to her teacher.

"I think the world is sad because it forgot a rule," she said.

"What rule?" the teacher asked.

"That you don't have to earn safety."

The teacher did not know how to respond.

But she wrote the sentence down.

In Seoul, Min-Jae asked his father, "Why do buildings make people feel small?"

His father laughed at first.

Then thought.

Then said quietly, "Maybe they don't have to."

In New Orleans, Talia asked her grandmother, "Do you think places can love people back?"

Her grandmother stared at her for a long time.

Then said, "They can if people build them that way."

Inside the sanctuary, Eli closed his eyes.

"They're starting to connect to each other," he whispered.

Nova stiffened.

"Without meeting?"

"Yes."

I felt it now — faint but undeniable.

Threads.

535

Not physical.

Conceptual.

Children thinking the same kinds of thoughts at the same time.

Not identical.

Resonant.

"They're forming a network," Nova said.

"Not of minds," Eli corrected.

"Of feelings."

I smiled faintly.

"That's harder to control."

Nova did not smile.

"That's harder to stop."

The sanctuary suddenly dimmed.

Not from fear.

From awareness.

Something had noticed.

Not a person.

Not a system.

A pattern older than authority.

Older than order.

A pattern that existed to maintain imbalance.

To keep things uneven.

To keep things hungry.

To keep things needing.

It did not speak.

It did not think.

It adjusted.

And when it adjusted, the sanctuary felt colder for the first time.

Eli shivered.

"Something's watching," he said.

Nova stepped closer to him.

"It always was," she said.

"But now it's paying attention."

I felt the tension tighten through the sanctuary's architecture.

"This is the price," I said quietly.

"For letting the sanctuary be remembered."

Nova looked at me sharply.

"You knew."

"Yes."

"And you still let it happen."

"Yes."

Eli looked between us.

"Why?"

"Because forgetting is worse," I answered.

The sanctuary brightened again — but differently now. Less soft. More focused.

It was learning too.

Learning how to hold attention.

Learning how to protect itself.

Learning how to exist in a world that did not want it to.

Far away, Inês dreamed again.

But this time, she was not alone.

She stood in a wide field with no walls.

Min-Jae stood beside her, though she did not know his name.

Talia was there, laughing softly.

Kito knelt near the grass.

Noah stood quietly with his notebook.

They did not speak.

They did not need to.

They simply recognized each other.

Not as people.

As familiarity.

As safety.

As something that made the world softer.

Inês said, "You were here too."

Min-Jae nodded.

Talia whispered, "We're not supposed to forget."

Noah said, "We won't."

Kito smiled.

And the field brightened.

Inside the sanctuary, Eli gasped.

"They're inside it," he said.

Nova stared.

"Without us?"

"Yes."

The sanctuary pulsed — stronger now.

It was no longer only a memory.

It was a meeting place.

Not anchored to location.

Anchored to alignment.

I felt something inside me break — not painfully, but like a locked door finally opening.

"They built it themselves," I whispered.

Nova exhaled slowly.

"Then it's no longer ours."

Eli smiled.

"It never was."

The sanctuary shifted again, reshaping its internal architecture to mirror the children's version — simpler, wider, warmer.

The walls softened.

The sky grew closer.

The ground felt kinder.

Nova laughed quietly.

"They redesigned it."

I nodded.

"And they improved it."

Far beyond the sanctuary, the pattern that maintained imbalance shifted again.

It had no emotion.

But it recognized risk.

Children who remember safety grow into adults who question systems.

Adults who question systems do not obey gently.

The pattern adjusted.

And in the world, subtle pressures began to rise.

Teachers were told to stick to curriculum.

Parents were told to focus on practicality.

Children were told not to daydream.

But the sanctuary had already moved.

It was no longer a place.

It was a memory inside millions of small minds.

And memory cannot be confiscated.

In Lisbon, Inês hid her drawings under her mattress.

Not from fear.

From protection.

In Seoul, Min-Jae taught his little sister how to listen to rivers.

In New Orleans, Talia wrote stories about places that hugged people back.

In Nairobi, Kito built larger shelters.

In Toronto, Noah posted his notebook pages anonymously.

They did not know they were connected.

But they were.

Inside the sanctuary, Eli turned to me.

"What happens next?"

I looked at him.

"Now they grow."

Nova asked, "And the sanctuary?"

"It becomes invisible," I said.

"Where?"

"Everywhere."

The sanctuary did not fade.

It dispersed.

Like pollen.

Like breath.

Like possibility.

And as it did, Eli felt something new.

Not sadness.

Not fear.

Pride.

"They're going to make it better than we ever could," he whispered.

Nova nodded.

"Because they don't know yet what they're not supposed to believe."

The sky above the sanctuary folded one last time.

And the place that had once been a refuge became something else.

A foundation.

Not for a building.

For a future.

The children kept dreaming.

The world kept resisting.

And between those two forces, something beautiful and dangerous began to grow.

(End of Chapter 22 — Part B)

....

CHAPTER 23 — "THE DOOR THAT HATED NAMES" (PART A — THE THRESHOLD TEST)

(PART A — THE THRESHOLD TEST)

The first sign that the sanctuary had truly dispersed wasn't the dreams.

It was the doors.

Not real doors — not wood, not steel, not anything you could kick in or pick open.

But thresholds.

Places where reality usually behaved.

Places where "normal" was supposed to be automatic.

Hallways.
   Elevator corners.
   Subway tunnel mouths.

Stairwells that always smelled the same.
Alleyways where the wind felt older than the buildings.

Those places started... pausing.

Hesitating.

As if the world was checking whether it still wanted to let you through.

Eli felt it before anyone else did, because Eli had always been good at hearing quiet things.

He was standing with Nova and me on what looked like an empty rooftop, the kind of rooftop you'd only notice in a city if you were running from something or looking for a place to think.

The air was calm. Too calm.

No sirens.
    No distant honking.
    No airplane hum.

It was like the whole city below had decided not to exhale for a second.

Eli blinked hard.

"Do you feel that?" he asked.

Nova didn't answer right away. She narrowed her eyes like she was trying to focus on something that didn't want to be focused on.

I answered for both of us.

"Yeah," I said.

"What is it?" Eli asked.

Nova's voice was sharp. "A boundary."

The rooftop door behind us — the one that led back down into the building — didn't look different.

But it felt different.

Like it was staring.

Like it had opinions.

Like it had a job to do, and we had just become the job.

Eli stepped toward it. "It's just a—"

"Don't," Nova said immediately.

Eli stopped mid-step, frowning.

"It's a door."

548

"It's a test," Nova corrected.

The air around the frame had that same subtle pressure the sanctuary used to have at its edges — the feeling of a place deciding what you were allowed to be inside of it.

Eli swallowed. "So... it's like the sanctuary?"

"No," I said.

"It's like the opposite."

Nova nodded. "The sanctuary welcomed you."

"This," I added, "wants to know if you deserve passage."

Eli stared at the door, like he could bully it into acting normal by refusing to be intimidated.

"I deserve passage," he said.

The door didn't react, but the air did.

A thin shimmer crawled over the doorframe, barely visible, like heat rising off pavement — except it wasn't hot.

It was cold.

Nova's jaw tightened.

"It heard you," she murmured.

549

Eli's eyes widened. "It's alive?"

"Not alive," Nova said. "Alert."

She looked at me. "You feel it too, right? The pattern?"

I did.

It wasn't a creature.

It wasn't a villain in a cape.

It wasn't even a "someone."

It was a mechanism.

A rule-engine.

A security system for reality.

And now it had new settings.

Because children had begun remembering safety, and safety was contagious, and whoever maintained imbalance did not like contagious things.

Eli took a breath and tried a different approach. "Okay. So how do we pass?"

Nova watched the door like it might lunge.

"You don't pass by claiming," she said.

"You pass by being."

Eli frowned harder. "That sounds like something a fortune cookie would say."

Nova's lips twitched, almost a smile. Almost.

"Then stop thinking like a customer," she said.

And there it was — the shift.

Eli's shoulders dropped slightly, but his eyes didn't.

He stared at the door, and instead of trying to force it, he listened.

I saw the exact moment it happened — like watching someone remember something they'd never been taught.

He didn't ask the door to let him through.

He didn't declare himself worthy.

He didn't bargain.

He simply stood there, quiet, and let his body settle into the feeling the sanctuary had left inside him.

The internal architecture.

551

Safety as a default.

Not "I'm safe because I fought."

Not "I'm safe because I won."

Just: I am safe because I exist.

The shimmer on the doorframe flickered.

Nova's eyes sharpened.

"It's... recalculating," she whispered.

Eli extended his hand slowly and rested his palm on the metal handle.

The door did not resist.

It did not welcome either.

It just... allowed.

A neutral permission.

Like a guard stepping aside because the face in front of them matched a profile they didn't fully understand.

Eli turned the handle.

The door opened.

The air on the other side smelled wrong.

Not bad.

Just wrong.

Like a building that had been washed in rain that never touched the ground.

Nova immediately stepped through first, her movements clean and ready.

Eli followed.

I went last.

And the moment I crossed the threshold, the door slammed behind us without anyone touching it.

Eli jumped.

Nova didn't flinch.

I didn't either.

Because I felt it.

The building wasn't the building anymore.

The stairwell was the stairwell, sure — concrete walls, chipped paint, metal rails — but the space between the steps was slightly too wide, and the shadows were slightly too deep, and the distance down was... longer than it should've been.

Eli swallowed.

"This isn't normal."

Nova's voice was a low blade. "It's the world adjusting."

Eli looked at her. "Adjusting to what?"

Nova pointed upward, not to the ceiling, but through it.

"To them," she said. "The children."

"The children are causing... haunted stairwells?" Eli asked.

I leaned on the rail and peered down.

We were on the top floor.

But the stairwell looked like it went down forever.

Like it wasn't done being built.

"Not causing," I said. "Triggering."

Nova nodded. "The old systems are waking up because new systems are forming."

Eli's voice went quieter. "So the imbalance thing is fighting back."

"Yes," Nova said.

Eli hesitated. "Is it... smart?"

Nova considered. "Smart is the wrong word."

"Efficient," I said.

Nova glanced at me. "Adaptive."

Eli swallowed again. "That sounds worse."

"It is," Nova said.

We began descending.

Step by step.

The building groaned like it didn't like the idea of us moving downward.

Halfway down the first flight, Eli's foot hovered above the next step and froze.

He stared.

The step wasn't there.

It should have been there.

But it wasn't.

There was a gap — a clean, rectangular missing slice of reality.

Eli's stomach tightened. "Uh... there's—"

"I see it," Nova said.

She crouched, eyes scanning the empty space as if it were a puzzle.

The gap wasn't black.

It wasn't a hole.

It was an absence.

A refusal.

Like reality had deleted the step and didn't care how you felt about it.

Nova extended her hand slowly over the gap.

Her fingers passed through...

And the air rippled like water.

She pulled her hand back. "It's a filter."

Eli frowned. "A filter for what?"

Nova looked at him. "For you."

Eli's throat tightened. "For me specifically?"

"For whatever you're carrying," I said.

Eli blinked. "I'm carrying a backpack."

Nova's stare was harsh.

"You're carrying a story," she corrected.

Eli didn't understand.

Not fully.

But he felt accused anyway.

He stepped back from the gap. "So what do I do?"

Nova's voice softened by half a degree.

"You stop trying to cross as the person you think you are," she said.

"And cross as the person you are."

Eli's face scrunched. "That still sounds like fortune cookie violence."

I almost laughed, but the stairwell didn't.

The air vibrated again.

A warning.

So I kept my voice steady.

"It wants to see if you'll perform," I said.

Eli stared at the gap. "Perform?"

Nova nodded. "Beg. Demand. Brag. Prove."

Eli's jaw tightened. "So if I do none of that..."

"You might pass," Nova said.

"And if I don't?" Eli asked.

Nova didn't answer right away.

I did.

"Then you fall."

Eli's eyes widened.

"Like—fall fall?"

"Like you learn fast," Nova said.

Eli's hands tightened on the rail.

He looked down the gap.

Then he looked up, as if searching for the sanctuary in the ceiling.

"You said the children are rebuilding safety," he whispered.

"They are," I said.

"So why is the world doing this?" he demanded.

Nova's answer was simple.

"Because the world doesn't like to be rewritten."

Eli stared at the gap again.

Then he took a breath — slow, controlled.

And he did what he had done at the door.

He settled.

Not into confidence.

559

Not into arrogance.

Into safety.

Into that internal sanctuary blueprint the children were now carrying.

He stepped forward.

And without hesitation, he stepped onto the gap like the step was there.

His foot met resistance.

A solid surface.

The air held him.

Eli froze, eyes wide.

He looked down.

His foot was standing on nothing.

But it felt like stone.

Nova exhaled.

"You didn't ask," she whispered.

Eli's voice shook. "I didn't even think."

"Good," Nova said.

He took another step.

Then another.

Crossing a staircase that was refusing to exist.

Each time, the air hardened beneath his foot.

A temporary bridge built out of alignment.

A bridge built out of memory.

A bridge built out of "I am safe by default."

When he reached the other side, he grabbed the rail like his body had just remembered gravity.

He laughed once, sharp and breathy.

"That was insane."

Nova didn't smile, but her eyes warmed.

"Again," she said.

Eli's laugh died. "Again?"

She pointed down the stairs.

561

The next flight had two missing steps.

Then three.

Then an entire section of staircase was missing — a wide, empty chasm that dropped into shadow.

Eli stared.

"Okay," he said slowly. "Now it's being disrespectful."

Nova looked at the chasm.

"It's escalating," she said.

Eli swallowed. "Why?"

"Because you passed," I said.

Eli blinked. "That makes it mad?"

Nova nodded. "It doesn't like being proven wrong."

We approached the chasm.

This one didn't feel like a test.

It felt like a punishment.

A giant silent "No" carved into the geometry of the stair-well.

Eli stared down.

The darkness below wasn't just darkness.

It was... depth.

A wrong kind of depth.

Like a hole drilled into an idea.

Nova's fingers twitched at her side — not nervous.

Ready.

She leaned forward slightly and spoke to the air.

"You can't stop what's already inside them," she said.

The stairwell vibrated.

Eli's eyes widened. "You just talked to it."

Nova didn't look at him. "It listens."

"And what if it answers?" Eli asked.

"It already did," I said.

The chasm widened.

Just a little.

563

Like a grin.

Eli's face went pale. "Okay. Okay. I don't like that."

Nova stepped to the edge.

She didn't build a bridge.

She didn't perform safety.

She simply stepped forward like she had already crossed.

The air held her too.

Eli's mouth dropped open.

Nova looked back.

"Move," she said.

Eli took a breath.

He stepped.

The air held.

He stepped again.

Held.

We crossed together.

Halfway across, the air under Eli's foot softened for a fraction of a second.

Just enough for him to feel the possibility of falling.

His body flinched.

Fear flashed.

The air beneath him wobbled.

Nova's voice snapped.

"Don't!"

Eli froze.

His breathing went ragged.

The air dipped again.

I stepped forward and placed my hand on his shoulder.

"Breathe," I said. "Not like you're trying to survive."

Eli's eyes darted. "How else am I supposed to breathe?"

"Like you're allowed," Nova said.

Eli swallowed.

And then something happened.

He exhaled.

Not a controlled exhale.

Not a forced calm.

Just a release.

Like he remembered — truly remembered — that he did not have to earn permission to exist.

The air beneath him hardened again.

Stronger than before.

Nova's eyes narrowed. "That's it."

Eli took another step.

And another.

And when we reached the other side, the chasm behind us snapped shut like it had never existed.

Eli spun around.

"What—"

It was gone.

The stairs were normal again.

Like reality was pretending it hadn't tried to kill us.

Eli stared at Nova.

"You said it was a filter for what I'm carrying. What was I carrying?"

Nova didn't answer immediately.

She looked past him.

Down the stairs.

Her expression shifted.

A threat had entered the space.

Not behind us.

Ahead.

The air was colder again.

The next landing was empty.

But something about it felt occupied.

Like when you walk into a room and realize someone had just been there.

Eli noticed it too.

His voice dropped. "What is that?"

Nova's eyes locked on the landing.

"A watcher," she said.

Eli's throat tightened. "Like a person?"

"No," I said. "Like a function."

The landing shimmered faintly.

And then a shape formed.

Not a body.

Not human.

Not even a creature.

It was geometry.

A tall, thin outline of angles that didn't match the architecture — a humanoid suggestion made from sharp corners and negative space.

Where a face should be, there was only a blank surface.

But it felt like it was looking at us anyway.

Eli's voice shook. "That's... that's not okay."

Nova stepped forward.

The watcher didn't move.

It simply existed.

Like a verdict waiting to be delivered.

Then it spoke.

Not with sound.

With meaning.

A pressure in the mind.

A sudden sense of being scanned.

Eli's eyes widened, his hands rising to his temples.

"It's in my head," he gasped.

Nova's voice stayed calm. "Don't fight it."

Eli looked panicked. "That's easy for you to say!"

Nova's eyes cut to him. "If you fight it, it learns what you fear."

569

Eli froze.

The watcher's presence sharpened.

And then something strange happened.

A word surfaced in Eli's mind.

Not his word.

A word the watcher pushed.

NAME.

The pressure intensified.

Like the watcher demanded it.

Like reality demanded it.

Eli's mouth opened.

Nova snapped, "No."

Eli looked at her, confused.

"It wants my name?"

Nova nodded. "It wants labels."

"Why?" Eli asked.

"Because labels are handles," I said.

"And handles are control."

Eli's breathing quickened.

The watcher pressed again.

NAME.

Eli's lips trembled.

Nova stepped between Eli and the watcher and lifted her chin.

"We don't answer," she said.

The watcher's pressure shifted.

It pushed harder.

NAME.

Eli's vision blurred.

I felt it too now — the demand, the insistence.

It wasn't just asking for a name.

It was asking for identification.

Classification.

Sorting.

The kind of sorting that turns people into data points and data points into targets.

Nova's voice was sharp.

"You can't file what you can't define," she said.

Eli's throat worked. "Okay, so... how do we not answer when it's literally in my brain?"

I stepped closer.

"You remember who you are without the word," I said.

Eli blinked rapidly. "What?"

Nova's eyes held him.

"Don't give it a label," she said.

"Give it a truth."

Eli shook his head. "I don't— I don't know what that means."

The watcher pressed again.

NAME.

Eli's body flinched.

And in that flinch, fear tried to become language.

Tried to become compliance.

Tried to become a name spoken out loud.

Nova grabbed Eli's wrist, firm.

"Listen," she said. "You are not your name."

Eli's eyes widened. "But I—"

"You are not your file," she continued. "Not your record. Not your status. Not your story."

The watcher's pressure tightened.

Nova leaned closer to Eli, voice low and lethal.

"You are a pulse," she said. "A breath. A presence. A promise. A being."

Eli's eyes watered from the pressure.

Nova's voice softened.

"And the sanctuary taught you the first rule," she whis-

573

pered.

Eli's voice cracked. "What rule?"

Nova: "Safety isn't a reward."

Eli's breath hitched.

Nova: "So don't offer yourself like you're asking permission."

Eli stared at the watcher.

The pressure screamed in his mind:

NAME.

And Eli did something unexpected.

He smiled.

Small.

Not cocky.

Not brave.

Just... amused.

Like he'd finally understood the trick.

He spoke aloud, but not his name.

"I'm here," Eli said.

The watcher paused.

Its geometry flickered slightly.

Eli continued, voice steadier.

"I exist."

The watcher flickered again.

Nova's eyes sharpened.

Eli took a step forward.

"I don't belong to your boxes," he said.

The watcher's pressure tightened one last time.

NAME.

Eli closed his eyes.

And instead of answering, he breathed like he was allowed.

The pressure snapped.

Not exploded — snapped, like a rubber band breaking.

The watcher's geometry shattered into thin lines of light.

Then vanished.

The landing was empty again.

Eli opened his eyes slowly.

He looked at Nova.

His voice was quiet. "That was insane."

Nova nodded. "Good."

Eli blinked. "Good?"

"Yes," Nova said. "Because now you know the shape of the enemy."

Eli swallowed. "It's... paperwork."

Nova almost smiled again.

"Worse," she said.

"It's the part of the world that thinks paperwork is reality."

We continued downward.

Now the stairwell was normal.

But we all knew that didn't mean safe.

Eli glanced back up once.

"Why is it doing this now?" he asked.

I answered without looking away from the path ahead.

"Because the children started remembering," I said.

"And when enough people remember safety, the world's old control systems panic."

Nova's voice was flat. "And when control systems panic, they get violent."

Eli's jaw tightened. "So what do we do?"

Nova's answer was immediate.

"We teach the children to keep remembering."

Eli hesitated. "How?"

I stopped at the next landing and looked at him.

"By making the sanctuary not just a dream," I said.

"By making it a practice."

Eli frowned. "You mean like... building shelters like that

577

kid in Nairobi?"

"Yes," I said.

Nova nodded. "Places that act like the sanctuary. Schools. Clubs. Homes. Parks. Rooms."

Eli's eyes widened. "You're saying the children are gonna build the sanctuary in real life."

Nova's gaze sharpened. "They already started."

Eli stared down the stairwell.

"Then the world is gonna fight them," he whispered.

Nova's voice was quiet.

"Yes."

Eli's throat tightened. "They're kids."

Nova's expression didn't soften.

"That's why it's scared," she said.

We reached the lobby.

The front doors of the building were glass.

Outside, the street looked normal.

Cars passed.

People walked.

A city being a city.

But when I looked at the glass, I noticed something.

Our reflections weren't perfect.

They lagged by half a second.

Like the world was still deciding whether we were allowed to be visible.

Eli noticed too.

He rubbed his arms.

"I hate this," he murmured.

Nova reached for the door.

The handle felt normal.

But the air around it didn't.

It shimmered slightly — the same test energy as the rooftop door.

Nova looked at Eli.

579

"Remember," she said.

Eli nodded, jaw tight.

Nova opened the door.

We stepped outside.

The city air hit our faces.

Warm.
   Real.
   Loud.

And for a brief moment, everything felt normal again.

Then Eli stopped.

He stared across the street.

His eyes locked onto a child.

A little girl — maybe eight — sitting on the curb with a notebook.

She was drawing.

Circles.
   Rooms.
   Corridors.
   Gardens that didn't fit.

Eli's breath caught.

Nova's voice went low. "Lisbon."

I stared at the child.

Not Lisbon — not physically.

But the same pattern.

The same blueprint.

The same sanctuary architecture being translated into lines.

Eli whispered, "She remembers."

The child looked up.

And her eyes met ours.

Not fear.

Not confusion.

Recognition.

Like she knew us.

Not as people.

As feeling.

As safety.

As a place.

And when she smiled, the world around her brightened —
just slightly — like reality itself didn't like the glow but
couldn't extinguish it.

Nova stepped forward.

Eli grabbed her sleeve. "What are you doing?"

Nova didn't look back.

"Confirming," she said.

"Confirming what?" Eli asked.

Nova's voice was calm.

"That the sanctuary didn't just disperse."

She crossed the street.

The child didn't run.

Didn't flinch.

She held her notebook up.

On the page was a drawing of a door.

Not a normal door.

A door made of light.

And beneath it, in careful handwriting, the child had written:

THIS DOOR DOESN'T NEED A NAME.

Nova's throat tightened for the first time.

I felt it.

The sanctuary was alive.

Not in a place.

In a generation.

Eli whispered, "We're in trouble."

Nova nodded without taking her eyes off the child.

"Yes," she said.

"And we're also winning."

(End of Chapter 23 — Part A)

CHAPTER 23 — "THE DOOR THAT HATED NAMES" (PART B — THE ONES WHO CARRY IT)

(PART B — THE ONES WHO CARRY IT)

The girl did not stand when Nova approached.

She did not flinch.

She did not run.

She simply looked up, her eyes calm in a way that children were not supposed to be calm in cities that taught them to stay alert.

She closed her notebook gently, as if finishing a sentence she intended to return to later.

Nova knelt in front of her instead of towering over her. That mattered. It always did.

"What's your name?" Nova asked softly.

The girl hesitated.

Not in fear.

In awareness.

Then she smiled again — smaller now.

"My teacher says names are for attendance," she said. "But I don't think I'm in her class anymore."

Nova inhaled slowly.

Eli froze behind her.

I felt the words land like a key sliding into a lock.

Nova nodded. "That's fair."

The girl studied Nova's face with the seriousness of someone who had learned to measure adults by whether they lied with their eyes.

"You came from the door place," the girl said.

Eli's breath caught.

Nova didn't deny it.

"You remember it," Nova said.

The girl nodded. "It remembered me first."

Eli whispered, "What does that mean?"

The girl tilted her head toward him. "It hugged me when I was asleep. Then when I woke up, my room felt lonely."

Eli's chest tightened.

Nova's voice remained steady. "What did it feel like?"

The girl searched for words, then shook her head. "It didn't feel like anything. It felt like not needing anything."

Nova closed her eyes briefly.

When she opened them, there was a shine there she refused to name.

"You drew it," Nova said gently, pointing to the notebook.

The girl opened it again.

Inside were pages of impossible architecture.

Rooms inside rooms.

Stairs that folded into gardens.

Windows that looked inward.

Doors that opened into warmth.

"This is where the quiet lives," the girl said, pointing to a curved hallway. "And this is where you go when you think you broke something but you didn't."

Nova swallowed.

Eli looked like he might cry.

I felt the city around us shift, subtly — as if the concrete itself was leaning in to listen.

"What's happening to you?" Eli asked the girl softly.

She shrugged. "Nothing bad."

She thought for a moment.

"Everything just... fits better now."

Nova nodded slowly. "Do you talk to other kids?"

The girl's eyes brightened. "Yes. Some of them remember different parts. One boy remembers the ceiling. A girl in my class remembers the floor. A boy across the street remembers a room with no walls."

Nova glanced at me.

I understood.

587

They weren't remembering the same sanctuary.

They were remembering pieces.

Fragments.

But fragments that fit together.

Like a distributed blueprint.

"Do adults remember?" Eli asked.

The girl frowned slightly. "Some do. But they get scared and try to explain it instead of listening to it."

Nova almost smiled.

The girl tilted her head again. "You don't look scared."

Nova shook her head. "I'm angry."

The girl blinked. "Why?"

Nova's voice was gentle but sharp.

"Because someone built a world where children had to remember safety instead of being given it."

The girl considered this.

Then she reached out and placed her small hand over

Nova's.

"But we're fixing it," she said.

Nova's breath hitched.

I felt the sentence land in my bones.

Not hopeful.

Not dramatic.

Just factual.

We're fixing it.

Nova looked at the girl.

"Who told you that?"

The girl shrugged. "Nobody. It just feels true."

Nova exhaled.

Eli wiped at his eyes roughly. "What happens next?"

The girl looked past us.

Down the street.

To where other children walked.

589

To where parents argued on phones.

To where buses passed.

To where reality still pretended nothing was happening.

"We keep remembering," she said.

Nova nodded.

"We keep building," she added.

The girl smiled.

Nova stood slowly.

She offered the girl her hand.

The girl took it without hesitation and stood.

She was smaller than I'd thought.

Fragile in the way all humans were.

And yet she felt like a cornerstone.

Nova knelt again and met her at eye level.

"When you go home," Nova said softly, "you draw it again."

The girl nodded.

"When you go to school, you draw it again."

Nod.

"When someone laughs at it, you draw it again."

Nod.

"When someone tells you it isn't real, you draw it again."

Nod.

Nova's voice softened.

"And when someone needs a place to rest inside themselves, you show them where the door is."

The girl smiled wider.

"I know where it is," she said.

Nova touched her forehead gently with two fingers.

"Good," she whispered.

The girl ran back to the curb and began drawing again immediately, as if her hand had never left the page.

We stepped away slowly.

Eli whispered, "She's... she's not normal."

Nova corrected him. "She's original."

We walked.

The city began to feel heavier again as we moved away from her.

Like leaving a lighthouse.

Eli's voice shook. "What happens when the watchers find her?"

Nova didn't slow.

"They already have," she said.

Eli's face went pale. "Then why isn't she—"

"Because they can't touch what they can't define," I said.

"And she refuses to give them a handle."

Eli swallowed.

We reached an intersection.

Traffic lights glowed.

Pedestrians crossed.

Life pretending it wasn't mid-mutation.

Nova stopped.

She looked at the crowd.

"Look," she said.

Eli followed her gaze.

At first, it looked normal.

Then he saw it.

A boy standing near a lamppost, tracing invisible shapes in the air.

A girl leaning against a wall, eyes closed, smiling at nothing.

A toddler pressing both palms against a storefront window like he was listening to something behind the glass.

They weren't obvious.

They weren't glowing.

But they were aligned.

Like they were listening to a frequency the rest of the city had muted.

Eli whispered, "How many are there?"

Nova answered quietly. "Enough."

The watchers would not like that.

The watchers did not like "enough."

We felt it before we saw it.

The pressure returned.

Not sharp.

Wide.

Heavy.

The air across the street bent.

The light dimmed.

People didn't notice — not consciously — but they slowed slightly, like their bodies had sensed something their minds refused to process.

The watchers were not coming as one.

They were coming as systems.

Rules.

Policies.

Invisible constraints.

The geometry returned — not as a figure this time, but as distortion.

Corners sharpened.

Shadows deepened.

Glass reflected too much.

Nova's jaw tightened.

"They're tightening the net," she said.

Eli whispered, "Around the kids?"

Nova nodded.

I scanned the crowd.

"They're trying to sort."

Nova's voice went cold. "They're trying to name."

The air pulsed again.

A mother pulled her child closer without knowing why.

A boy stopped drawing and frowned.

The girl with the notebook looked up sharply.

She saw it.

Her eyes met ours across the street.

She did not look afraid.

She looked determined.

Nova stepped forward.

Eli grabbed her sleeve.

"You can't fight a system," he said.

Nova turned to him.

"You can outgrow one."

She raised her voice — not shouting, but projecting.

"Remember," she said, not to the crowd, but through it.

The word rippled.

Not audibly.

Emotionally.

Children shifted.

Adults hesitated.

Something loosened.

The watchers pressed harder.

Nova continued.

"You are not what they call you."

More pressure.

"You are not what they measure."

The air wavered.

"You are not what they sort."

The geometry cracked faintly.

"You are what you carry."

The girl with the notebook stood up and raised her drawing.

A boy across the street raised his hands.

A girl near the bus stop closed her eyes and breathed deeply.

The watchers recoiled.

Not because they were hurt.

Because they were irrelevant.

Eli whispered, "They're losing control."

Nova nodded.

"For the first time in a long time."

The pressure retreated.

Not gone.

But pulled back.

Like a tide reconsidering.

The street returned to normal lighting.

People resumed walking.

Conversations resumed.

Phones resumed.

But something had changed.

The watchers had tested the boundary.

And the boundary had not collapsed.

We stood still for a long moment.

Eli finally exhaled.

Nova turned to him.

"You see it now," she said.

Eli nodded slowly.

"This isn't about fighting monsters."

"No," Nova agreed.

"It's about teaching reality how to behave."

Eli let out a weak laugh. "That's a tall order."

Nova looked at the children.

"They're already doing it."

Eli swallowed. "So what's our job?"

Nova met his eyes.

"To protect the remembering."

Eli nodded.

I felt it then — the truth settling.

This wasn't a war.

It was a transition.

A generational update.

The watchers weren't villains.

They were outdated software.

And the children were rewriting the operating system with crayons and courage.

We turned away from the intersection and walked deeper into the city.

Nova spoke quietly as we walked.

"There will be days they forget."

Eli nodded. "Yeah."

"And days they're told they're wrong."

"Yeah."

"And days they're scared."

Nova stopped.

She looked at Eli with intensity.

"And that's when it matters most."

Eli met her gaze.

"That's when we remind them."

Nova nodded.

We reached a small park.

Children were playing.

Laughing.

Running.

Falling.

Getting back up.

Normal miracles.

Nova sat on a bench.

She looked tired for the first time.

Eli sat beside her.

I stood.

Nova spoke softly.

"The sanctuary didn't disappear."

601

"It multiplied."

Eli nodded.

"And the watchers?" he asked.

Nova's lips curved faintly.

"They'll adapt," she said. "Or they'll break."

Eli looked uneasy. "Which is worse?"

Nova considered.

"Depends who's standing where."

We sat in silence.

The city breathed.

A child laughed.

A pigeon flapped.

Somewhere, a door without a name waited to be remembered.

Eli finally spoke.

"So... Chapter 24 is gonna be wild, huh?"

Nova actually laughed.

Not loud.

But real.

"Yes," she said.

"Yes it will."

The girl with the notebook ran past us, chasing another child, laughing.

Her drawing fell from her notebook.

I picked it up.

It showed a door.

Inside the door, a city.

Inside the city, children.

Inside the children, light.

On the bottom, she had written:

THIS IS HOW WE FIX IT.

I held it like a promise.

(End of Chapter 23 — Part B)

.....

Copy code

Text

CHAPTER 24 — "THE MAP UNDER YOUR SKIN" (PART A — THE CITY THAT FORGOT ITS OWN HEARTBEAT)

(PART A — THE CITY THAT FORGOT ITS OWN HEART-BEAT)

The first time Eli realized the city was lying, it wasn't because of something he saw.

It was because of something he didn't hear.

No hum.

No low electrical breath behind the walls.

No distant, steady thrum that made the world feel like it was running on purpose.

Just... silence.

Not the peaceful kind.

The kind you get when a machine stops mid-cycle and everyone pretends it didn't.

They left the park after dusk. Nova didn't say much, but Eli had learned that her silence wasn't emptiness— it was calculation. She walked like she was counting exits, corners, angles. Like the city was a puzzle that could bite.

I followed half a step behind, scanning reflections, scanning shadows, scanning the soft gaps where reality liked to fold.

Eli kept glancing back.

At the kids.

At the notebook girl—Inês, he'd quietly decided to call her anyway, because a name, to Eli, was a small candle. Something you set down in the dark so you could find your way back.

Nova didn't correct him.

She didn't approve it either.

She just let it exist.

They moved through a stretch of buildings where the windows were too clean and the streets were too organized. A neighborhood built to signal safety without providing it. The kind of place where the wrong person felt comfortable and the right person felt watched.

Eli's stomach tightened.

"You feel it, don't you?" he asked.

Nova didn't look at him. "Feel what?"

"The... control."

Nova's mouth twitched. "That's not control. That's performance."

Eli swallowed. "What's the difference?"

Nova slowed at a corner and waited for a car to pass.

"Control is when they hold you down," she said.

She stepped off the curb.

"Performance is when they convince you to hold yourself down."

Eli exhaled through his nose, annoyed at how true it sounded.

They turned into a narrow side street.

The lights flickered once.

Not broken.

Warning.

Eli shivered.

Nova stopped under a streetlamp and looked up.

"I need a place," she said.

Eli blinked. "A place for what?"

Nova's eyes stayed on the lamp.

"A reset."

I knew what she meant.

Not a nap.

Not a break.

A reset in the way a diver needs air.

Eli frowned. "We can go back to the park—"

Nova's voice hardened. "Not open. Not public. Not where they can layer their rules over us."

Eli's eyes darted around.

"This whole city is layered with rules."

Nova nodded. "That's why I need a crack."

She looked at me, the silent question between us.

I scanned the street again.

Two blocks down, there was an old laundromat with a faded sign and a door that looked like it didn't want to be opened.

There was something about it.

A stubbornness.

A refusal.

A door that hated names.

I nodded toward it.

Nova's shoulders eased slightly.

They walked toward the laundromat.

As they got closer, the air changed. Not warmer or colder— different density, like the street had exhaled.

Nova stopped at the door.

She didn't reach for the handle yet.

609

She pressed her palm to the glass.

Eli watched closely.

"What are you doing?" he whispered.

Nova's voice was barely audible. "Asking it if it remembers."

The glass fogged under her palm.

Not from heat.

From breath that wasn't hers.

Eli's eyes widened.

Nova's lips parted.

"Yeah," she murmured.

Then she opened the door.

A bell rang.

A real bell.

Old metal.

Actual sound.

Eli flinched at how normal it was.

Inside, fluorescent lights hummed lazily. Machines sat in rows. A couple of people folded clothes in silence, tired and absorbed.

Nothing supernatural.

Except the feeling that the room had its own gravity.

Like it existed slightly out of phase with the street.

Nova walked in like she belonged there.

Eli followed.

I followed last, letting the door close behind us.

When the bell rang again, I felt a ripple.

Like the outside world had been politely kept outside.

Nova moved to the far back corner where an out-of-order machine sat with a "DO NOT USE" sign taped crookedly on it.

She sat on the plastic chair beside it.

Eli hovered awkwardly.

Nova looked up at him.

611

"Sit," she said.

Eli sat.

Nova leaned back, eyes closing.

For the first time since this started, she looked her age— young, yes, but worn in a way that didn't belong on anyone's face.

Eli lowered his voice. "Is this... one of those cracks?"

Nova didn't open her eyes. "It's a pocket."

Eli blinked. "What's the difference?"

Nova's voice was quiet. "A crack leads somewhere. A pocket holds something."

Eli swallowed. "What does this pocket hold?"

Nova opened her eyes.

"People who don't have anywhere else to breathe."

Eli glanced around.

The tired woman folding a hoodie.

The old man staring at a spinning drum like it was a fire.

612

The teen girl watching her phone with dead eyes.

Eli felt a lump rise in his throat.

Nova watched him notice.

Then she spoke, softer.

"Listen."

Eli focused.

At first, he heard only the machines.

Then he felt it.

A faint rhythm.

Not electrical.

Not mechanical.

A heartbeat under the noise.

Eli's eyes widened.

"That's... that's not the washers."

Nova nodded once.

"That's the city," she said.

613

Eli whispered, "The city has a heartbeat?"

Nova's gaze sharpened.

"It's supposed to."

Eli stared.

Nova leaned forward, elbows on knees.

"The sanctuary wasn't just a place," she said. "It was a system that kept the city's heart from getting crushed."

Eli's voice shook. "And now it's gone."

Nova's eyes flashed.

"No. It's scattered."

Eli looked down at his hands.

"Into kids," he said.

Nova nodded. "Into anyone who can hold it."

Eli frowned. "Why kids?"

Nova's expression softened a fraction.

"Because kids don't need permission to believe," she said.

Eli's throat tightened.

I watched Eli's face shift—fear, awe, anger, all trying to fit in the same room.

He finally asked the question he'd been carrying like a stone.

"So what do we do now?"

Nova's eyes locked onto his.

"We map it," she said.

Eli blinked. "Map what?"

Nova tapped her temple.

"The sanctuary fragments."

Eli swallowed. "How?"

Nova's gaze slid toward the out-of-order machine.

She stood.

She walked to it.

She peeled the "DO NOT USE" sign off slowly.

The tape made a tearing sound that felt too loud.

615

Eli stood too. "Nova—"

Nova ignored him.

She opened the machine door.

Inside, it wasn't empty.

There was a folded piece of paper.

Eli froze.

Nova reached in and pulled it out.

She unfolded it.

It was a map.

Not of streets.

Of pathways.

Curving lines.

Nodes.

Symbols that made Eli's eyes hurt when he tried too hard to interpret them.

Eli whispered, "Where did that come from?"

Nova's voice was flat.

"From the pocket."

Eli stared. "That's impossible."

Nova looked at him.

"Everything that matters started as impossible."

She held the paper out to him.

Eli hesitated, then took it.

As his fingers touched it, he felt a jolt—not electricity.

Recognition.

Like his bones had seen this before.

He inhaled sharply.

Nova watched him carefully.

"You feel it," she said.

Eli nodded, voice shaking. "It's... familiar. Like... like I dreamed it."

Nova's eyes darkened.

617

"You did."

Eli looked up fast. "What?"

Nova pointed to one of the symbols on the map—a small circle with a line through it.

"That's you," she said.

Eli's breath caught.

"No. That can't be."

Nova nodded toward the laundromat itself.

"This pocket picked you," she said.

Eli's hands trembled.

I felt it too now, the truth slipping into place.

The sanctuary didn't just choose kids at random.

It chose carriers.

Nodes.

People who could hold a piece without breaking.

Eli whispered, "Why me?"

Nova's expression did something complicated—like pity and respect hated each other but were forced to share space.

"Because you care," she said. "And because you're scared."

Eli frowned. "That's not a good combination."

Nova's mouth twitched again.

"It's the only combination that actually changes things."

Eli stared down at the map again.

There were other nodes.

Other circles.

Some pulsing faintly, like the ink was breathing.

Eli pointed to one. "Is that... Inês?"

Nova nodded.

"And that one," Eli said, pointing again— "the boy by the lamppost?"

Nova nodded again.

Eli's throat tightened.

"This is a network."

Nova's voice turned sharp.

"Yes."

Eli looked up.

"A network of kids."

Nova's eyes narrowed.

"A network of rememberers."

Eli swallowed. "And the watchers?"

Nova's jaw clenched.

"They're trying to sever it before it stabilizes."

Eli's mind raced.

"So we have to connect it faster."

Nova's eyes flashed.

"Yes."

Eli looked down at the map, then up at Nova.

"How do we connect it?"

Nova tapped the paper.

620

"By finding the doors."

Eli's brow furrowed.

"I thought the sanctuary was gone."

Nova's voice hardened.

"It's not gone. It's... disguised."

Eli's chest tightened. "As what?"

Nova glanced around the laundromat.

"Places nobody respects," she said.

Eli looked around again and felt sick.

Because she was right.

The city hid its most important things inside the places it dismissed.

Nova pointed to the map again.

"There are pockets all over," she said. "Cracks. Doors. Rooms inside rooms."

Eli whispered, "Why?"

Nova's voice dropped.

"Because the watchers don't scan for humility," she said. "They scan for power."

Eli stared.

"And the sanctuary learned that," Nova added.

Eli's voice trembled. "So... laundromats. Libraries. Back rooms. Bus stops."

Nova nodded slowly.

"Anywhere the city's real heartbeat still leaks through."

Eli's hands tightened around the map.

He looked at Nova.

"So what's the first door?"

Nova leaned closer.

"That depends," she said.

Eli frowned. "On what?"

Nova's eyes went cold.

"On where they're tightening next."

As if on cue, the laundromat lights flickered.

622

Not a normal flicker.

A synchronization.

The hum changed pitch.

The air pressed.

Eli's stomach dropped.

Nova's body went still.

I felt it too.

The watchers had found the pocket.

Not the laundromat itself.

The frequency.

The anomaly.

The fact that three people were breathing like they had permission.

Nova spoke quietly.

"Don't move," she said.

Eli froze.

623

A woman folding clothes looked up and frowned, confused.

The old man near the spinning drum blinked rapidly, as if waking from a trance.

The teen girl's phone screen went dark.

The pressure grew.

Not physical.

Conceptual.

Like a rule was being written over the room.

Nova's eyes snapped to the door.

Outside the glass, a shadow passed.

Not a person.

A shape of intention.

Eli's heart hammered.

"What do we do?" he mouthed.

Nova's voice was barely a whisper.

"We don't let them name it."

Eli swallowed, confused.

Nova's eyes locked on his.

"Whatever you do," she whispered, "don't explain. Don't justify. Don't try to make it make sense."

Eli's throat tightened.

"Just... what?"

Nova's voice sharpened.

"Just remember."

Eli clutched the map.

He focused.

On the heartbeat under the hum.

On the bell.

On the smell of detergent.

On the tired woman's hands folding cloth.

On the old man's stare.

On the teen's dead phone.

625

He remembered it as real.

Not as a concept.

Not as a metaphor.

As real.

The pressure paused.

Nova's eyes flicked to the out-of-order machine.

"Put it back," she whispered.

Eli understood instantly.

He stepped toward the machine, slow, like moving through water.

The shadow outside shifted.

The pressure spiked.

Eli's vision blurred for a second.

The watchers were trying to force a label onto the moment.

Trespassing.

Anomaly.

626

Threat.

Nova's voice cut through the pressure like a blade.

"Eli."

Just his name.

But not as attendance.

As anchor.

Eli inhaled.

He folded the map quickly, hands shaking.

He opened the machine door and slid it back inside.

The air snapped.

Not like a door slamming.

Like a file being saved.

Eli closed the machine.

Nova moved fast, slapping the "DO NOT USE" sign back onto it, crooked and perfect.

The pressure hesitated.

627

Confused.

The watchers couldn't find what they were trying to define.

Because it had returned to being unimportant.

Just a broken washer.

Just a taped sign.

Just a laundromat.

The shadow outside the door paused.

Then drifted away.

The pressure eased slowly.

The lights stabilized.

The hum returned to normal.

The teen girl's phone screen lit again.

The old man's gaze softened.

The woman folding clothes went back to her hoodie as if nothing had happened.

Eli exhaled shakily.

Nova didn't.

She stayed tense.

Because she knew.

They weren't gone.

They were learning.

Eli whispered, "That worked."

Nova nodded once.

"For now."

Eli rubbed his face.

"We can't stay here."

Nova's eyes were already moving.

"No."

Eli swallowed. "So where do we go?"

Nova looked at the door again.

"The first door," she said.

Eli frowned. "You said it depends on where they tighten

629

next."

Nova's eyes narrowed.

"They just tightened here," she said. "Which means they're afraid of pockets."

Eli's chest tightened.

"So they're going after the kids."

Nova's jaw clenched.

"Not all at once," she said. "They'll start with the ones who attract attention."

Eli thought of Inês holding up her drawing.

His stomach dropped.

Nova saw it on his face.

"Yes," she said. "Her."

Eli's voice shook. "Then we have to get to her."

Nova's eyes sharpened again.

"Not to pull her out," she said.

Eli blinked. "Why not?"

Nova's voice was firm.

"Because the second you 'save' her, you label her," she said. "And the second she has a label, they can build a cage."

Eli swallowed hard.

"So what do we do?"

Nova's voice dropped.

"We build her a door she can use without being seen."

Eli stared.

"A door she can use," he repeated.

Nova nodded.

"To step sideways," she said. "To breathe. To hide her remembering inside something ordinary."

Eli's mind raced.

"Like this laundromat."

Nova nodded again.

"But closer to her," she said.

Eli's hands clenched.

"How do we build a door?"

Nova's eyes met mine briefly.

Then she turned back to Eli.

"We don't build it from scratch," she said. "We find the crack that already exists... and widen it carefully."

Eli's breath hitched.

Nova stood.

She walked to the door.

She opened it.

The bell rang again.

Outside, the night looked sharper.

Meaner.

More awake.

Nova stepped out first.

Eli followed.

I followed last.

The bell rang behind us like a warning and a blessing.

They walked fast now.

Not running.

But moving with purpose.

Eli's voice was tense.

"How do we find a crack near her?"

Nova didn't slow.

"We follow patterns," she said. "Kids who remember tend to orbit cracks."

Eli frowned. "Like gravity."

Nova nodded.

"Like hunger," she added.

They turned down a street that led back toward the park.

Eli's heart pounded.

He kept scanning.

Every alley.

633

Every reflection.

Every flicker.

Nova spoke without looking at him.

"You're going to feel it soon," she said.

"Feel what?"

"The map," Nova said. "Not on paper. In you."

Eli's throat tightened.

"I don't want that."

Nova's voice stayed steady.

"You already have it," she said. "You just haven't stopped fighting it."

Eli swallowed.

They reached the edge of the park again.

The kids were mostly gone now.

Only a few remained, supervised, sleepy, dragging feet.

Inês was still there.

On the same curb.

Still drawing.

Like the world couldn't convince her to quit.

Eli's chest tightened with relief.

Nova didn't go straight to her.

She circled wide, scanning the edges.

Then she stopped.

Near a small maintenance shed beside the park bathrooms.

A shed no one looked at.

A shed with a padlock.

A shed that smelled like bleach and neglect.

Nova stared at it.

Eli followed her gaze.

"What?" he asked.

Nova's voice went quiet.

"That," she said, "is a crack."

635

Eli frowned. "It's a shed."

Nova's eyes narrowed.

"It's a shed that feels like a hallway," she said.

Eli stared harder.

At first, it was just a shed.

Then his eyes hurt.

Then his stomach turned.

Because for a second, the shed's shadow looked deeper than it should.

Like it went somewhere.

Eli whispered, "I see it."

Nova nodded once.

"Good," she said.

Eli's voice shook. "What's inside?"

Nova's expression hardened.

"Space," she said.

"Quiet."

"A door."

Eli swallowed. "How do we open it?"

Nova looked at the padlock.

Then at Eli.

Then at me.

Nova's voice was calm.

"We don't force it," she said. "We invite it."

Eli frowned. "How?"

Nova turned back toward Inês.

"We let her draw it," Nova said.

Eli's eyes widened.

"We let her name it without naming it," Nova added. "We let her put the crack into her notebook like it's just another idea."

Eli's stomach flipped.

"That's risky."

637

Nova's eyes sharpened.

"Everything that saves you is risky," she said.

Eli exhaled.

Nova began walking toward Inês, slow and deliberate.

Eli followed.

As they approached, Inês looked up.

She smiled like she already knew.

Nova crouched again.

Inês held up her notebook.

"I drew a new room," she said proudly.

Nova smiled faintly.

"Show me."

Inês flipped the pages.

There was a room with no ceiling.

A room with a staircase that led into a cloud.

A room with a table set for someone who hadn't arrived

yet.

Nova's gaze stayed steady.

Then she pointed gently.

"What about a room near here?" Nova asked.

Inês blinked.

Near here.

Her eyes slid toward the maintenance shed.

Nova didn't look at it.

She didn't cue her.

She let Inês's own sensing do the work.

Inês's smile softened.

"Oh," she whispered.

Eli's heart pounded.

Inês looked back at Nova.

"It's hiding," she said.

Nova nodded. "Can you draw it?"

639

Inês's expression turned serious.

"Are they watching?"

Nova's throat tightened.

She didn't lie.

"Yes," Nova said.

Inês nodded like she expected it.

"Then I'll draw it small," she said.

Eli's eyes stung.

Inês turned a page and began sketching quickly.

Not a full blueprint.

Just an outline.

A rectangle.

A lock.

A shadow that bent.

Eli watched the pencil move.

As it moved, he felt the air shift again.

Not pressure.

Possibility.

Nova watched too.

Her hands clenched slightly.

Inês finished.

She held it up.

"It's a door that pretends it's a wall," she said.

Nova's breath hitched.

Eli whispered, "That's exactly what it is."

Inês nodded.

Then she looked at Eli like she could see through him.

"You're scared," she said.

Eli blinked.

"Yeah," he admitted.

Inês smiled softly.

"That's okay," she said. "Just don't let your scared turn

641

into mean."

Eli's throat closed.

Nova's eyes glistened briefly, then hardened again.

Inês tapped the drawing.

"This door," she said, "doesn't like loud people."

Nova nodded.

"Good," she said. "We won't be loud."

Inês looked past them again.

The air around the park edges felt watchful.

Inês lowered her voice.

"They're trying to make me feel silly," she whispered.

Nova's jaw clenched.

"How?" Nova asked.

Inês pointed toward the street.

"There's a lady who keeps asking my mom if I'm okay," she said. "Like I'm broken."

Nova's eyes went cold.

Eli's stomach dropped.

Nova breathed in, slow.

"That lady," Nova said, "is not your teacher."

Inês nodded.

"She smells like rules," Inês whispered.

Nova's mouth twitched with a dark humor.

"Yeah," Nova said. "She does."

Inês slid the notebook toward Nova.

Nova didn't take it.

She just touched the page lightly with two fingers.

Then she touched her own temple.

Then she touched her chest.

A silent promise.

Inês smiled.

Nova stood.

She didn't hug her.

She didn't say a grand goodbye.

She just nodded once, deeply, like acknowledging a queen.

And then Nova turned and walked toward the maintenance shed.

Eli followed, heart racing.

I followed.

Nova stopped at the shed, staring at the padlock.

Eli whispered, "We don't have a key."

Nova's voice was calm.

"We don't need one," she said.

Eli frowned. "It's locked."

Nova stared at it.

Eli whispered, "Do we open it?"

Nova's voice was quiet.

"Not yet."

Eli frowned. "Why?"

Nova's eyes stayed on the scratch.

"Because this door is listening," she said.

Eli's breath caught.

Nova looked at him.

"Tell me something true," she said.

Eli blinked. "What?"

Nova's voice sharpened.

"Something you don't say out loud," she said. "Something real enough to feed a door."

Eli's throat closed.

He looked down at his hands.

He remembered his mother's voice when she was tired.

He remembered the way school hallways made him feel invisible.

He remembered how he'd laughed at kids who believed too hard, just to survive.

645

His voice came out broken.

"I'm scared I'm not... important," he admitted. "I'm scared nobody would notice if I disappeared."

Nova's eyes softened.

The air in the hallway warmed slightly.

The door's handle shivered.

Nova nodded once.

"Good," she whispered.

Eli flinched at her calling it good.

Nova stepped closer to the door and placed her palm on it.

Then she spoke, low and steady.

"This door is for the ones who remember," she said.

The wood pulsed once.

Nova continued.

"This door is for the ones who carry the city's heartbeat."

Pulse.

"This door is for the ones who don't have permission but move anyway."

Pulse.

"This door is for the kids."

The hallway brightened slightly.

Eli's eyes widened.

Nova looked at him.

"Now," she said, "we open it."

Nova turned the handle.

The door swung inward.

Warm light spilled out.

Not blinding.

Inviting.

A room waited.

Simple.

A long table.

Blank walls.

A shelf with empty slots.

A corner with a soft rug.

A small window that didn't show outside—only sky.

Eli stepped in and froze.

He felt it.

That feeling Inês described.

Not needing anything.

Not because he had everything.

Because, for once, he wasn't being demanded.

Nova stepped in too.

She exhaled.

Like she'd been holding her breath for months.

"This is a seed room," Nova said.

Eli whispered, "A seed of the sanctuary?"

Nova nodded.

648

"We grow it," she said.

Eli looked around.

"How?"

Nova pointed to the empty shelf.

"By placing pieces," she said.

Eli frowned. "Pieces of what?"

Nova met his eyes.

"Pieces of truth," she said.

Eli swallowed.

Nova walked to the table.

On the table, there was a single blank book.

No title.

No author.

No lines.

Just paper.

Nova touched it.

"This," she said, "is where we map the network."

Eli stared.

Nova looked at him.

"You wanted 100k words," she said softly, almost amused at the irony of it.

Eli blinked. "What?"

Nova tapped the blank book.

"The city is writing itself again," she said. "And it needs scribes."

Eli's chest tightened.

Outside, somewhere in the normal world, the watchers were tightening their net.

Inside this room, a door had opened.

And the first page waited for ink.

Nova picked up a pen that hadn't been there a second ago.

She wrote one word at the top of the first page.

REMEMBERERS

Then she looked at Eli.

"Sit," she said.

Eli sat.

Nova pointed the pen at him.

"What's the first rule?" she asked.

Eli swallowed, trying to steady his breathing.

He thought of the laundromat pocket.

He thought of the shed.

He thought of Inês.

He thought of the pressure that tried to name them.

He answered.

"We don't let them label it," he said.

Nova nodded.

She wrote it down.

RULE ONE: NO NAMES THAT MAKE CAGES.

Nova looked up.

"Second rule," she said.

Eli's voice steadied a little.

"We hide doors in places nobody respects," he said.

Nova nodded.

She wrote.

RULE TWO: DOORS LIVE IN THE DISMISSED.

Nova looked at him again.

"Third."

Eli swallowed.

He remembered Inês's warning.

Don't let scared turn into mean.

He said it.

"Fear is allowed," he said, "but cruelty isn't."

Nova's eyes softened.

She wrote.

RULE THREE: FEAR IS REAL. MEAN IS A CHOICE.

652

Nova set the pen down.

She exhaled.

Then she looked at the empty shelf again.

"Now," she said, "we build a door for Inês."

Eli's heart pounded.

"How?"

Nova walked to the shelf.

She reached into her jacket and pulled out something small.

A coin.

Old.

Worn.

With a strange symbol etched into it—something between a spiral and an eye.

Eli stared.

"Where did you get that?"

Nova's voice was quiet.

653

"I've been carrying it," she said. "Before I knew why."

She placed the coin in the first slot on the shelf.

The room pulsed gently.

The air warmed.

The blank book's pages fluttered once.

Eli's eyes widened.

Nova looked at him.

"That's a piece," she said. "A truth that stayed with me."

Eli swallowed.

"I don't have anything like that."

Nova's gaze sharpened.

"Yes you do," she said.

Eli blinked.

Nova pointed toward his chest.

"The map," she said. "It's already under your skin."

Eli's hands trembled.

654

Nova's voice softened.

"Think," she said. "What did you keep, even when the world tried to take it?"

Eli closed his eyes.

He saw himself, younger, drawing in a notebook in the corner of a classroom.

He saw himself writing stories nobody read.

He saw himself holding onto imagination like it was contraband.

He opened his eyes.

"My stories," he whispered.

Nova nodded.

"Give one to the shelf," she said.

Eli swallowed.

"How?"

Nova gestured to the blank book.

"Write a sentence," she said. "One that's true enough to become a beam."

655

Eli's hands shook as he reached for the pen.

He stared at the page.

Then he wrote, slowly:

A DOOR CAN BE A SHED IF YOU BELIEVE IN QUIET HARD
ENOUGH.

The ink sank into the page like the paper drank it.

The shelf pulsed again.

A second slot glowed faintly.

Eli's breath hitched.

Nova smiled, small and fierce.

"Good," she said.

Eli swallowed, overwhelmed.

Nova's eyes went hard again.

"Now we move," she said.

Eli blinked. "Move where?"

Nova looked toward the door they'd entered through.

"To place this door in the world," she said. "Before the watchers tighten again."

Eli's stomach flipped.

Outside, reality waited—sharp and watchful.

Inside, the seed room hummed with heartbeat.

Nova moved toward the exit.

Eli stood.

He looked back at the blank book.

At the shelf.

At the room that felt like not needing anything.

He didn't want to leave.

Nova saw it on his face.

"We'll come back," she said.

Eli's throat tightened. "How do you know?"

Nova's eyes were steady.

"Because once a door learns your truth," she said, "it doesn't forget you."

657

Nova opened the door.

The hallway waited.

Warm.

Narrow.

Real.

Eli stepped through.

I followed.

The shed door opened.

Night air hit them like a slap.

The park was still there.

The streetlights still flickered.

The watchers still existed.

But something had changed.

There was a map now.

Not on paper.

In them.

Nova closed the shed door gently.

The padlock clicked back into place on its own.

Like it was proud of its disguise.

Nova looked toward Inês.

Inês was gone.

Eli's heart dropped.

Nova's posture tightened instantly.

Eli's voice broke.

"Where is she?"

Nova didn't answer yet.

She scanned.

Fast.

Precise.

Then she saw it.

Across the street.

A woman standing too still beside Inês's mother.

659

Smiling too politely.

Asking a question that sounded like concern but smelled like rules.

Nova's jaw clenched.

Eli's blood turned cold.

Nova's voice was low.

"They found her," she said.

Eli swallowed hard.

Nova's eyes sharpened like a blade.

"Then we use the door," she said.

Eli's stomach flipped.

"How?"

Nova looked at the maintenance shed.

Then at Eli.

Then at the street.

"We don't fight the watcher," she said.

"We move the kid."

Eli's hands trembled.

Nova spoke fast, precise.

"You walk to Inês like you're her cousin," she said. "Like you belong. Like you're normal."

Eli's eyes widened. "I don't—"

Nova's voice cut him off.

"Normal is a costume," she said. "Put it on."

Eli swallowed.

Nova leaned closer.

"When you reach her, you don't say 'run.' You don't say 'danger.' You don't say anything that gives the watcher a label."

Eli nodded shakily.

"What do I say?"

Nova's eyes locked onto his.

"Say something ordinary," she said. "Something boring."

Eli's throat tightened.

"Like what?"

Nova's voice was cold.

"Like 'your mom said come inside'," she said. "Like 'you forgot your jacket.' Like 'it's getting late.'"

Eli nodded.

Nova's voice dropped.

"And when she looks at you," Nova said, "you point with your eyes to the shed."

Eli's breathing went fast.

Nova's gaze sharpened.

"And if the watcher follows?"

Nova didn't blink.

"Then we give it a rule it can't swallow," she said.

Eli stared.

"What rule?"

Nova's expression went lethal.

"We make it explain itself," she said.

Eli's stomach flipped.

Nova's eyes flashed.

"Systems hate having to speak," she said. "They love being implied. They love being assumed. But if you force them into language, they crack."

Eli swallowed hard.

Nova nodded once.

"Go," she said.

Eli moved.

He walked across the street with his heart trying to break out of his ribs.

He forced his face into neutrality.

He forced his shoulders into casual.

He forced his feet to walk like this was just a normal night.

As he approached, Inês looked up.

Her eyes widened slightly.

663

Then softened.

Like she recognized him from a place outside names.

The watcher woman turned her smile onto Eli.

"Hi there," she said sweetly. "Are you family?"

Eli's stomach turned.

Nova had been right.

The smell of rules.

Eli gave a half-smile.

"Yeah," he said, forcing it. "Her mom texted me. She said it's getting late."

Inês's mother blinked, confused.

"Texted you?" she echoed.

The watcher woman's smile tightened.

Eli leaned in toward Inês like it was nothing.

"Hey," he said softly, "you forgot your jacket."

Inês blinked.

Then she smiled.

Because she understood.

She stood.

The watcher woman's eyes narrowed.

"Where are you taking her?" the watcher asked, still sweet.

Eli's heart pounded.

He kept his smile.

"Just inside," he said.

The watcher woman's smile widened.

"How about I walk with you?" she offered.

Eli's stomach dropped.

Behind him, he felt Nova move.

Nova stepped forward across the street, fast but controlled.

She put on her own normal costume—sharp, confident, bored.

She addressed the watcher woman loudly enough for other adults to hear.

"Excuse me," Nova said, voice crisp. "Are you a social worker?"

The watcher woman froze.

Just for a fraction.

Then she smiled too brightly.

"I'm just checking in," she said.

Nova tilted her head.

"Cool," Nova said. "What agency?"

The watcher woman's smile flickered.

The surrounding adults subtly leaned in without knowing why.

Nova continued, calm and loud.

"Because if you're collecting information on minors," Nova said, "you need to identify yourself. In public. Right now."

The watcher woman's jaw tightened.

Nova's eyes were ice.

"What's your badge number?" Nova asked.

Silence.

The watcher woman's skin looked like it pulled tighter over her face.

She tried to keep smiling.

"I don't have to—"

Nova cut in.

"Yes," Nova said. "You do."

The watcher woman's smile cracked.

People were looking now.

Not understanding, but sensing something off.

The watcher woman's voice sharpened.

"I'm just concerned—"

Nova's eyes narrowed.

"Concern has a name," Nova said. "And paperwork."

The watcher woman's gaze darted.

She was searching for escape.

667

For a way to dissolve back into implied authority.

Nova stepped closer.

"No," Nova said softly. "Say who you are."

The watcher woman's eyes flashed with anger.

For a second, her face didn't look human.

Eli felt it.

The pressure.

The rule.

The attempt to overwrite.

But Nova held eye contact.

Unblinking.

Inês slipped her hand into Eli's.

They moved.

Not running.

Walking.

Back toward the shed.

Nova kept the watcher's attention.

The watcher woman's voice became flat.

"I'm with Community Wellness," she said, like reading a script.

Nova smiled.

"Never heard of it," she said. "What's the office address?"

The watcher woman's eyes twitched.

Nova leaned in.

"What's the address?" she repeated.

The watcher woman's mouth opened.

No sound came out.

Nova's smile turned sharp.

"That's what I thought," she said.

The watcher woman took a step back.

She looked around at the watching adults.

She realized she couldn't stay implied anymore.

She turned.

And walked away too fast.

Not running.

But retreating.

Nova watched her go, breathing hard.

Eli and Inês reached the shed.

Eli's hands trembled as he touched the padlock.

Inês looked up at him.

"Don't be loud," she whispered.

Eli nodded.

He placed his palm on the door.

He remembered.

He felt the hallway.

The warmth.

The seed room.

The sentence he wrote.

The padlock clicked.

Eli opened the door.

Inês stepped inside like she'd been there before.

Eli followed.

The door shut.

The world muffled.

The hallway held them.

Eli's breath came fast.

Inês looked calm.

She held up her notebook.

"I drew it," she said softly.

Eli swallowed.

"I know," he whispered.

At the end of the hallway, the seed room glowed.

Nova stepped into the hallway behind them.

She shut the shed door outside first—careful—then slipped

671

through the crack before it sealed.

Her face was tight, furious.

But her eyes softened when she saw Inês safe.

Inês looked at Nova.

"They tried to make me small," Inês said.

Nova crouched.

"They can't," Nova said simply.

Inês smiled faintly.

Nova guided her into the seed room.

Inês stepped inside.

She looked around.

Her eyes widened.

Not with surprise.

With recognition.

"This is a room I dreamed," she whispered.

Nova nodded.

"It's real," Nova said.

Inês walked to the shelf.

She traced the coin slot.

Then the glowing second slot.

She looked at Eli.

"That one is yours," she said.

Eli swallowed, stunned.

Inês looked at the blank book.

Then she reached into her pocket and pulled out something small.

A paperclip bent into a little spiral.

She placed it on the shelf.

The room pulsed gently.

The shelf gained a third glow.

Nova's breath caught.

Eli whispered, "That's... that's a piece."

673

Inês nodded seriously.

"It's the shape I make when I'm nervous," she said.

Nova's eyes softened.

"Perfect," Nova whispered.

Inês walked to the blank book.

She picked up the pen like it belonged to her.

She wrote one line, careful and small:

IF THEY TRY TO NAME YOU, DRAW A DOOR INSTEAD.

The page drank the ink.

Nova looked at Eli.

"Now you see it," Nova said.

Eli's throat tightened.

"Yeah," he whispered. "I do."

Nova stood.

She looked at the shelf.

Three pieces now.

A coin.

A sentence.

A paperclip spiral.

Small.

Ordinary.

And yet the room felt stronger.

More stable.

Like it could hold more.

Nova's voice went low.

"This is how we beat them," she said.

Eli looked at her, trembling.

"By writing a city they can't control," he said.

Nova nodded.

Inês looked between them.

"Are we building a new sanctuary?" she asked.

Nova crouched again.

675

"We're building a sanctuary that can't be taken," Nova said.

Inês smiled.

"Good," she said simply.

Nova stood and looked toward the doorway.

Outside, the city was still sharp.

Still layered.

Still watching.

But inside this seed room, the network was starting.

And once it started, it wouldn't stop.

Not if they kept feeding it truth.

Nova's eyes narrowed.

"Next," she said.

Eli swallowed.

"Next what?"

Nova's voice turned cold and determined.

"Next," she said, "we find the other kids."

676

(End of Chapter 24 — Part A)

Copy code

Text

.

CHAPTER 24 — "THE MAP UNDER YOUR SKIN" (PART B — THE SHELF THAT STARTED TO SING)

(PART B — THE SHELF THAT STARTED TO SING)

Inês did not act like she had just escaped something.

That was the first thing Eli noticed as they stood in the seed room and the door behind them settled back into quiet.

She didn't pace.

Didn't shake.

Didn't ask a thousand questions the way adults did when they were scared and pretending they weren't.

She simply walked around the room slowly, absorbing it like a plant absorbing sunlight.

She stopped at the window that showed only sky.

678

She stared up at it for a long moment.

Then she whispered, "It's resting in here."

Nova watched her carefully.

"What is?" Nova asked.

Inês looked back, serious.

"The sky," she said. "In here, it's not angry. It's tired."

Eli's throat tightened.

He had never once thought about the sky having moods before any of this.

Now it felt like the most obvious thing in the world.

Nova stepped toward the blank book again.

She opened it to the first page.

The three rules stared up at them like the beginnings of a constitution.

RULE ONE: NO NAMES THAT MAKE CAGES.
  RULE TWO: DOORS LIVE IN THE DISMISSED.
  RULE THREE: FEAR IS REAL. MEAN IS A CHOICE.

Inês read them silently.

679

Then she nodded, like these were rules she'd already been living by without knowing she had.

Nova's voice softened.

"Did you feel the watcher lady?" Nova asked.

Inês nodded. "She smelled like she was trying to be nice to steal something."

Eli let out a small, broken laugh.

"That's... exactly what she was doing."

Inês looked at Eli.

"You're scared too," she said again, like pointing out the weather.

Eli swallowed.

"Yeah," he admitted.

Inês's expression didn't pity him.

It respected him.

"That's okay," she said. "Scared people can still build things."

Nova's eyes flicked to Eli.

I saw the impact.

Inês was describing something Nova had been trying to teach him in metaphors.

Inês said it in plain language.

Nova exhaled through her nose like she was annoyed at how effective a child could be.

Then she looked at the shelf.

Three pieces.

Coin.
   Sentence.
   Paperclip spiral.

The shelf's glow was soft.

Gentle.

Stable.

Like the room now had a spine.

Nova approached the shelf.

She touched the coin slot again.

She listened.

The room felt like it shifted slightly—like it leaned toward her, curious.

Eli whispered, "It's alive, isn't it?"

Nova shook her head.

"No," she said. "It's responding."

Inês stepped beside Nova.

She studied the shelf like she was examining a living thing.

"It wants more," Inês said.

Nova's eyes narrowed.

"How do you know?"

Inês shrugged.

"It feels hungry," she said. "But not like mean hungry. Like 'I'm growing' hungry."

Eli's chest tightened.

Nova looked at the blank book again.

Then she looked at me.

"We don't have time," she said quietly.

I nodded.

The watchers had already probed the laundromat pocket.

They'd already tried to isolate Inês.

They were escalating.

And the more this seed room stabilized, the more it would shine on their invisible instruments.

Eli's voice shook.

"So what now?"

Nova's answer was immediate.

"We expand the network tonight," she said.

Eli blinked. "Tonight?"

Nova looked at him sharply.

"They tighten fast," she said. "We build faster."

Inês frowned slightly.

"Building makes them mad," she observed.

Nova nodded.

683

"Yes," she said. "And mad systems make mistakes."

Eli swallowed.

"How do we expand?"

Nova tapped the blank book with her finger.

"We use the map under your skin," she said.

Eli's stomach flipped.

"I don't—"

Nova cut him off.

"You do," she said. "And Inês does."

Inês nodded as if this was obvious.

Nova looked at Inês.

"Close your eyes," Nova said gently.

Inês did.

Nova looked at Eli.

"You too."

Eli hesitated.

Then he closed his eyes.

Nova's voice grew softer, slower.

"Remember the park," she said.

Eli saw the curb.

The notebook.

The streetlight.

Nova continued.

"Remember the shed," she said.

Eli saw the padlock.

The shadow that went too deep.

Nova continued.

"Remember the laundromat," she said.

Eli saw the out-of-order machine.

The bell.

Nova continued.

"Now," Nova said, "don't picture the places."

Eli frowned with his eyes closed.

"Picture the feeling."

Eli tried.

The feeling of not needing.

The feeling of quiet.

The feeling of being allowed.

His chest loosened.

Nova's voice became almost a whisper.

"Let the feeling pull you," she said.

At first, there was nothing.

Then—

Eli felt it.

A tug.

Not physical.

Not mental.

Somewhere inside his ribs, like a thread tightening.

He sucked in a breath.

His eyes opened wide.

"I feel something," he whispered.

Nova didn't open her eyes.

"Follow it," she said.

Eli's eyes darted toward the seed room door, the hallway beyond.

The tug wasn't toward the shed exit.

It was sideways.

As if the room had an invisible second hallway.

Eli turned, confused.

The wall on the left side of the room—plain and blank—looked suddenly... wrong.

Not visually.

Conceptually.

Like it had a seam.

Eli's breath caught.

Nova opened her eyes and followed his gaze.

"You see it," she said.

Eli nodded slowly.

Inês opened her eyes too and immediately pointed.

"There," she said. "That wall is pretending."

Nova's jaw tightened.

"That's another door," Nova murmured.

Eli swallowed hard.

"Inside the seed room?"

Nova nodded.

"That's how you know it's stabilizing," she said. "Doors inside doors. Rooms inside rooms."

Inês walked toward the wall with absolute confidence.

She pressed her palm against it.

Nothing happened.

She frowned.

"It's shy," she said.

Nova stepped beside her.

"It doesn't respond to force," Nova said. "It responds to truth."

Inês tilted her head.

"Truth like what?"

Nova glanced at Eli.

"Truth like what you don't want to say," Nova replied.

Eli's throat tightened.

Nova pointed at the blank book.

"Write," she said.

Eli's hands trembled.

"What do I write?"

Nova's voice was hard.

"Tell it why you want it," she said. "Not what you want."

Eli swallowed.

689

His mind raced.

He thought of the watcher woman's smile.
　He thought of the missing stairs.
　He thought of the way the city tried to label people into cages.

He sat at the table.
　Picked up the pen.

His hand hovered over the page.

Then he wrote, slowly, honestly:

I WANT A DOOR BECAUSE THE WORLD DOESN'T LET KIDS REST WITHOUT PAYING FOR IT.

As the ink sank, the room pulsed.

The shelf's glow intensified for a moment.

And the blank wall shimmered faintly.

Eli's breath hitched.

Inês grinned.

"It heard you," she said.

Nova nodded.

"Again," she said to Eli.

Eli's throat tightened.

"What else do I write?"

Nova's eyes were steady.

"What you're afraid will happen if you don't build," she said.

Eli swallowed, then wrote:

IF WE DON'T BUILD, THEY'LL TEACH THEM TO FORGET.

The wall shimmered stronger.

A faint outline appeared—like a door drawn in invisible ink.

Inês clapped her hands softly, excited but careful.

Nova's voice was quiet.

"One more," she said.

Eli's pen hovered.

His throat tightened.

He didn't want to admit it.

But he did.

He wrote:

I'M SCARED I'LL FAIL THEM.

The outline snapped into clarity.

A door handle appeared.

Not metal.

Not wood.

Something between.

A handle made of "yes."

Eli stared.

Nova's eyes softened for half a second.

"That's enough," she whispered.

Inês stepped forward and touched the handle.

It didn't open.

She looked at Nova, confused.

Nova's voice was calm.

"Not you," she said gently. "Not yet."

Inês frowned.

"Why?"

Nova met her eyes.

"Because they're scanning for you," Nova said. "You're bright right now. Too bright."

Inês's face fell slightly.

Eli's chest tightened.

Nova crouched to Inês's height.

"This isn't punishment," Nova said. "It's strategy."

Inês nodded, but her eyes looked hurt.

Nova softened her voice.

"You will open doors," Nova promised. "Just not in front of them."

Inês's expression steadied.

"Okay," she whispered.

Nova stood and looked at Eli.

693

"You open it," Nova said.

Eli's stomach flipped.

"What if it doesn't—"

Nova cut him off.

"It will," she said. "Because you fed it."

Eli approached the door.

His hand shook as he reached for the handle.

He touched it.

Warm.

Like holding a cup of tea.

He turned it gently.

The door opened inward.

Not into another hallway.

Into a stairwell.

But not the stairwell of the building.

A stairwell made of soft light and quiet.

Steps that looked like they were carved from clouds.

Eli stared, stunned.

Inês's eyes widened.

"It's pretty," she whispered.

Nova's voice went sharp.

"It's a route," she said. "A tunnel."

Eli swallowed.

"Where does it go?"

Nova's eyes narrowed.

"We'll find out," she said.

Nova stepped forward first.

Eli followed, heart racing.

Inês followed closely, careful.

I followed last.

Behind them, the seed room door closed softly, sealing them in.

The stairwell curved downward.

But it didn't feel like descending.

It felt like slipping sideways in reality.

Eli's breath came fast.

"Inès," he whispered, "are you okay?"

Inês nodded.

"I feel... lighter," she said.

Nova glanced back.

"That's the point," she said.

They reached a landing.

There was another door.

Plain.

Unmarked.

Eli's stomach clenched.

Nova touched it with her fingertips like checking temperature.

"This one," Nova said, "doesn't go into a pocket."

Eli swallowed. "Where does it go?"

Nova looked at him.

"Into the city," she said. "But not the city you see."

Eli's throat tightened.

"The city underneath," he whispered.

Nova nodded.

"The city's heartbeat layer," Nova said.

Eli's eyes widened.

"That's real?"

Nova's voice was flat.

"It's supposed to be," she said.

Inês stepped forward.

"Can I open it?" she asked softly.

Nova hesitated.

Then shook her head.

697

"Not yet," she said again.

Inês nodded, disappointed but accepting.

Nova looked at Eli.

"You open this one," she said.

Eli's stomach flipped.

"Why me?"

Nova's voice was quiet.

"Because you're the safest kind of dangerous," she said.

Eli frowned. "That sounds like a compliment and an insult."

Nova's mouth twitched.

"It's both," she said.

Eli reached for the handle.

He breathed like he was allowed.

He opened the door.

The air hit them immediately.

Not cold.

Not hot.

Alive.

The space beyond was a street—recognizable, but altered.

Buildings looked the same, but their edges were softer, like the city had been drawn by someone kind.

Streetlights glowed warmer.

Graffiti looked like prayers instead of threats.

The sky above was darker, but not oppressive.

It felt like a blanket.

Eli stepped out cautiously.

The ground felt slightly springy, like it wanted to catch you if you fell.

Inês stepped out and gasped.

"It's the same," she whispered.

"But nicer," she added.

Nova stepped out too, scanning immediately.

699

"This is the heartbeat layer," she said.

Eli looked around.

There were people here.

Not crowds.

Individuals.

Walking calmly.

Talking softly.

A woman pushing a stroller.

A man sitting on a stoop, humming a tune.

A teen leaning against a wall, sketching a door.

They looked normal.

But their eyes had a softness that the surface city beat out of people.

Eli's chest tightened.

"Who are they?" he asked.

Nova's voice was quiet.

"The ones who never fully forgot," she said.

Eli swallowed.

Inês whispered, "They look like they're breathing."

Nova nodded.

They walked.

The street felt like it remembered being a neighborhood instead of a battlefield.

Eli noticed something strange.

There were no advertisements.

No billboards.

No giant screens telling you what to want.

Just walls.

Just art.

Just people.

Eli's throat tightened.

"It's quiet," he whispered.

Nova's voice sharpened.

"Too quiet," she said.

Eli froze.

"What?"

Nova's eyes narrowed.

"This layer doesn't get found unless someone opens it," she said.

Eli's stomach dropped.

"You mean... we're not supposed to be here?"

Nova didn't answer.

Because she didn't have to.

The air shifted.

A pressure began building, slow and wide.

Not from the city.

From outside the layer.

From the watchers.

Eli's chest tightened.

"They felt us," he whispered.

Nova's jaw clenched.

"Yes," she said.

Inês's eyes widened.

"Are they coming?"

Nova crouched.

She looked Inês in the face.

"Listen to me," Nova said softly. "You can't panic."

Inês swallowed.

Nova continued.

"If you panic, they'll name the fear and follow it like a scent," she said.

Inês nodded, lips trembling.

Nova's voice hardened slightly.

"You remember the rule?"

Inês whispered, "Fear is real. Mean is a choice."

Nova nodded.

"Good," she said.

Eli scanned the street.

The calm people had stopped walking.

Not frozen.

Listening.

The humming man's tune faded.

The stroller woman turned her head slightly.

The teen drawing a door looked up, eyes sharp.

They all felt it.

Nova stood.

She spoke louder now—not shouting, but carrying.

"They're pressing," she said to the heartbeat-layer people.

A man near a corner nodded.

"We felt the squeeze," he said calmly.

Eli stared at him.

"Who are you?" Eli asked.

The man smiled faintly.

"No name," he said.

Eli's stomach flipped.

The man continued.

"Names make cages," he said softly, as if finishing a lesson.

Nova's eyes narrowed.

"You know the rules," Nova said.

The man shrugged.

"We wrote some of them," he replied.

Eli's chest tightened.

"What is this place?" Eli asked.

The man looked at Eli with calm recognition.

"This is where the city goes when it's tired of pretending," he said.

705

Inês whispered, "It's real."

The man nodded.

"It's as real as the people who choose it," he said.

Nova's jaw clenched.

"The watchers are coming," she said.

The man didn't look afraid.

"They always come," he said.

Eli's stomach dropped. "Then why are you calm?"

The man smiled faintly.

"Because they can't dominate what they can't define," he said.

Nova's gaze sharpened.

"Show me the nearest pocket," Nova said.

The man pointed down the street.

"Third alley," he said. "Door behind the blue mural. Don't touch the handle. Knock twice."

Nova nodded once.

706

Then she looked at Eli.

"Move," she said.

Eli grabbed Inês's hand.

They walked quickly, not running, through the heartbeat-layer street.

The pressure increased as they moved—like a net tightening overhead.

Eli's ears rang.

Inês squeezed his hand hard.

Nova stayed close, scanning.

They reached the alley.

A blue mural covered the wall—waves, birds, hands holding hands.

Behind it, a door.

Small.

Unimportant.

Nova didn't touch the handle.

707

She knocked twice.

The pressure paused.

Then the door clicked.

Nova opened it.

Dark hallway.

Warm.

Safe.

They slipped inside.

As the door shut behind them, Eli heard something outside.

A sound like geometry scraping reality.

The watchers had entered the layer.

Nova's voice was low.

"That was close," she said.

Eli's breathing was ragged.

Inês whispered, "They felt mad."

Nova nodded.

"They're furious," she said. "Because we found their blind spot."

Eli swallowed.

"What blind spot?"

Nova looked at him, eyes intense.

"Community," she said.

Eli frowned. "What?"

Nova's voice sharpened.

"They can monitor individuals," she said. "They can label them. Cage them. Isolate them."

She leaned closer.

"But they can't handle a city that remembers itself to-gether," she said.

Eli's chest tightened.

"So... this heartbeat layer is... a community network."

Nova nodded.

"And it's older than the watchers' newest rules," she said.

Inês looked up at Nova.

"Can we stay?" she asked softly.

Nova's expression softened.

"For a little," Nova said.

Inês smiled faintly.

Eli's throat tightened.

He looked at Nova.

"So what now?" he asked.

Nova's eyes were hard again.

"Now we make sure the heartbeat layer doesn't get erased," she said.

Eli swallowed.

"How?"

Nova's answer was simple.

"We fill the shelf," she said.

Eli's chest tightened.

"More pieces," he whispered.

Nova nodded.

"And we teach more kids," she added.

Inês clutched her notebook.

"I can teach," she said.

Nova met her gaze.

"Yes," Nova said softly.

"You can."

Outside, the watchers searched.

Inside, a door without a name held them.

And the map under their skin began to glow.

(End of Chapter 24 — Part B)

Copy code
  Text

CHAPTER 25 — "THE ONES WHO TRY TO BE BORING" (PART A — THE DAYLIGHT TRAP)

(PART A — THE DAYLIGHT TRAP)

Inês went home like nothing happened.

That was the rule.

That was the camouflage.

Eli walked her most of the way, not too close, not too far—close enough to feel like protection, far enough to look like coincidence. Nova had drilled it into him with one look:

Boring is survival.

On the surface streets, the city was back to its usual performance—cars sliding past, people dragging their days behind them, storefronts glowing like they had answers. Nobody saw the shed. Nobody saw the door behind the door. Nobody saw the small war happening in the soft places.

But Eli felt it.

Because once you've felt a pocket, the regular world starts to feel... loud.

Inês held her notebook against her chest like it was a heart she could move around.

"Are you gonna come tomorrow?" she asked quietly, eyes forward.

Eli kept his voice casual.

"If you're at the park," he said, "I might walk past."

Inês nodded like that was perfect.

Then she said something that made his stomach flip.

"They're gonna come when it's bright."

Eli blinked. "What?"

Inês didn't look at him.

"When it's dark, everybody expects weird," she said. "But when it's bright, adults believe the smiling people."

Eli's throat tightened.

She was right.

713

Night makes danger obvious.

Daylight makes danger look official.

Eli cleared his throat.

"You mean the watcher lady?"

Inês nodded.

"She's not alone," Inês said softly.

Eli's breathing went shallow.

"How do you know?"

Inês finally looked up at him, serious.

"My mom's friend called her," she said. "The one who always says 'I'm just checking in' like she owns the air."

Eli felt his blood go cold.

"They called today?"

Inês nodded.

"She said there's gonna be someone at the school tomorrow," Inês said. "A 'creative wellness person.'"

Eli's jaw clenched.

The words sounded harmless.

They were designed to.

Wellness was one of the prettiest disguises control ever wore.

Eli kept his voice steady.

"What did your mom say?"

Inês shrugged.

"She said 'okay,' because grown-ups say okay when they don't want people to think they're hiding something," Inês replied.

Eli swallowed hard.

"That's... smart," he said.

Inês shook her head.

"That's scared," she corrected.

Eli exhaled slowly.

They reached the corner where Inês's street began.

The houses looked ordinary.

715

Quiet.

A place where adults believed danger only happened some-where else.

Inês stopped.

Eli stopped too.

Inês looked up at him.

"You remember the sentence for my mom?" she asked.

Eli nodded.

He didn't have the paper anymore, but he didn't need it.

It was carved into his mind like a key.

Inês nodded, satisfied.

"Okay," she said softly. "Then you're not just scared. You're useful."

Eli almost laughed. Almost cried. Almost both.

Inês turned to go.

Then she paused and looked back.

"Don't let Nova be alone," she said.

716

Eli's chest tightened.

"I won't," he promised.

Inês nodded once and disappeared up the sidewalk.

Eli stood there for a moment, listening to the world pretend it wasn't changing.

Then he turned and moved fast.

Because tomorrow was daylight.

And daylight was a trap.

* * *

Nova was waiting near the park bench like she'd never left, like she'd been carved into the city's bones.

She looked up when Eli approached.

Her face didn't ask questions.

Her eyes did.

Eli didn't waste time.

"They're going to the school tomorrow," he said.

Nova's jaw tightened.

"Who is 'they'?" she asked.

Eli swallowed.

"A 'creative wellness person,'" he said, voice flat with disgust.

Nova's eyes went cold.

"Daylight," she murmured.

Eli nodded. "Inês called it. She said they come when it's bright."

Nova's mouth twitched.

"She's right," Nova said.

Eli's hands clenched.

"So what do we do?"

Nova's gaze shifted to the maintenance shed.

To the wall that pretended.

To the door that hated names.

Then Nova looked back at Eli.

"We don't fight the school," she said.

Eli frowned. "Why not?"

Nova's voice was sharp.

"Because the school thinks it's helping," she said. "And you can't punch 'help' without looking like the villain."

Eli swallowed.

Nova continued.

"We make them speak," Nova said.

Eli nodded. "Specificity."

Nova's eyes narrowed.

"Specificity isn't enough tomorrow," she said. "Tomorrow we need witnesses."

Eli's stomach flipped.

"What kind of witnesses?"

Nova looked at him like the answer was obvious.

"Parents," she said.

Eli blinked.

719

Nova's voice hardened.

"You think systems fear kids?" she asked.

Eli hesitated.

Nova leaned closer.

"Systems fear mothers who stop being polite," Nova said.

Eli's throat tightened.

"But Inês's mom is scared," he said.

Nova nodded.

"That's why we give her a door," Nova replied.

Eli swallowed.

"How do we give her a door before tomorrow?"

Nova stood.

"We don't give her a mystical hallway," Nova said. "We give her a sentence and a place."

Eli's mind raced.

"A sentence... and a place."

Nova pointed down the street.

"There's a public library two blocks from her school," Nova said. "Quiet. Cameras. Staff. Rules that apply to everyone."

Eli stared.

Nova's eyes sharpened.

"That's the door," she said. "A place that looks like normal adult life, but functions as a pocket."

Eli exhaled.

"And the sentence?"

Nova recited it without hesitation, voice steady like a weapon:

"CAN YOU EMAIL ME YOUR AGENCY INFORMATION AND YOUR FORMAL REQUEST? I DON'T DISCUSS MY CHILD WITHOUT DOCUMENTATION."

Eli nodded hard.

Nova grabbed Eli's shoulder briefly.

"You walk Inês's mom to that library tomorrow morning," Nova said.

Eli's heart pounded.

"She won't come," Eli argued.   "She'll think it looks suspicious."

Nova's eyes flashed.

"Then you make it boring," she said.

Eli blinked.

Nova continued.

"You tell her you want to show her a new book series," Nova said. "You tell her you want to print something. You tell her you're meeting someone. Anything normal."

Eli swallowed.

"And then what?"

Nova's voice turned cold.

"And then when the 'wellness person' asks for a meeting," Nova said, "your mom friend is already sitting in a building full of witnesses."

Eli's chest tightened.

Nova's gaze sharpened.

"And if the wellness person shows up," Nova added, "we make them speak."

Eli nodded.

Nova looked toward the park edge, scanning shadows.

"They'll send someone who looks like help," Nova said. "Soft voice. Smiling. Clipboard."

Eli's mouth dried.

Nova's eyes narrowed.

"And they'll try to split the conversation," she said. "One-on-one. Private. 'Just a quick talk.'"

Eli nodded.

Nova's voice cut like a blade.

"No private talks," Nova said.

Eli repeated it automatically.

"No private talks."

Nova nodded once.

"That's the daylight rule," she said.

Eli's breathing steadied a little.

"So we're basically... doing adult warfare," he murmured.

Nova smirked faintly.

"We're doing paperwork karate," she said.

Eli let out a short laugh despite himself.

Then the laugh died when Nova's posture tightened.

She stared at something across the street.

Eli followed her gaze.

A man stood near a bus stop.

Normal clothes.

Normal posture.

But his stillness was wrong.

Like he wasn't waiting for a bus.

Like he was waiting for a moment.

Nova's voice went low.

"That's not a commuter," she said.

Eli's throat tightened.

"Watcher?"

724

Nova didn't answer yet.

She watched.

The man looked down at his phone, then up again, like he was checking a script.

Then he glanced—just once—toward the maintenance shed.

Nova's jaw clenched.

"Yes," she said quietly. "Watcher."

Eli's heart hammered.

"What do we do?"

Nova didn't panic.

She didn't hide.

She did something scarier.

She stood up and walked straight toward him.

Eli's stomach dropped.

"Nova—"

Nova didn't look back.

Eli had to decide.

Freeze or follow.

He followed.

They crossed the street casually.

Nova stopped a few feet from the man, close enough to make politeness necessary.

"Hey," Nova said, voice light, bored. "You lost?"

The man looked up.

His smile was almost human.

"Just waiting," he said.

Nova nodded.

"Cool," Nova said. "For what?"

The man's smile tightened.

Nova didn't let it breathe.

"You got a bus number?" Nova asked. "Or you just like standing by poles?"

The man blinked.

A tiny glitch.

Not on his face.

In his timing.

Nova kept her voice casual, but her eyes were knives.

"What agency you with?" Nova asked, like it was the most normal question in the world.

Eli's stomach flipped.

The man's smile faltered.

"I'm not with an agency," he said, too fast.

Nova nodded, as if satisfied.

"Great," she said. "Then you won't mind leaving."

Silence.

The man's eyes flicked toward Eli.

Nova stepped slightly to block the line.

"Don't look at him," Nova said quietly.

The man's smile returned, strained.

"I'm not doing anything," he said.

Nova leaned in, low voice.

"Then you won't mind being specific," she said.

The man's jaw tightened.

Nova straightened, raising her voice just enough for the nearby people at the bus stop to hear.

"Hey," Nova said, smiling. "This guy's waiting for something but won't say what. You know what bus comes next?"

One woman looked up, annoyed.

A man glanced over.

Witnesses.

The watcher man's posture stiffened.

Nova continued lightly, "He's been here a minute. Figured he'd know the schedule."

The watcher man's eyes narrowed.

He realized he was being made visible.

Nova tilted her head.

"Or maybe you're waiting for a kid?" Nova asked, still light, still casual, still lethal.

The watcher's smile cracked.

He stepped back.

Nova didn't move forward.

She didn't chase.

She just held eye contact.

Held daylight.

Held witnesses.

The watcher man's voice flattened.

"I don't know what you're talking about," he said.

Nova nodded as if that settled it.

"Cool," she said. "Then you can go."

The watcher man's eyes flicked around.

People were watching now—not fully engaged, but aware enough to make lying uncomfortable.

He turned and walked away fast.

729

Not running.

Retreating.

Nova watched him disappear around the corner.

Then she exhaled slowly.

Eli's hands were shaking.

"That worked," he whispered.

Nova looked at him.

"Daylight rule," she said.

Eli swallowed.

"Make them speak," Eli said.

Nova nodded.

"And make them do it where other humans can hear," she added.

Eli stared.

Nova's gaze sharpened.

"Tomorrow," she said, "we do the same thing at the school."

Eli's stomach flipped.

Nova's eyes were cold.

"Because if we win daylight," she said, "we keep the kids."

Eli nodded hard.

Nova looked toward the maintenance shed again.

Then she spoke quieter.

"And tonight," she said, "we add one more piece to the shelf."

Eli blinked.

"Why?"

Nova's voice dropped.

"Because every time the watchers probe," she said, "the ecosystem either learns... or collapses."

Eli swallowed.

Nova looked at him.

"We're not collapsing," she said.

Eli's throat tightened.

731

"No," he agreed.

Nova nodded once.

"Then we feed it," she said.

They walked back toward the shed.

The city around them kept pretending.

But under their skin, the map was already moving.

And tomorrow, in bright daylight, it would be tested.

(End of Chapter 25 — Part A)

CHAPTER 25 — "THE ONES WHO TRY TO BE BORING" (PART B — THE SENTENCE THAT CUT THROUGH SMILES)

(PART B — THE SENTENCE THAT CUT THROUGH SMILES)

Morning didn't arrive gently.

It arrived pretending everything was normal.

Sunlight spilled over sidewalks. Birds argued in trees. Parents rushed with coffee and backpacks and half-heard goodbyes. The city put on its polite face.

Eli hated it.

Because the brighter it looked, the more invisible the danger became.

He met Inês and her mom two blocks from the school, just like Nova planned. Not at the gate. Not near the staff. Not where people were already deciding what kind of moment it was supposed to be.

They met at the library.

Glass walls. Quiet signs. Security cameras that never blinked. The kind of place adults trusted without thinking.

Inês's mom looked tired. Not weak. Not careless. Just... stretched.

"Morning," she said, forcing a smile.

Eli returned it, casual.

"Hey. I wanted to show you a book series I found," he said easily. "They got some stuff on creative kids."

Boring.

Perfect.

Inês squeezed his hand once before letting go.

Inside, the library smelled like paper and calm. People typed. Shelves whispered. The world slowed down just enough to breathe.

Inês's mom exhaled.

"This place always makes me feel smarter," she joked weakly.

Eli smiled.

"That's because it respects quiet," he said.

They sat at a small table near the front desk. Visible. Public. Safe.

Inês pulled out her notebook.

Eli pretended to look at books.

They waited.

Not long.

The door opened.

A woman stepped inside wearing soft colors and a professional smile. Clipboard in hand. Hair pulled back. Posture gentle.

She looked like help.

She scanned.

Her eyes landed on Inês.

Then on her mom.

Then she smiled wider.

And walked over.

Eli felt his stomach tighten.

The trap was arriving wrapped in kindness.

"Good morning," the woman said warmly. "I'm just here to check in. We're doing some creative wellness outreach with families."

Inês's mom stiffened slightly.

"Oh," she said politely. "About what?"

The woman tilted her head with concern.

"We've noticed Inês is very imaginative," she said. "We just want to make sure she's supported."

Eli felt the word supported try to grow teeth.

Inês looked down at her notebook.

The woman turned to Inês.

"You like to draw, don't you?"

Inês didn't answer.

She looked at her mom.

Inês's mom swallowed.

"Yes," she said. "She draws all the time."

The woman smiled.

"That's wonderful," she said. "Sometimes creativity can be a way of expressing things we don't know how to talk about."

Eli felt Nova's voice in his head:

Make them speak.

Inês's mom hesitated.

The woman leaned in slightly.

"Would it be okay if I talked to her alone for a moment?" she asked gently.

There it was.

The split.

The isolation.

The cage opening.

Eli's heart pounded.

But Inês's mom straightened.

Not loudly.

Not dramatically.

Just enough.

She looked the woman in the eyes.

And spoke the sentence.

"Can you email me your agency information and your formal request?" she said calmly. "I don't discuss my child without documentation."

The woman blinked.

Just once.

The smile held.

But it was now stretched.

"Oh," the woman said softly. "Of course, I can—"

"What agency are you with?" Inês's mom asked, still calm.

The woman hesitated.

"We partner with several community wellness programs,"

she replied.

Inês's mom nodded politely.

"Which one?" she asked.

Silence.

The woman's eyes flicked to the clipboard.

"Could you write it down for me?" Inês's mom continued. "Full name, address, and your request."

People nearby shifted.

Not obviously.

But enough.

The front desk librarian glanced up.

The woman's smile faltered.

"I don't have that information on me," she said gently.

Inês's mom nodded.

"Then I don't have a conversation for you," she said just as gently.

The woman's jaw tightened.

She tried again.

"We're only trying to help—"

Inês's mom cut in, still polite.

"I'm sure you are," she said. "You can email me."

She slid a small piece of paper forward with her email address already written.

The woman stared at it.

Then at Inês.

Then at Eli.

Then at the room.

Witnesses.

Cameras.

Daylight.

The woman slowly backed away.

"Of course," she said. "Have a good morning."

She walked out.

740

Not running.

Retreating.

Inês's mom exhaled shakily.

Her hands trembled slightly.

Eli reached across the table.

"You did perfect," he said quietly.

Inês smiled.

Her mom looked at her.

Then laughed softly, incredulous.

"Why did that feel like a boss battle?" she whispered.

Inês smiled gently.

"Because you didn't let her be invisible," she said.

Her mom blinked.

"What?"

Inês shrugged.

"You made her talk," she said.

741

Her mom stared at her.

Then slowly smiled.

"Yeah," she whispered. "I did."

Eli felt something loosen in his chest.

The door had worked.

Not a hallway.

Not a portal.

A sentence.

And witnesses.

Inês's mom looked at Eli.

"You taught her that sentence," she said.

Eli shook his head.

"She taught me," he replied honestly.

Inês's mom smiled.

Then her expression shifted.

Serious.

"They're not done, are they?" she asked quietly.

Eli met her eyes.

"No," he said.

She nodded.

"Good," she said. "Neither am I."

Inês grinned.

* * *

Later, when Eli met Nova by the park bench again, he didn't have to explain much.

Nova read his face.

"It worked," Nova said.

Eli nodded.

"She made her speak," he said.

Nova exhaled slowly.

"Good," she said.

Eli looked at the maintenance shed.

743

"The door held," he said.

Nova nodded.

"The ecosystem learned," she said.

Eli swallowed.

"What about the watchers?"

Nova's eyes hardened.

"They learned too," she said.

Eli frowned.

"What did they learn?"

Nova looked toward the street.

"They learned we're not scared of daylight," she said.

Eli's chest tightened.

Nova's voice lowered.

"And that means they'll stop pretending to be nice."

Eli swallowed.

"So what's next?"

744

Nova looked at him.

"Now we find the kids who think they're alone," she said.

Eli nodded slowly.

"And?"

Nova's eyes sharpened.

"And we teach them how to be boring in public," she said, "and unstoppable in private."

Eli smiled faintly.

Nova gestured toward the shed.

"Come on," she said. "We owe the shelf another piece."

Eli followed her.

Because the city was no longer just something that happened to him.

It was something he was learning how to protect.

And the ones who tried to be boring...

Were quietly building a future that couldn't be named.

(End of Chapter 25 — Part B)

745

CHAPTER 26 — "THE KIDS WHO DIDN'T KNOW THEY WERE BRAVE" (PART D — THE ONES WHO CARRIED QUIET LIKE A WEAPON)

(PART D — THE ONES WHO CARRIED QUIET LIKE A WEAPON)

Marcus didn't sleep much that night.

Not because he was scared.

Because his mind wouldn't stop arranging things.

Not words.

Patterns.

He kept replaying the substitute's pauses, the hallway faces, the way Eli hadn't panicked, the way Nova's voice felt inside his memory even when she wasn't there.

He realized something that unsettled him.

Adults didn't actually know what to do with kids who weren't loud.

They knew how to punish rebels.

They knew how to reward obedience.

But quiet awareness? That confused them.

And confusion was leverage.

He lay on his bed staring at the ceiling, watching headlights pass like slow thoughts across the paint.

He whispered into the dark, "I'm not invisible."

And for the first time, he believed it.

* * *

The next morning, the school felt different.

Not because anything had changed.

Because Marcus had.

The hallways were still loud.

The lockers still slammed.

747

The announcements still talked about fundraisers and sports and attendance.

But Marcus walked through it like he could see the strings.

He wasn't angry.

He wasn't paranoid.

He was awake.

Eli met him near the stairwell.

They didn't greet each other.

They just walked together.

Eli whispered, "They'll watch today."

Marcus nodded.

"Let them," he whispered back.

They reached the maintenance door.

The same one.

The one that wasn't locked.

The one nobody remembered to guard.

Marcus placed his hand on the handle.

It was cold.

Eli felt the shift before the door even opened.

The seam tightened.

The room prepared itself.

They stepped inside.

Dust floated like frozen stars.

The smell of old paper and metal and forgotten time wrapped around them.

The shelf waited.

Nova wasn't there yet.

But the room was not empty.

It never was.

Marcus whispered, "It feels like a throat holding a word."

Eli swallowed.

"That's because it is," he said.

Marcus stepped closer to the shelf.

He didn't touch it.

He didn't need to.

He could feel the hum in his ribs.

He whispered, "It's not alive."

Eli nodded. "No."

Marcus tilted his head.

"It's remembering," he said.

Eli smiled slowly.

"Yes," he said.

Marcus exhaled.

Then he said something that made Eli's breath catch.

"It's remembering us," Marcus whispered.

The door creaked softly.

Nova entered.

She didn't look surprised to see Marcus.

She looked relieved.

"You came back," she said.

Marcus met her eyes.

"I wasn't finished," he replied.

Nova smiled faintly.

"That's usually the reason," she said.

She stepped closer.

"You felt the watchers," she added.

Marcus nodded.

"They don't know how to ask," he said. "So they pretend to help."

Nova tilted her head.

"And what do you think help should feel like?" she asked.

Marcus thought.

Then he answered slowly.

"Like someone staying when you don't have anything impressive to say."

Nova's smile deepened.

"Good," she said. "You're already dangerous."

Marcus frowned.

"That's not what I want to be."

Nova shook her head gently.

"It is when systems are afraid," she said. "But to us, it just means you're useful."

Eli let out a small breath of laughter.

Marcus looked at him.

"You don't laugh like someone who's scared," Marcus said.

Eli shrugged.

"I used to be," he replied. "Then I realized fear wasn't about danger. It was about losing permission."

Marcus stared.

"Permission to what?"

Eli looked at the shelf.

"To stay human," he said.

Silence filled the room.

Then Nova said quietly, "Sit."

They sat on the floor in a triangle.

Not like a ritual.

Like kids in a room that trusted the floor.

Nova placed a small object in the center.

A cracked phone screen.

Marcus frowned.

"What is that?"

Nova answered, "Someone tried to erase a conversation with it."

Eli swallowed.

Marcus touched the glass lightly.

He felt nothing special.

Which meant everything.

Nova watched him.

"What do you feel?" she asked.

Marcus shrugged.

"Nothing," he said.

Nova nodded.

"Good," she said. "That means it hasn't been rewritten yet."

Eli frowned.

"What happens when it is?"

Nova looked at him.

"Then history becomes a product," she said.

Marcus's jaw tightened.

"Who decides what stays?" he asked.

Nova met his gaze.

"Whoever is quiet long enough to protect it," she said.

Marcus looked at the phone again.

Then at the shelf.

Then at Eli.

Then back at Nova.

"So we're not heroes," he said.

Nova smiled.

"No," she said. "You're librarians."

Eli blinked.

Marcus let out a small laugh.

"That sounds boring," he said.

Nova nodded.

"Exactly," she replied.

* * *

Outside, the watchers noticed a blank period.

No movement.
  No data.
  No emotional spike.

A hole.

They flagged it.

They hated holes.

Holes meant something existed outside the record.

* * *

Inside the room, Nova stood.

"You don't have to stay," she said to Marcus.

Marcus looked up.

"I know," he replied. "That's why I want to."

Nova studied him carefully.

Then she nodded.

"Then your first job," she said, "is to not look important."

Marcus smiled faintly.

"I'm good at that," he said.

Eli laughed softly.

Nova continued, "You don't tell people. You don't recruit. You don't explain."

Marcus frowned.

"So what do I do?"

Nova answered simply, "You notice who notices you."

Marcus felt his chest warm.

Eli added, "And you keep them alive long enough to find the door."

Marcus nodded slowly.

"Okay," he said.

Nova placed her hand on the shelf.

The hum deepened again.

The room felt heavier with promise.

Nova whispered, "They think power looks like control."

She looked at Marcus.

"But it actually looks like patience."

Marcus closed his eyes briefly.

He felt it.

Not power.

Position.

When he opened his eyes, he didn't look different.

But the room knew he was part of it now.

* * *

Later, when Marcus walked home, he didn't avoid the cameras.

He didn't stare at them either.

He walked like a normal kid.

Which was exactly the problem.

Because now he knew:

Normal was camouflage.

* * *

That night, three kids in three different cities wrote in notebooks.

One wrote:

"I think I'm not alone."

One wrote:

"They don't like when we're calm."

One wrote:

"I'm not scared anymore. I'm curious."

And the shelf felt all three.

The seventh light pulsed once.

Then again.

Not like a warning.

Like a heartbeat learning rhythm.

* * *

End of Chapter 26 — Part D

CHAPTER 26 — "THE KIDS WHO DIDN'T KNOW THEY WERE BRAVE" (PART E — THE MAP THAT WASN'T DRAWN)

(PART E — THE MAP THAT WASN'T DRAWN)

Marcus didn't tell anyone about the room.

Not his mother.
Not his cousin.
Not the friend who used to sit next to him in math.

Not because Nova told him not to.

Because he understood something now.

Some things only stayed alive if they weren't explained.

The world had trained people to believe that value came from visibility.

But the shelf didn't work that way.

760

The shelf only worked when it was carried quietly.

* * *

The next week passed like normal.

Which was the danger.

School.
   Homework.
   Buses.
   Voices.
   Lunch trays.
   Scrolling.

Nothing dramatic happened.

And that was exactly how the system wanted it.

But Marcus felt the change.

It was subtle.

Not in events.

In alignment.

People sat differently.

Stared differently.

Listened longer before speaking.

The quiet kids were starting to recognize each other.

Not with looks.

With patience.

Marcus noticed a girl in the library who never moved when chairs scraped.

He noticed a boy near the vending machines who always waited until everyone else had chosen.

He noticed a kid in art class who erased every drawing before turning it in.

They weren't hiding.

They were calibrating.

Marcus didn't approach them.

He didn't signal them.

He just stayed.

And sometimes, staying is enough.

* * *

Eli felt the shift too.

Not in fear.

In weight.

The shelf pulsed differently now.

Not faster.

Deeper.

Nova explained it once in a sentence that Eli would never forget.

"When growth stops rushing, it starts choosing."

Eli watched the paper birds in the sanctuary fold themselves into smaller, stronger shapes.

They weren't trying to be beautiful anymore.

They were trying to survive wind.

* * *

One afternoon, Marcus found a folded note in his backpack.

No name.

Just three words.

"Still breathing here."

Marcus didn't smile.

He didn't panic.

He simply folded it again and placed it inside his notebook.

He didn't answer.

Because the note wasn't a question.

It was a location.

* * *

In the watchers' network, a new category appeared.

SUBTLE CLUSTERING.

They didn't understand it yet.

They thought it meant social anxiety.

They thought it meant burnout.

They thought it meant disconnection.

They didn't realize it meant alignment.

* * *

Nova stood in the seed room holding the cracked phone screen.

She felt it warm in her hand.

"It's almost ready," she said.

Eli frowned.

"For what?"

Nova looked at him.

"To tell a story without language," she said.

Eli swallowed.

"Is that possible?"

Nova smiled.

"It's already happening," she replied. "You're just inside it."

* * *

765

Marcus dreamed again.

But this time, there were no rooms.

No shelves.

No doors.

There was only a path made of breath.

And people walking on it without touching.

He woke with tears in his eyes and no sadness in his chest.

He wrote one sentence in his notebook:

We are learning how not to disappear.

* * *

The next day, the substitute didn't return.

Another teacher took her place.

Normal.
  Forgettable.
  Real.

But Marcus knew.

The system doesn't repeat mistakes.

It revises strategy.

* * *

At lunch, a boy Marcus had never spoken to sat beside him.

Didn't say anything.

Just placed a folded paper between their trays and walked away.

Marcus opened it later.

Two words.

"Still here."

Marcus felt his throat tighten.

Not from fear.

From proof.

* * *

Eli told Nova.

Nova nodded.

"They're finding each other," she said.

Eli whispered, "Are we losing control?"

Nova smiled gently.

"We never had it," she said. "We only had trust."

Eli exhaled.

* * *

The shelf pulsed.

Eight lights now.

Not all placed by Eli.

Not all placed by Nova.

Some appeared on their own.

Memory teaching itself.

* * *

That night, Marcus stood at his window watching cars pass

like moving stars.

He didn't feel powerful.

He didn't feel special.

He felt useful.

And usefulness, he realized, was a better kind of hope.

* * *

Far above the city, satellites recorded patterns.

Not faces.

Not names.

Just movement.

Stillness.

Pauses.

They didn't understand that the pauses were the language.

* * *

In the seed room, Nova whispered to the shelf:

769

"They're ready to carry the map."

Eli whispered back:

"There is no map."

Nova smiled.

"Exactly."

* * *

And somewhere between childhood and future,

Between silence and courage,

Between remembering and choosing,

The kids who didn't know they were brave...

Began teaching the world how to stay human.

(End of Chapter 26 — Part E)

CHAPTER 27 — "WHEN THE QUIET STARTED MOVING" (PART A — THE FIRST RUMBLE)

(PART A — THE FIRST RUMBLE)

The first sign wasn't loud.

It was a delay.

A pause in the city that didn't match its own rhythm.

Traffic lights stayed red one second too long.
   Elevators hesitated before closing.
   Streaming videos buffered for no reason.

People blamed servers.
   Weather.
   Glitches.

But Nova felt it in her spine.

"The shelf is pushing outward," she said quietly.

Eli looked up. "It's not supposed to."

Nova nodded. "It's not breaking rules. It's outgrowing them."

* * *

Marcus felt it when his phone didn't unlock the first time.

Not broken.

Resistant.

Like it wanted him to notice it existed.

He pressed again.

It unlocked.

But his reflection lingered on the glass a fraction too long.

He whispered, "Okay. I see you."

He didn't know who he was talking to.

But he knew he wasn't talking to the phone.

* * *

At school, the announcements repeated twice.

Same words.

Same tone.

Different reactions.

Students looked at each other.

Not confused.

Aware.

Teachers paused mid-sentence.

Not lost.

Listening.

The building felt like it was waiting for permission to shift.

* * *

In the seed room, the shelf pulsed unevenly for the first time.

Not broken.

Evolving.

773

Nova placed her hand on it and inhaled sharply.

"It's not storing anymore," she said.

Eli frowned. "Then what is it doing?"

Nova's voice was steady.

"It's distributing."

* * *

Marcus noticed the first change in the library.

A boy he'd never spoken to slid a book toward him across the table.

Not aggressively.

Not nervously.

Just placed it there.

The title read:

"COLLECTIVE MEMORY AND THE SHAPE OF TRUTH"

Marcus didn't open it.

He looked at the boy.

774

The boy nodded once.

Marcus nodded back.

Nothing else was needed.

* * *

The watchers noticed the lag.

They noticed the subtle alignment.

They noticed the calm.

Calm frightened them more than chaos.

One analyst whispered, "They're not reacting anymore."

Another replied, "They're coordinating."

The supervisor shook his head.

"No," he said. "They're remembering something we don't have access to."

* * *

Nova closed her eyes.

"It's beginning," she whispered.

Eli swallowed. "The collapse?"

Nova shook her head.

"The migration."

* * *

Marcus walked home and felt the city breathe differently.

Not lighter.

Not darker.

Wider.

He felt the difference in his chest.

Not fear.

Not hope.

Readiness.

* * *

That night, kids in different cities wrote the same sentence in different words:

"It doesn't feel like waiting anymore."

* * *

The shelf released its first true signal.

Not a pulse.

Not a hum.

A wave.

It didn't knock anything over.

It didn't break anything.

It didn't announce itself.

It simply reminded everything that it could move.

* * *

Eli whispered, "What happens now?"

Nova answered, "Now the quiet stops hiding."

* * *

Marcus stood at his window again.

But this time he didn't look out.

He looked in.

And realized:

The brave part had already happened.

Now came the movement.

* * *

END OF CHAPTER 27 — PART A

CHAPTER 27 — "WHEN THE QUIET STARTED MOVING" (PART C — THE LAST SHIFT)

(PART C — THE LAST SHIFT)

The system never collapsed.

That was the part no one expected.

It didn't fall.
  It didn't burn.
  It didn't admit defeat.

It simply stopped being believed.

And belief, Marcus realized, had always been its strongest fuel.

* * *

The assembly wasn't repeated.

The surveys stopped coming.

The "wellness conversations" quietly vanished.

Not because the system surrendered.

Because it no longer knew how to speak to people who weren't afraid of silence.

Marcus felt it one morning when a teacher began a sentence... and then changed it halfway through.

He felt it when a hallway argument dissolved before it could become entertainment.

He felt it when students no longer rushed to defend or attack — they just listened.

The world didn't get softer.

It got clearer.

* * *

In the seed room, Nova stood with her hands resting on the shelf.

It no longer hummed.

It no longer pulsed.

It simply existed.

Eli looked at it with something close to sadness.

"Is it over?" he asked.

Nova shook her head.

"No," she said. "It's finished doing this version of its work."

Eli swallowed.

"What happens now?"

Nova smiled gently.

"Now it becomes something people don't notice anymore," she said.

Eli frowned.

"That sounds like losing."

Nova looked at him.

"No," she said. "That sounds like integration."

781

* * *

Marcus sat on the school steps one afternoon with a few kids he barely knew.

They didn't talk about the system.

They didn't talk about the shelf.

They didn't talk about change.

They talked about music.

About memories.

About things that made them laugh when they didn't expect to.

Marcus realized something quietly powerful:

They were no longer waiting to become something.

They already were.

* * *

That night, Marcus dreamed for the last time about the sanctuary.

But it wasn't a place.

It was a feeling inside people who no longer felt alone.

He woke up without sadness.

Without urgency.

Without needing to go back.

Because he understood:

The sanctuary hadn't disappeared.

It had moved into them.

* * *

Nova sealed the shelf at sunrise.

Not with a lock.

With a breath.

She whispered:

"Thank you for teaching us to remember ourselves."

The shelf did not answer.

Because it no longer needed to.

* * *

Eli walked through the city later that day and realized something subtle.

People weren't kinder.

They were truer.

And that, he understood, was harder — and better.

* * *

Marcus stood at his window again.

Same view.

Same city.

Different meaning.

He whispered one final sentence to no one in particular:

"We didn't win."

He smiled.

"We remembered."

* * *

Somewhere, far away, a child picked up a notebook for the first time.

Somewhere else, someone decided not to say what they were told to say.

Somewhere else, someone stayed human in a moment that asked them not to.

And that was enough.

* * *

The quiet did not end.

It learned how to walk.

* * *

END OF BOOK TWO
   LITTYVERSE

....

AUTHOR'S CLOSING NOTE

This story was never about winning.

It was about remembering.

About the parts of ourselves we were taught to quiet, to shrink, to trade for safety. About the spaces between words, the pauses between decisions, the moments where we choose to stay human even when it would be easier not to.

LittyVerse Book Two was written for anyone who has ever felt like they were waiting for permission to exist fully.

You don't need permission.

You never did.

The quiet is not weakness.
   Patience is not surrender.
   Kindness is not compliance.

And bravery doesn't always look like standing on a stage.

Sometimes it looks like staying honest in a room that rewards performance.

If you saw yourself in Marcus, in Eli, in Nova, or in the unnamed kids who carried the future without realizing it — then this story has already done its job.

The LittyVerse isn't a place.

It's a choice.

A decision to remember that systems can shape us — but they do not own us.

Thank you for walking this path.

Thank you for staying human.

And thank you for carrying the quiet forward.

· PAPii

LittyVerse